PRAISE FOR KATE WHITE

I Came Back for You

"*I Came Back for You* is an elegant and gripping whodunit as much as it is a moving deep dive into love, grief, and a mother's search for justice. Kate White brings her formidable talent to bear in this haunting, unputdownable novel. I read it in one sitting and can't stop thinking about it."

—Lisa Unger, *New York Times* bestselling author of *Close Your Eyes and Count to 10*

"In *I Came Back for You*, Kate White delivers a quietly explosive mystery about a daughter's final days through the eyes of a mother desperate to understand the daughter she lost. Bree returns to the place she hoped never to see again, chasing answers about her daughter's death—and the version of the young woman she never got to fully know. What follows is a taut, deeply felt whodunit filled with grief, reckoning, and painful truths that come to light only when it's too late to ask the questions. A five-star story that lingers."

—Kimberly Belle, international bestselling author of *The Expat Affair*

"A heartbreaking premise, a deeply emotional story, and an intense ride through one mother's nightmare, *I Came Back for You* is a whip-smart thriller from the amazing Kate White. With characters so alive they leap off the page, the story is sharp, sophisticated, and full of intrigue. A fabulous read from the unsettling opening to the explosive end."

—J.T. Ellison, *New York Times* bestselling author of *Last Seen*

"Utterly compelling. *I Came Back for You* is the kind of story that just keeps building with every flip of the page. I couldn't stop reading."

—Chad Zunker, Amazon Charts bestselling author of *In His Wake*

The Last Time She Saw Him

"*The Last Time She Saw Him* delivers a lush setting with textured characters and a twisty plot that keeps you jumping from one suspect to the next."

—The Big Thrill

"An engrossing murder mystery with an engaging main character who is determined to do right by the man she loved but couldn't marry . . . We admire her for her perseverance and her dedication to unmasking the killer . . . This is yet another win that Kate White will be able to claim in her long list of intriguing and complex psychological thrillers."

—Bookreporter.com

Between Two Strangers

"Kate White's formidable talent for turning the screws of suspense is on full display in this deliciously addictive chiller. With her perfect pacing and gift for simmering tension, White deftly pulls back the delicate layers of secrets and lies, page by thrilling page. Whip-smart, elegant, and utterly immersive, *Between Two Strangers* is as impossible to predict as it is to put down."

—Lisa Unger, *New York Times* bestselling author of *Secluded Cabin Sleeps Six* and *Last Girl Ghosted*

"A high-caliber thriller that satisfies on every level and is just begging to be adapted into a miniseries."

—Bookreporter.com

"Another fine performance . . . The writing sizzles, the mystery of the inheritance is intriguing, and the characters are vivid. Readers who have yet to read White's fiction are in for a real treat; longtime fans know what to expect. For domestic thriller devotees, White delivers the goods."

—*Booklist*

"A suspenseful novel you won't soon forget . . . Original, unpredictable, and one of the best thrillers I have read in many months."

—*BookTrib*

"*Between Two Strangers* is fantastic and so artful. It's Kate White's most suspenseful novel ever. I was on the edge of my seat—it crackles."

—Adriana Trigiani, *New York Times* bestselling author of *The Good Left Undone*

Have You Seen Me?

"Arms linked, breath held, we drop alongside Ally Linden into Kate White's dagger-sharp, whip-smart new thriller *Have You Seen Me?*, the same questions burning like neon signs in our minds . . . As nimbly plotted as *Before I Go to Sleep*, as winning as the best of Mary Higgins Clark, *Have You Seen Me?* showcases Kate White at her formidable best."

—A. J. Finn, #1 *New York Times* bestselling author of *The Woman in the Window*

"A well-honed thriller . . . White skillfully maintains the pace . . . Even the most jaded reader will be satisfied."

—*Publishers Weekly*

"Intense, nonstop suspense . . . You won't want to miss the stunning conclusion."
—Bookreporter.com

"Provides the twists and shocks that any reader of domestic thrillers expects and savors, but she also manages to use some of our expectations to create clever dead ends . . . An engaging novel that turns some clichés of recent thrillers on their heads."
—*Kirkus Reviews*

"This gripping psychological suspense tale is hard to put down."
—*Booklist*

"White is a master at creating sympathetic characters, and from the first pages of the novel through to its impressive twist ending, Ally is likable, relatable, and compelling."
—The Big Thrill

"Kate White has done it again. Her latest novel, *Have You Seen Me?*, stars Ally, who shows up at her old job with no memory of why she shouldn't be there. White starts with a bang and keeps the suspense high throughout, weaving together a labyrinth of buried memories and disturbing revelations that blur the lines between what's true and what's not. An addictive, up-all-night stunner."
—Kimberly Belle, internationally bestselling author of *Dear Wife*

"Well-executed . . . The smaller the town, the bigger (and dirtier) its secrets."
—*Kirkus Reviews*

The Second Husband

"Immersive, spellbinding thriller about a woman questioning everything—including her husband. In Kate White's perfectly plotted novel, it's impossible to predict what will happen next."
—Samantha Downing, internationally bestselling author of *My Lovely Wife*

"Intricately plotted and suspenseful, *The Second Husband* is a terrific book, packed with surprises and a nail-biting conclusion."
—Sarah Pekkanen, *New York Times* bestselling coauthor of *The Golden Couple*

"*The Second Husband* is suspense at its most addictive. The pages turn in a blur. You won't put this one down."
—Michele Campbell, internationally bestselling author of *It's Always the Husband*

"Kate White continues to build her fan base with another page-turner, the perfect read for the beach, the mountains, and everywhere in between. Besides an intriguing mystery, White creates interesting characters that may remind us, for better or worse, of family and friends in our own lives . . . There are many twists and turns."
—Woman Around Town

"This thoroughly involving psychological thriller promises a startling conclusion and delivers it."
—*Booklist*

"White establishes a pervasive uneasy tone, ending chapters with cliff-hangers and small revelations that propel this domestic suspense tale to an intense penultimate scene."
—*Library Journal*

The Fiancée

"A tense, simmering, fast-paced mystery, Kate White's latest captivating thriller explores the secrets that lurk just under the surface of a picture-perfect facade. I raced through this story about a close-knit family's annual gathering at an idyllic estate that quickly turns deadly. *The Fiancée* kept me guessing until the very end, never sure who to trust—or where the danger was hiding."

—Megan Miranda, *New York Times* bestselling author

"Kate White's newest thriller, *The Fiancée*, is a perfect poolside or beach read, as this psychological thriller has everything a great summer read needs! Told in an almost locked-room style, as we are secluded at a wealthy family's sprawling estate, this mystery looks at what appears to be a picture-perfect family . . . the constant threatening feeling in the air propels this psychological thriller to a truly surprising climax."

—The Nerd Daily

"A twisty family drama."

—*Library Journal*

"A skillfully constructed page-turner . . . Expert pacing, characters readers can love to hate, and an intelligent heroine make this a winner. White consistently entertains."

—*Publishers Weekly*

"Kate White's *The Fiancée* is exactly what we all need right now: a fast-paced, perfectly woven murder mystery, with a hearty dash of family drama. This one must not be missed!"

—Aimee Molloy

The Secrets You Keep

"This can't-put-it-down murder mystery from the former editor of *Cosmo* follows an author pushed to the brink by escalating chaos. Crazy dreams guaranteed."

—*Cosmopolitan*

"A psychological thriller that doubles as a cautionary tale, *The Secrets You Keep* marks another success for a prolific author and casts an intelligent, if grim, eye on love—love that can warm, and love that can burn."

—*Richmond Times-Dispatch*

"White weaves a story that is mesmerizing and thrilling . . . Mystery lovers will be well served with this novel, as it grabs the reader instantly and can be devoured in one afternoon."

—*Booklist*

"White keeps the suspense high to the end."

—*Publishers Weekly*

"White's latest is a fast-paced mystery with suspenseful intrigue throughout . . . sure to please those looking for a gripping mystery."

—*Romantic Times*

"Kate White ratchets up the suspense by not revealing the identity of the killer until the very end. It is quite a shocker, making *The Secrets You Keep* a riveting psychological thriller that shows White . . . at the very top of her game."

—Bookreporter.com

"This terrific story is full of mysteries, twists, turns, thrills, and chills that only Kate White could come up with and put together like the perfect puzzle that causes readers' pulses to race."
—*Suspense Magazine*

"True to form, Kate White's *The Secrets You Keep* kept me up way past my bedtime, anxiously turning the pages. Taut, tense, and utterly gripping, I could not go to sleep until I found out whodunit."
—Jessica Knoll, *New York Times* and *USA Today* bestselling author of *Luckiest Girl Alive*

"Suspenseful, twisty, and sharply observed, Kate White's clever psychological thriller lures us into the life of vulnerable narrator Bryn, whose marriage is not what she thought it was. The uncertainty develops as the stakes ramp up ever higher, and I was holding my breath as I turned the last few pages."
—Gilly Macmillan, *New York Times* bestselling author of *What She Knew*

I
CAME
BACK
FOR
YOU

ALSO BY KATE WHITE

Stand-Alone Fiction

Hush

The Sixes

Eyes on You

The Wrong Man

The Secrets You Keep

Have You Seen Me?

The Fiancée

The Second Husband

Between Two Strangers

The Last Time She Saw Him

Bailey Weggins Series

If Looks Could Kill

A Body to Die For

'Til Death Do Us Part

Over Her Dead Body

Lethally Blond

So Pretty It Hurts

Even If It Kills Her

Such a Perfect Wife

Nonfiction

Why Good Girls Don't Get Ahead . . . But Gutsy Girls Do: Nine Secrets Every Career Woman Must Know

I Shouldn't Be Telling You This: How to Ask for the Money, Snag the Promotion, and Create the Career You Deserve

The Gutsy Girl Handbook: Your Manifesto for Success

I CAME BACK FOR YOU

a novel

KATE WHITE

THOMAS & MERCER

This is a work of fiction. Names, characters, organizations, places, events, and incidents are either products of the author's imagination or are used fictitiously. Otherwise, any resemblance to actual persons, living or dead, is purely coincidental.

Text copyright © 2026 by Kate White
All rights reserved.

No part of this book may be reproduced, or stored in a retrieval system, or transmitted in any form or by any means, electronic, mechanical, photocopying, recording, or otherwise, without express written permission of the publisher.

Published by Thomas & Mercer, Seattle
www.apub.com

Amazon, the Amazon logo, and Thomas & Mercer are trademarks of Amazon.com, Inc., or its affiliates.

EU product safety contact:
Amazon Media EU S. à r.l.
38, avenue John F. Kennedy, L-1855 Luxembourg
amazonpublishing-gpsr@amazon.com

ISBN-13: 9781662533976 (hardcover)
ISBN-13: 9781662533990 (paperback)
ISBN-13: 9781662533983 (digital)

Cover design by Mumtaz Mustafa
Cover image: © Andrea Epstein / ArcAngel Images; © satoru sakuraba / Shutterstock; © Francesco Ungaro / Unsplash

Printed in the United States of America

First edition

I CAME BACK FOR YOU

Chapter 1

When Sebastian explains one morning that he needs to go away for a few days and asks if I'll mind staying here alone, I tell him not to worry, that I'll be fine.

But that's a lie.

Alone still scares me, even after all this time. The dark does, too, especially the kind of utter darkness we have here in the countryside, where at night the only outdoor light comes from the moon and the wide, filmy swath of the Milky Way. But I tell myself that maybe I *can* manage by myself, that I have to at least try. I hate being such a baby at this point in my life.

"Bree, what if you come, too?" Sebastian says a little later in the day. "I know you've got a deadline, but there's a desk in the basement I could bring up to the guest room."

That would solve the problem, of course, and it's only a thirty-minute flight to Buenos Aires from the Carrasco airport in Uruguay, but I insist it's best for him to go on his own. His father's blood pressure has skyrocketed, and his mother desperately wants Sebastian to have a face-to-face talk with his dad and convince him to finally cede full control of his leather goods company to the youngest son, Roberto. My presence would be a distraction, I'm sure.

Besides, even with a desk in our room, I'd never get any work done. I like his parents and appreciate their warmth toward me, especially knowing they weren't fans of Sebastian's ex-wife, but their large, lovely home can be chaotic. In addition to the two of them, there's a live-in housekeeper; two dogs; a cat; and now his older brother, Manuel, who moved back "temporarily" after his divorce. To say nothing of the endless stream of pastry-bearing friends and relatives, all speaking a language I'm only now getting a handle on.

Being caught in so much commotion can sometimes leave me slightly frantic, like I'm having one of those travel nightmares in which I can't find the right gate or I've shown up at the wrong airport altogether.

"Thank you, Bas," I say, using a nickname only I have for him, because his family prefers *Seba*, "but why don't I go next time instead. This way you can really focus on your father."

And it's not like I'll be totally alone. Our housekeeper and caretaker, Maitena and Jorge, will be here every day. Their cottage is on the same property, less than a quarter of a mile from our house.

I've also got Poco, the forty-pound brown-haired rescue mutt Bas adopted several years ago. He barks at the sight of a gecko shooting up a tree trunk, meaning he's not going to let anyone get close.

The first day goes surprisingly well. After Sebastian departs for his midmorning flight, I bring my laptop outside to the table on the *galería*, a type of veranda that runs across the back of the single-level, white stucco house topped with terra-cotta roof tiles. From here I can look out onto endless rolling green fields dotted with shrubs and copses of eucalyptus trees, and finally blue-gray hills against an enormous sky. The only buildings in sight are one other chacra—the word for *country house*—over a mile in the distance, and some concrete sheds on a neighboring sheep farm.

The view has captivated me from the moment I visited the property two years ago. It's tranquil but at the same time expansive, and I find myself alternately soothed and stirred by the sight of it, whether I'm eating meals out here with Bas or working on my own.

I'm a freelance book editor, and though I find much of what I do rewarding, the novel I'm currently handling has been particularly gratifying. The author's writing is powerful and her story compelling, but the book has needed both strong line editing and cutting to help the themes emerge more clearly.

For most of the day, I lose myself in my work. It's April, the first full month of autumn in Uruguay, but the temperature is in the seventies, and I love the feeling of warmth on my skin as I work. Poco has spent much of the day lying sweetly at my feet as if he's sensed my nervousness.

Sebastian calls at five to say hi. I see him instantly in my mind's eye, sitting in his family's wood-paneled den. Though he's not movie-star gorgeous like some of the young Argentinian men I've passed on the streets of Buenos Aires, he's an attractive, well-built fifty-one-year-old—two years younger than I am—with a slightly craggy face, dark-brown eyes, light stubble, and an intriguing bump on his nose.

"Poco taking good care of you, *cariño*?" he asks.

"Oh yeah, the guy hasn't left my side since you've been gone."

"You're not going to let him sleep on my pillow, are you?" he asks, and I hear the smile in his voice.

"Not a chance, sweetheart. Unless he gargles with a quart of hydrogen peroxide first."

Bas chuckles, and I feel a silly rush of pleasure at the sound. As we've settled into life at the chacra, I've found my sense of humor creeping back after all these years. I can't imagine ever being truly *funny* again, the way my friends claimed I could be at times, but it's nice to be appreciated for the mildly amusing asides I toss out now and then.

"You haven't had the big talk yet, have you?" I ask.

"No, my mother wants to do it when my dad gets home from work tomorrow. I would have liked to have gotten the conversation over with, but she thinks it's best if things seem to flow organically. Then he won't feel ambushed."

"That makes sense. And are you still planning to meet with your team tomorrow?"

Bas runs a small Spanish-language book packaging company, and since he can work remotely, he travels to BA for business just once a month, and only for the day, unless I'm making the trip with him.

"Yes, we're going to look at some proofs, brainstorm, and then go out to lunch at Las Lilas. Speaking of work, how's the book going?"

"I'm finally done, just reviewing my edits now. It's five thousand words shorter than when I started, but I swear I heard the book sigh in gratitude."

We chat for another few minutes, mostly with Bas sharing funny updates about Manuel's feeble attempts at online dating. This is the first time in eighteen months that we've been apart for longer than a day, and as we sign off, I realize I miss him even more than I imagined I would. Just two more days, I think, and so far, I *am* doing fine.

But not long afterward, I feel the first real prick of unease. The sun has sunk in the sky, and though I occasionally catch sounds of Maitena moving around the kitchen, it feels unnaturally still.

I gather up my work and head inside, with Poco trailing right behind. Maitena's in the great room setting the table. She's a lovely woman in her mid-fifties, easygoing like almost everyone I've met in this country, and always gracious to me, even though I seemed to materialize out of nowhere.

"Ah, perfecto," I exclaim, spotting a platter with the spinach-and-Parmesan tart she promised to make tonight.

"*Bueno, gracias,*" she says, smiling. Her dark hair is tied back with a red ribbon today, and she looks even more youthful than usual. "*¿Necesita algo más?*"

"*No, nada más, gracias.*"

She wishes me good night, and seconds later I hear her exit the house. After I finish eating, I lock all the doors, set the security alarm, and read for a couple of hours on the couch, then head to the bedroom. Some nights Poco waits a bit before joining Bas and me, but tonight he enters the room at the same time and jumps onto the foot of the bed.

"Come up closer if you want," I say once I'm under the duvet. "I promise not to tell."

As if understanding, he crawls to the spot next to me and presses his shaggy body against mine. I drape an arm over him in gratitude.

Though I wake a few times during the night, straining to hear in the darkness, the only sounds I pick up are Poco's snoring and the creak of the eucalyptus trees near the back of the house.

There, I tell myself in the morning. *I did it.*

But just before lunch, things start to unravel. Though Poco joined me when I first brought my work outside, he's since disappeared. He's probably off in the fields, I decide, chasing the small wild guinea pigs that roam the property. At one point I stroll into the kitchen to make a second espresso and notice that he hasn't touched the food in his bowl.

I check the bedroom, where I've heard Maitena vacuuming.

"*¿Sabes donde está Poco?*" I ask.

No, she tells me, she doesn't know where he is right now. After calling him from the galería without success, I search the house. While checking the great room, I hear a faint whimpering, and once I've followed the sound, I find Poco wedged behind the couch.

"Poco, what *is* it?" I ask, wiggling my hand into the space and gently petting him. Without raising his head, he lifts two mournful eyes to better see me. It's clear he's sick, maybe with a tummy ache.

A second later a scarier thought jolts me. *Snake.* Though I've never seen one on the property, Bas warned me when I first came here that yararás, a type of venomous pit viper, have been known to travel down from the hills to this region.

I call out for Maitena, alert her to the situation, and she summons Jorge. Poco, we agree, needs to be seen by the vet right away. The always competent Jorge manages to dislodge Poco from behind the couch and carefully loads him into the back of the car wrapped in a blanket. I join Jorge in the front seat, and the two of us set out on the bumpy twenty-five-minute drive. I send Sebastian a text, looping him in, and hear back almost instantly.

> Poor Poco. I'm still in my meeting but please call the minute you know something, okay?

For sure

Once we arrive at the *clínica veterinaria*, Jorge does most of the talking, and since it's tough for me to understand the exchanges, he repeats everything back to me in slower Spanish. The vet, a small man with wavy black hair, looks concerned, but after examining Poco, he says his vital signs are good and there aren't any injuries or puncture marks indicating a snakebite.

"*¿Tienen veneno para ratas en la casa?*" he asks, and Jorge explains that, yes, there's rat poison on the property but it's protected in bait stations. The vet says that Poco most likely ate or drank something nasty rather than poisonous, but as a precaution he wants to induce vomiting and observe him for at least twenty-four hours.

"Muchas gracias," I tell him, and kiss Poco's head. The vet promises to phone later with an update.

As soon as I'm in the car, I call Bas on WhatsApp and fill him in.

"So, the vet isn't too worried?" he asks anxiously when I'm done.

"He doesn't seem to be, so you shouldn't worry, either. Just focus on the meeting with your dad, okay?"

"Thanks, cariño. I'll call you later."

Like Bas, I feel awful about Poco, but as the kilometers pass, a sense of dismay invades my concern. Poco, the dog with a constitution of a damn ox, has gotten sick during the one time Bas is away overnight. I'm going to be all by myself tonight, maybe tomorrow night, too.

When we reach the property, Jorge drops me at the house and asks if there's anything I need before he heads to the cottage.

"*No, gracias, no necesito nada más,*" I tell him, forcing a smile.

I return to the galería and finish reviewing my work on the book. I also respond to a few emails, including one from my best friend, Ellie, a book editor who came up in publishing at the same time I did and followed, all the way to the end, the career path I imagined for myself but never finished—editorial assistant, associate editor, senior editor, executive editor, and then finally head of an imprint at a major publishing house. She's not only been wonderful about staying in touch during the time I've been living with Bas, but she's got a gift for offering the right words of support year after year. I know I can count on her not to tell me that a flickering lamp or the feather from a red-tailed hawk is a sign that the daughter I will never see again is keeping an eye on me from some other realm.

Finally, at six, there's a message from the vet. Poco is better, drinking a little water, and might be well enough to return home tomorrow. Knowing Bas is probably talking to his father now, I text him the news instead of calling, and I also shoot a text to Jorge.

Not long afterward, the scent of sautéing chicken and onions wafts from the house. I look up and realize the day has turned to dusk. The only sound is the far-off yawn of cars on the highway leading toward miles of Uruguayan beach towns, including Punta del Este.

As I gather up my laptop and folders, preparing to go inside, I feel my body humming anxiously. I should have gone with Bas, I tell myself.

"*¿Quisiera comer al aire libre?*" Maitena asks when she sees me enter the great room. She's wondering if I want to eat on the galería since the weather this evening is particularly pleasant.

"*No, gracias. Aquí, por favor,*" I say, nodding to the dining table. There's no way I'm sitting out there by myself tonight.

She smiles, retreats to the kitchen, and returns with the chicken dish, rice, and a simple *ensalada verde*. I pour myself a glass of red wine. While I eat, I hear her cleaning up in the kitchen, and when she comes back to say good night, there's a crazy moment when I consider asking her to stay in the guest room tonight. But what in the world would she think of me if I floated that request?

As soon as I hear her leave through the kitchen, I not only lock up but also begin flicking on lamps and sconces throughout the entire house. I tell myself that I'm being insane, that even if thieves want to break into a house in the general area, they'll select one of the fancy estancias around here instead of our chacra.

Bas calls at eight thirty, just as I'm making myself a cup of herbal tea.

"So, how did it go?" I say, eager for his news.

"To our complete shock, he agreed almost instantly to retire. What's the English expression? *Like taking candy from a baby?* Needless to say, my mother's in heaven about it."

"That's wonderful, sweetheart. Deep down, he must have known it was time."

"Yes, I think he was waiting for someone to give him permission . . . How about Poco? Any news?"

"Not beyond what I told you."

"And how about you, Bree? I realized that without the dog, you might be nervous."

"Just a little," I say. Bas knows the broad outlines of my history, but I've never spelled out to him how much the dark freaks me out. I wonder what he'd think if he could see the house from the highway right now, glittering like a cruise ship sailing north toward Rio.

"Well, you'll only have one more night alone. Friends of my parents want to take them out Wednesday night to celebrate, so I'm going to catch a midday flight mañana instead of coming back Thursday."

"Fabulous," I say, feeling a ridiculous rush of relief. "I've really missed you."

"Same here, cariño."

After we say our goodbyes, I settle on the couch with my Kindle. I tell myself to savor the evening—the tea, the peaceful silence, the lingering smell of old woodsmoke from the hearth.

But then, just as my eyes finally focus on a page of text, I hear it: the purr of a car engine. And nearby, not on the highway. Someone is coming up the long dirt driveway.

It's Maitena and Jorge's twenty-something-year-old son, I tell myself. Sometimes he visits in the evening. But never this late.

Has someone made a wrong turn? I wonder, rising from the couch. Most of the driveways that are off the main road, the ones to farms and chacras, don't even have the name of the property posted.

I hear the car come to a stop. The driver will have reached the locked wooden gate just below the house.

For a few seconds I stand with my ears perked, waiting for another sound. The driver backing out, recognizing he's come down the wrong road. But it's silent.

I pick up my phone and tap Jorge's number. A half dozen rings and then only voicemail. I try Maitena's mobile next, but also without luck. I hurry into the kitchen and glance out the window, gazing through the trees toward the cottage. It's dark, except for the security light above the back door. Where in God's name are they?

I squeeze my head in my hands. How can this be happening? I could hit the panic button on the alarm fob, but it would take forever for anyone from the security company to arrive.

I return to the great room, still straining to hear. Is the driver just sitting in the car, watching the jerky movements of my shadow behind the curtains?

And then another sound comes. Not of the car backing out but *footsteps*. Softly scuffling along the gravel in front of the house.

Holding my breath, I tiptoe toward the thick wooden door. Whoever's out there is now standing just on the other side—I can *feel* it. And then there's a rap on the wood. My heart nearly explodes in my chest.

"Who is it?" I call out.

No reply.

"Who's *there*?"

"Bree, it's me. Logan."

Instinctively, my hand flies to my mouth in shock. I reach out and inch open the door, needing to make sure before I swing it all the way.

And then there he is, standing right in front of me, bathed in a small halo of light. My ex-husband. A man I last set eyes on seven years ago.

Chapter 2

The sight of Logan Chase is so utterly improbable that there's a moment when I wonder if I've imagined it. But I know I haven't. Your imagination needs thoughts or images to spark off, and I almost never allow Logan inside my head anymore.

My next thought: Something truly horrible must have happened, and he's come all this way to break the news in person and spare me the anguish of hearing it over the phone. But no, it can't be that, either. Because the only horrible thing Logan could share has already happened—eight Octobers ago.

"Hello, Bree," he says, offering a cautious smile. "I hope I didn't scare you."

"It's more that I'm flabbergasted. What—what are you doing here?"

"It's a fairly long story. Is it okay if I come in?"

I inhale deeply, absorbing his presence, or at least what I can make out from the light cast by the wrought-iron sconces on either side of the door. He's wearing jeans and a blue V-neck sweater—cashmere, I suppose—under an unzipped lightweight jacket. The tip of a boarding pass pokes out from one of the jacket pockets.

"Of course." Because what else am I going to say? He's come for a reason, and I need to hear what in the world it is. Maybe he has health or financial issues he thinks I should know about, or his sister-in-law's sick again. "You've rented a car, I take it?"

"Yeah, and I left it down by the gate. Will I be blocking anyone?"

"No, it's okay there."

I open the door even wider and gesture with my hand for him to enter. My pulse is still racing—not from fear anymore but the pure shock of his being here.

He steps inside. Now that he's in better light, I see that he looks remarkably close to how he did when I last saw him, though his thick brown hair is silvery gray at the temples, and the crease that had begun to form between his blue-green eyes has deepened, like a tiny slice in his forehead. He's probably a few pounds heavier, too, but it's barely noticeable.

"Have you driven all the way from Montevideo?"

"No, from the Punta del Este airport. But it was a forty-minute wait at the car rental counter—the guy was apparently on his dinner break—and then I kept getting lost, even with GPS . . . Where's your partner—Sebastian?"

"In BA for a few days."

He sweeps a hand through his hair and advances into the great room. I can see now that he's tired, even a little frayed around the edges. But he's doing his best to be chipper. I wouldn't expect anything less.

"Do you want something to drink?" I ask, and not just to be polite. I need to sit, I realize. The last ten minutes have knocked the wind out of me. "Soda? A beer?"

"I'd love some water right now . . . It's just good to be out of the car. And it's good to see you, Bree."

As I lead him through the house, I sense him swiveling his head behind me, checking out the place. I described it briefly on the phone to him just after I'd moved here, and texted a couple of pictures per his request, but I know the house is far more impressive in person.

When we reach the kitchen, I lift my chin toward the table and tell him to have a seat, but he takes a bit more time to look around. Though the room wouldn't be everyone's favorite—it's old-fashioned in style, with wooden beams running along the ceiling, white plaster walls, and a terra-cotta-tiled floor—Bas wanted something similar to the original kitchen.

"Very impressive," Logan says, and I can tell from his tone that he means it. "Sebastian did this himself after his uncle died?"

"No, he's not *that* handy, but he provided a lot of input. It's more Argentine in style than Uruguayan. Spanish Colonial isn't much of a thing here."

He slips out of his jacket and finally drops into a chair at the wooden table.

"Have you had anything to eat tonight?" I ask almost instinctively.

Another smile, this one a bit sheepish. "No, unless you count the lovely Aerolíneas Argentinas first-class snack of stale cashews and mineral water."

"Why don't I make you a plate," I say. "There's some leftover food from dinner."

So now I've both welcomed him inside *and* invited him to have a meal. But the past seems too past for me not to be considerate. Besides, Logan being Logan, he'll find it easier to share with a plate of food in front of him.

"That'd be great, thanks."

I pour him a glass of *agua con gas*, which I assume he still prefers over still, and then, following a moment's deliberation, a small glass of red wine for each of us. After I reheat some of the chicken and rice on a plate in the microwave, I set it in front of him and sit in the chair opposite.

This is surreal, I think. And unsettling.

Logan raises his wineglass in salute. The skin on his fifty-nine-year-old hands is crinkly in places, I notice, probably sun damaged. He mentioned in an email a year or so ago that he was still an avid jogger.

"This looks delicious," he says. "Did you make it?"

"No, our housekeeper did."

He sighs contentedly, grabs his fork, and takes a bite with still-familiar gusto. For someone who owns and runs a restaurant-management company, Logan was never what you'd call a total foodie, but he likes to cook and relishes eating even more.

"Wait, is this chicken stroganoff?" he asks once he's swallowed.

"Not a favorite anymore?"

"Still a favorite. But I was thinking you'd be knee-deep here in empanadas and *cordero* with chimichurri sauce."

"Oh, there's plenty of that, too."

He chuckles and takes another bite. I've now done all the waiting I can stand.

"So," I say, "why don't you tell me what you're doing here, over five thousand miles from home?"

He dabs at his mouth with a napkin, then levels his eyes on mine.

"I could ask the same of you, Bree," he says.

"Very funny, but we've already been *over* that ground."

And we have. After I decided to move in with Sebastian, putting an end to the crazy, once-a-month-and-never-enough-time-together commute we'd been doing between Manhattan and Buenos Aires, I informed Logan immediately of my plan. In the years since our divorce, we've loosely stayed in touch, communicating a couple of times a year, by email or phone, about things like his sister-in-law's cancer treatment and a few investments we still hold together. And though it might have been secretly satisfying to catch him off guard and announce months after the move, "Oh, I'm actually not on the Upper West Side anymore; I live on a small farm called El Bosquecillo in the Uruguayan countryside," that seemed too heartless to do.

"Believe it or not, I had business in Buenos Aires this week," he says. "Curt and I are looking at a steak restaurant there that we might bring to the States, to various locations. And since I was so close, I thought I'd come to see you."

He takes another bite of the stroganoff, sets the fork down, and rests his elbows on the table, cupping one hand over the other. Maybe it's that gesture, still so familiar, or being in a kitchen together after all this time—or both—but I'm swept back almost instantly to the night we met, sitting at someone's long wooden dining table in Tribeca.

I was twenty-four at the time and a guest at a dinner party given by friends of a guy I'd been seeing casually for a month or two. The hosts had a messy but charming loft-style apartment with a huge kitchen/dining area. Logan had come alone, and for the first half of the evening, he'd mostly listened, keeping his eyes focused intently on people as they spoke.

When the conversation shifted from politics to food—including food as foreplay—he suddenly seemed in the mood to engage, and announced, "Well, food can be a total *anti*-aphrodisiac as well." He proceeded to tell a story about trying to dazzle a woman by making shrimp étouffée, a type of stew, but he'd done the roux sauce all wrong so that the flour and wine hardened like plaster of paris around each piece of shrimp. It made a crunching sound when they chewed, and the woman had ended up chipping a tooth.

People laughed, in part because of *how* he'd told the story, pausing in places for dramatic effect and chuckling at his own incompetence. At one point he'd glanced down the table and held my gaze so tightly that my date turned to look at me, obviously wondering if Logan and I were already acquainted.

So I wasn't all that shocked when he called a few days later, having wormed my number out of my date's friends. He reintroduced himself and then got right to the point.

"Why don't you let me cook you dinner one night," he said.

"Shrimp in body casts?" I asked.

I heard him laugh softly.

"Only if that's your preference."

"No, something less crunchy, I think. I'd like to keep all my teeth."

Though he had a bad-boy vibe, a trait I'd vowed to steer clear of going forward, I was in the mood for a short summer fling, and he seemed like the perfect candidate. Three nights later he made me the best *spaghetti alle vongole* I'd ever tasted, and I went to bed with him hours later.

"And you decided to show up without even calling?" I ask him now.

"I was afraid if I called from BA, you'd discourage me from coming—though as soon as I was in Punta, I *did* try, but the call wouldn't go through on my phone."

The story sounds completely lame, but that's beside the point now. Maybe . . . maybe he's marrying Lisa, his girlfriend of the past year or so, and he's decent enough to want to tell me to my face. To my surprise, the thought roils me. Lisa isn't the coworker he was screwing during the last months of our marriage, but she was once a colleague of his, and in my mind, I've let her become a vague icon of his infidelity. My ex's betrayal doesn't hold a candle to what had happened to us the year before, but it hurt indescribably, creating a pile-on of pain that often took my breath away.

No, he's smart enough not to show up at my door to talk about Lisa.

And then, like a flower blooming in a fast-motion video, I finally realize what his mission tonight is all about, something I should have known from the moment I saw him. He thinks that if we speak in person, he can finally convince me to go back next week to Cartersville, the small city in upstate New York where all that pain got its start. He's been lobbying for months on this front.

Before I can press him, there's a rapping on the back door, and we jerk simultaneously in surprise.

"Señora, soy Jorge," a male voice calls out. "¿Esta todo bien?"

I jump up from the table, unbolt the door, and swing it open. Jorge's black hair stands on end like he's been in bed until now, and I realize that's why the cottage was dark and my phone calls went unanswered, though he's clearly seen the car by now.

He glances briefly at me and then redirects his gaze toward Logan, his eyes widening in surprise.

"*Sí, todo bien,*" I say. "*Mi amigo Logan—de Estados Unidos—está aquí.* Logan, Jorge. Jorge, Logan."

Logan starts to rise from the table, but Jorge raises a hand and tells him, *"No se moleste."* I thank him for checking on me and wish him good night. I'm sure he's wondering what the hell is going on, but at least he knows I'm not in any danger.

"That's your caretaker?" Logan asks as I take my seat at the table again.

"Yes, but he has his own small farm on the property. He worked for Sebastian's uncle for years . . . So, you were saying?"

"Right. The bottom line is that once I had the idea of coming here in my head, I couldn't stop myself. I was so close, and I wanted to see you."

"You mean you wanted to *talk* to me, don't you? About the reception."

He lets out a sigh. "It would really be good to have you there."

The reception is being held next Thursday night on the Carter College campus, in honor of gifts Logan mulled over for years and finally made to the school: two full-tuition creative writing scholarships and the funds necessary for the renovation of the office of the campus literary magazine, *The Muse*. These relate to our daughter, Melanie, who died during the first semester of her junior year there.

Though he's given these gifts in my name, too, I have no intention of attending the event. In fact, I'm revolted by the very thought of being in Cartersville again. And he knows it.

"You'll be fine without me, Logan," I say. "And won't Steve and Kirsten be there?" I'm talking about his brother and sister-in-law.

"Kirsten now has surgery planned for that week. Nothing scary and not related to the cancer—that's still in remission—but it can't be put off. And besides, theirs isn't the support I need most."

I throw up my hands. "You *have* my support. But it's going to have to be in spirit, not in person. I never gave you any reason to think otherwise."

Logan shakes his head, his earlier cheerfulness seeping away. *"Please."*

"I can't, Logan."

He probably thinks this is my way of punishing him. But it isn't—at least I don't think so. When I discovered he'd been cheating on me with a thirtysomething employee less than a year after Mel died, divorce seemed like my only option. He asked for forgiveness, saying grief had rendered him both desperate for consolation and utterly stupid, but I couldn't imagine trying to claw myself out from under my own crushing despair while being on constant hanky-panky patrol, endlessly digging through his pockets for signs of additional bad behavior.

In the years since, however, I've let a lot of the anger go and tried my best *not* to be punishing. Logan's actions were heart-wrenching but, in hindsight, not fully impossible for me to comprehend. Maybe grief makes you do the darndest things, even blow up your marriage. Still, there was no way I wanted to be friends with him.

"If you aren't there, though, the whole event will seem off," he says. "You're her *mother*."

"Logan, stop," I say, anger spiking in me. "You've no right to judge me on this. And I'm sorry if you've come all this way for nothing besides chicken stroganoff. If you're worried how things will look, I can write a short statement for the program. And as I told you, I have some poems of Mel's that I'd love for you to include, along with the photos you're using."

They're actually haikus. Mel seemed to love the five-syllable, seven-syllable, five-syllable structure.

He drums his fingers on the table, looking uncharacteristically flustered. "I'm sorry to have pressured you this way, Bree. It's just I remember you being so willing to go back there in the past."

"Don't you *get* it?" I say. Against my will, my eyes prick with tears. "I went to Cartersville when I was trying to make sure the police were doing all they could, and once that was done, I never wanted to see the town again. If I go back now, I know I'll lose ground. I've finally started to feel the tiniest bit whole again."

For a few seconds, he says nothing—simply studies me.

"Understood," he says at last. "But there's something else I need to discuss. And it's really the main reason I came."

"What *is* it?" I say, feeling my stomach clutch. "Are you okay, Logan?"

"It's not about me. It's about the monster who took Mel's life."

My anger spikes again, like a firecracker going off this time. "Don't tell me there's been some kind of appeal."

"No, worse. There's a chance he's not the one who murdered her."

Chapter 3

A moan escapes my lips, an involuntary sound like something from a wounded animal.

"No," I protest. "That's not true, and you can't possibly believe it."

"I didn't *want* to believe it, Bree, I swear," Logan says. "But it seems like it might be credible. You need to look at this letter—it was meant for both of us."

He tugs a brown leather wallet from his back pocket and withdraws a folded piece of white paper from where the bills are stored. Once he's opened the letter, he slides it across the table to me. I see right away that the letterhead is for a law firm, but not one I recognize, and the date at the top is eight days ago. I take a ragged breath and start to read.

> Dear Ms. Winter and Mr. Chase:
>
> I'm sorry to have to insert myself in your life again, but there's some information I need to pass along to you. As you recall, I was the lawyer who represented Calvin Ruck at his trial in Plattsburgh. He and I had not been in touch in recent years—in fact, I'm no longer with the public defender's office—but he reached out to me a short time ago. He informed me that he had recently been diagnosed with pancreatic cancer, had only a short time to live, and wanted me to come to

the Clinton Correctional Facility in Dannemora so that he could pass along critical information.

During my visit to Dannemora, he finally admitted to murdering the two women he'd been convicted of killing in Plattsburgh, Sailor Abbott and Amanda Kline, and he also claimed to have killed two other female college students, one from Ohio and another from Pennsylvania, who both have been missing for close to a decade. At his request, I immediately shared this information with the authorities in all three states involved, and included where Ruck claimed the remains of the missing women could be found. He refused to speak to the police directly.

During our meeting, Ruck also stated—vehemently—that though he had been in the Cartersville area at the time of your daughter's death, he was never in Pebble Creek Park and didn't murder her. Since he was forthcoming about the other homicides, it's possible he was telling the truth in this case, though the police will draw their own conclusions.

I am sorry for whatever pain and upheaval this causes in your life, but I felt it was essential for you to know.

Sincerely,
David Schmidt

By the time I finish reading, I have the bitter taste of bile in my throat. I push the letter away and snicker, another sound that escapes of its own volition.

"Ruck's a fucking liar," I exclaim. "He said when he was arrested that he never murdered anyone, but he *had*. He claimed he wasn't near

Cartersville, but his cell phone showed otherwise. And now he's treating us to one more appalling lie."

"That was my first thought, too," Logan says, "but I called Schmidt as soon as I got this, and I have a bit more information for us to go on. The police in Ohio and Pennsylvania have now uncovered the remains of the two women, using the details Ruck provided. One girl had been a student at the University of Akron, the other at the University of Pittsburgh, and they disappeared within months of each other—during a time, it turns out, Ruck was living in Ohio. The campuses are only a couple of hours apart, but since they're in two different states, authorities never connected the cases."

"Okay, so that part's true," I scoff. "That doesn't mean the rest is."

"But why would Ruck confess to four murders, including two previously unknown ones, but deny responsibility for one he'd already been accused of?"

I shake my head in disbelief at Logan's naivete—over a madman who smashed our daughter in the back of the head; ripped her clothes apart, leaving her pants at her ankles; and then strangled her to death.

"Because he's a sadist, and he probably wanted to have some fun torturing us before he died," I exclaim. "Remember that horrible way he used to stare at me during the trial?"

The memory alone is enough to sicken me: Ruck, sitting in his rumpled brown suit at the defense table, would sometimes turn his head ever so slightly and try to make eye contact with me and the two other mothers, letting his lips form the hint of a bloodcurdling smile.

"I know. It's just—"

"And it doesn't even compute. We're supposed to accept that a serial killer with the same MO used to kill Mel was staying near Cartersville for over a week, but that he isn't the one responsible for her death." Blood rushes to my head. "No, I'm not buying it for a second."

Logan reaches across the table and lays a hand over mine. My breath catches. It's been a whole year longer than seven since we were physically intimate, and the feel of his skin is jarring.

"Bree, I'm so sorry to upset you," he says gently. "But I felt I needed to let you know all this. And that's the real reason I've come. I wasn't planning to head to BA until after the reception, but I decided to move up the trip and tell you this in person."

My hand, the one under his, feels an urge to twitch, and I let it. Logan clearly notices and pulls his own hand away. I know he was just being thoughtful, but I don't want him touching me.

"Thank you, I appreciate your efforts," I say, softening my tone. I surely can't blame him for this brand-new nightmare. "And I know it isn't easy for you, either."

He lifts a shoulder in a half shrug. "Nope. But I've had a few days to process things—and to be honest, the trip here helped."

Of course. Logan, a medalist in cross-country running during both high school and college, did marathons during most of our marriage, and for him, motion was always a kind of balm when life got crazy. And he needed it more than ever after Mel died. At first, we were weirdly in sync, like two people trapped in one of those horrifying bullet rides at a carnival. But while I soon found myself sucked into a sinkhole of depression, totally immobilized, he became a gushing fire hose of grief and fury—flailing around the apartment, jogging endless miles a day, always desperately trying to stay busy. To say nothing of fucking his employee.

His drive to set up the scholarships in Mel's name has seemed like the last gasp of all that frantic forward motion.

Resting my elbows on the table, I massage my forehead roughly with my fingertips. I'm flooded with so many emotions right now—exasperation, rage, sadness, confusion, as well as discombobulation from having my former husband sitting across from me—that I can hardly sort them apart or light on one for long. I have no clue how to handle any of this.

"What are you going to do?" I ask finally.

Logan lifts both his shoulders this time and then glances quickly at his watch.

"Hit the road, I guess. The hotel I booked is in Punta del Este, which according to GPS, is only forty minutes from here."

"When do you fly back?"

"Tomorrow tonight around nine. I paid for an extra night at the hotel so I could hang there during the day."

I make a nearly instant decision, not giving myself time to debate it.

"You should stay here tonight, Logan," I say. "It's offseason, which means the roads will be deserted at this hour. If you have any kind of car trouble, you'll never find anyone to help, and even if you did, they wouldn't speak any English."

That's not an exaggeration. Though I don't relish the idea of him here in my home for a night—with Bas away, no less—it's really not wise for him to be driving at this hour.

"Thank you, but it's too much to expect, Bree," Logan says. "Really."

"It's not a problem. We have a guest room with its own bath at the other end of the house."

His shoulders sag a little, as if in relief. "If you're sure it's okay, I'll gladly accept. I didn't sleep well last night, thinking of having to lay all this on you, and I'm pretty fried."

"Okay, then. But that's not what I meant before. What are you going to do about the letter?"

"You want to hear tonight?"

"Of course I want to hear," I snap, then quickly lift my hands, palms forward, as an apology.

He nods and takes another swig of wine before speaking.

"I called the state police right before I came down here. Tim Caputo, the guy we dealt with the most, has retired, but the younger detective, Brian Halligan, is still there, and he'd already spoken to David Schmidt. And unless he was just blowing smoke at me, the situation has his full attention. He's going to meet with me when I'm in Cartersville for the reception."

"Will he make an attempt to speak to Ruck, despite the odds?"

Logan's expression turns even grimmer. "Ruck is dead. He died five days after Schmidt went to see him."

The news jolts me even more than I would have thought. I suppose I should be elated that the universe is rid of him, but this means Ruck, thirty-eight at the time of his arrest, won't spend decades rotting in Dannemora.

"So now what?" I ask.

"Halligan plans to comb through the New York State files again and also take a look at the files from Ohio and Pennsylvania. As of now, he's betting that Ruck was yanking our chain, just like you said, but he wants to review everything and see if something doesn't make sense."

"Doesn't make sense how?"

"He wants to compare Mel's file to the two new ones and also see if the similarities between her case and the Plattsburgh ones were less remarkable than the cops thought at the time."

That's ridiculous, I think. The Plattsburgh college student Ruck killed first, Sailor Abbott, was struck on the head with something hammer-like and repeatedly strangled, just like Mel was, and that was exactly what happened to Amanda Kline, murdered three weeks after Mel.

"Those similarities seemed pretty damn remarkable at the time," I say. "Are we supposed to now believe it was all a coincidence?"

"Not necessarily."

Suddenly, I suspect where he's going. "Wait, you're not about to say there could have been a copycat, are you? Someone who knew Ruck's pattern and used it?"

Logan shakes his head. "No, only Sailor was dead by that point, and there was little publicity about her murder farther downstate. That's why the cops didn't put two and two together at first. We should know more in a few days, once Halligan has looked at everything."

"All right." Though nothing's all right about it. And I hate how we sound like guests on a true crime podcast, when it's our *daughter* who's dead.

"Look, Bree, why don't we table this for now?" Logan suggests. "The letter's for you—a copy I made—but you can stick it in a drawer and not look at it again. I'm happy to be the point person with the cops on this, and I can keep you abreast as much or as little as you like."

"I need some time to consider it," I say, rising from the table. "Why don't you finish your meal, and I'll check on the guest room."

"Sure, thanks."

For the next few minutes, I concentrate on nothing but mundane tasks: putting a fresh towel in the guest bathroom, turning down the bedspread, opening the window a crack to let fresh air into the room. *Try not to think right now,* I tell myself. *Just put one foot ahead of the other.*

When I return to the kitchen, Logan is at the sink, washing his plate. Another kitchen memory floods my brain: Logan and I had been dating for six months, and one weekend, with both roommates out of town, we had my apartment all to ourselves. Logan made the most perfect coq au vin for dinner on Saturday night.

"God, I could eat this seven days a week," I exclaimed.

"Actually, that can be arranged," he said slyly. "Why don't you move in with me?"

His words were a shock since I'd had no clue he was that invested. It took me only a few seconds to say yes, because by then I'd realized I wanted something beyond a fling with him—and I'd begun to sense he was more than a bad boy.

Unaware of my presence, Logan sets the plate carefully into the rack. Though he's still in good shape, I notice for the first time that his posture isn't what it once was, that his shoulders curl a little. Is it simply from age—or because he hasn't been able to outrun grief as well as he thought he could?

Finished, he turns and finds me in the room. "Will Sebastian mind that I stayed?" he asks.

"Not in the least."

It's a dig of sorts—*Sebastian won't mind because he knows there isn't a chance in the world I'd fall back in your arms.*

"I'll need to get my bag from the car," he says.

"I'll go with you to open the gate."

I grab my phone and jacket, and we walk side by side down the dirt drive. As I deal with the driveway lock, using the flashlight on my phone, I notice Logan glancing up at the sky. The late-afternoon clouds have been chased away, and there's nothing up there now but black sky and endless sprays of bright-white stars.

"Wow," he says. "And is that Orion?"

"Yes, but he's upside down in this part of the world. It still throws me a little."

I swing open the gate.

"You want a lift?" he asks.

"No, I'll walk up behind you."

Back inside, I show him to the guest room, explaining a few details. I realize as I speak that I'm standing an unnatural distance away from him, but I don't have any stage directions for a moment like this one.

After we wish each other an awkward good night and Logan shuts the door behind him, I grab Schmidt's letter from the kitchen and hide it under a stack of books in my office so Maitena won't stumble upon it. Then I move about the house, switching off some of the lights I'd left blazing.

God, what if Sebastian had been home tonight? It would have been awkward for sure, but he would have handled things with total equanimity. Though I would have hated for him to read Schmidt's letter and be exposed to those gruesome details.

We met two and a half years ago at a publishing event in New York, introduced by a former colleague of mine who'd known him for years. Following Mel's death, I'd left my job as executive editor at a small publishing house and worked only freelance from then on, too distraught and shell-shocked to play the corporate game any longer, but I'd finally begun to make a stab at networking again, mainly so my career wouldn't dry up altogether. Though I was fine financially, thanks to the divorce settlement and a decent-size trust left to me by my late parents, I was afraid that if my work evaporated, there would be nothing left to keep me sane.

Our attraction had been close to instant, which stunned me. I was fifty then, and as far as I knew, I was going to spend the rest of my life alone. When we were still speaking a half hour after the colleague walked off, and Sebastian suggested—in that beguiling accent of his—that we grab dinner, I told myself that the only fair thing would have been to hold up a sign that read "Enter at Your Own Risk." But some mix of loneliness, lust, and a creeping desire to return to the land of the living wouldn't let me do it.

That dinner led to another and another, and then several long, wonderful phone conversations after he returned to BA. He seemed worldly and suave, but at the same time down-to-earth and grounded. He'd been a nerd through much of his early life, he told me, and didn't come into his own until his twenties.

"My parents got me a cat when I was three years old, and I called her *Escuela*," he said as way of explanation.

"But that sounds like a lovely name," I'd said.

"It means *school*," he replied, laughing. "That's all I could think of then, wanting to go."

By date four, after a month apart, sex was on the table, of course, and the thought terrified me. I'd already imagined what it would be like to go to bed with him, to re-experience pleasures I'd long given up for dead, but actually doing so seemed like something else entirely.

When I admitted to him that it had been almost six years since I'd made love with anyone, he'd smiled and said, "Well, I look forward to showing you it was worth the wait."

That was enough to convince me. He turned out to be not only a passionate lover but also a very patient, giving one.

After an intense year of long-distance dating, we started discussing the idea of my moving to Buenos Aires. He was deeply in love with me, he said, and though the clearest thought I could allow in my head right then was that I wanted to end the torturous commute between two continents, I soon realized that—against the odds—I was pretty sure I loved him, too.

On one of my visits to Argentina, when we were deciding between me sharing his apartment or us getting our own, he brought me to Uruguay to show me the house his uncle had left him and that he'd just finished renovating.

"What if we live *here*—at least for now?" I'd said as the weekend wound down.

"Are you serious?" he'd asked. "Because nothing could please me more."

I *was* serious. He'd mentioned already that it was easy enough for foreigners to obtain residency. It would be just the two of us in this tranquil place of rolling fields. I'd already known I couldn't pick up where I'd left off in life, that old routines would never offer solace again, but I sensed that living quietly here with such a tender, easygoing man would bring its own kind of comfort.

I wash my face, plug in the night-light in the bathroom, and leave the door to that room ajar. Fear of the dark is something I experienced as a child—an issue my parents thought might have developed after a distant cousin told me a terrifying story about an old woman who lived in attics and crept into bedrooms at night—and though it abated over time, it kicked in again after Mel died. If Sebastian has trouble falling asleep from the faint glow, he's never complained.

It's not until I've slid under the duvet that the night's events really catch up with me, leaving my stomach in painful knots.

I know Logan has meant well: following up with the lawyer, calling the state police, traipsing thousands of miles to break the news to me. But he's a fool if he falls for what Ruck said. What that monster probably wanted, as he lay close to death, was to have us twisting in the wind, desperate to know the truth and never free to move on.

I refuse to let him do that to me.

Chapter 4

When I wake, it's still pitch black outdoors, and though my eyelids are heavy, I can tell right away that I'll never fall back to sleep. Rather than get up, though, I lie in the twisted sheets, letting my thoughts untangle. As memories from last night work their way into my consciousness, I groan into the pillow. My ex-husband here in my home . . . The letter . . . Ruck's appalling lie . . . It all really happened.

But Sebastian will be back today and so will Poco, and Logan will be gone.

Just outside the window nearest me, an owl hoots a couple of times. Then other sounds sneak into the room. Footsteps and clinking, someone moving around the kitchen, it seems. I roll quickly on my side and peer at the clock. It's 6:12, later than I realized.

It must be Logan in there, making himself an espresso before he hits the road. Is he planning to take off without saying goodbye, leaving a note instead? I can't decide whether that behavior would suit me or seriously piss me off.

I struggle out of bed and quickly change into the jeans and turtleneck sweater I tossed onto the armchair last night. Then I pad barefoot to the kitchen. To my shock, it's Maitena who's there, removing something from the oven. Hearing me, she spins around, grasping a baking sheet of freshly made medialunas.

"Ah, Bree, *buen día*," she says.

I wish her a good morning, too, and before I can ask why she's here so early, she mentions that Jorge told her I had a guest, and she wanted to make sure that there was something to serve for breakfast besides yogurt. She says she will make a frittata, too, if I'd like.

I've never had reason to think Maitena's a busybody, but my gut tells me that part of her mission this morning is to get a sense of what I'm up to with my mystery guest, perhaps being protective of Sebastian.

"Gracias, pero no necesita," I explain. I go on to tell her that my friend is leaving shortly, and we will be fine with coffee and the medialunas, which look wonderful, I add. She thanks me, scoots the pastries into a basket, and after placing it on the table, takes her leave through the back door. She probably thinks I was chasing her out, and I am. I don't want her bustling around when I say goodbye to Logan.

As soon as she's gone, I leave the kitchen to finish dressing. While making my way back to my bedroom, I glance down the side corridor that leads to the guest suite. The carved wooden door is still closed, and I don't detect any movement behind it. Logan had said he wanted to get an early start today, but I'm hardly about to poke my head into his room and make sure he's up.

And then, in an instant, it's a Saturday morning eight years ago, just before five thirty, and I'm lurching down a hallway in our New York City loft. Unable to fall back to sleep, I'd gotten up super early for me and was drinking tea in the kitchen when the call came in from a Detective Caputo with the New York State Police. He asked if I was Bree Winter. Caught off guard, I confirmed the fact tentatively, as if I wasn't quite sure, and then he inquired if my husband was available, too.

"What's this about?" I'd asked, overwhelmed with dread.

"We'd like to speak to you and your husband together if that's possible," he'd said.

As I'd started to run, calling out Logan's name, the mug had slipped from my hands and shattered on the floor.

I slide my feet into a pair of loafers and then brush my teeth. My body's still jittery from the news about Ruck, but at the same time I'm groggy, so once I've returned to the kitchen, I make an espresso, then settle into a chair at the table. Maitena's opened a kitchen window, and outside a group of monk parakeets are already chattering among themselves.

"Good morning," Logan says from behind me. I twist around. It's almost as much of a shock to set eyes on him now as it was last night. And just as unsettling.

"Hi . . . Can I make you an espresso?"

"That would be great."

He's wearing his jeans again and a different sweater—a light-yellow crewneck. And though he's left it unzipped, he's already got his jacket on.

"Would you like orange juice, too?" I ask as I start to make the espresso.

"No, just coffee's fine."

"And have a medialuna if you want," I say, pointing to the basket. "They're like croissants but doughier."

"Um, sure, thanks."

When I'm done making his drink, I hand him the small cup and saucer, and our hands brush awkwardly. After downing the espresso in three sips, he helps himself to a medialuna.

"I guess I'll be off, then," he says, sticking the pastry in his jacket pocket. "Thanks for putting me up. I really appreciate it."

"Well, I appreciate you sharing the news in person. Look, I know Ruck was lying, but I want to stay in the loop on this, so can you give me updates? Email's fine."

"Will do. And you'll send me some of Mel's poems before the weekend?"

"Yes."

He goes to speak, hesitates, then starts again.

"It's been good to see you, Bree. And—I like your hair. It's so different than when I saw you last, but it looks great."

It had been long during our marriage, past my shoulders. After Mel died, I barely touched it and sometimes went for days without shampooing, let alone using a hairbrush. It was so good not to think about it, but in time I came to see that my haggard look only increased the amount of pity people projected toward me. I finally started paying attention again, and four years ago, I had it cut much shorter and styled. At the same time, I resumed the blond highlights I'd gotten in the past.

"Thank you."

And then, minutes later, he's pulling away. Jorge has already opened the gate, so I simply watch from the portico as the small Chinese-made rental car bumps down the long dirt driveway. Finally, all I see is the cloud of dust the car has left in its wake.

I *do* appreciate him sharing the news about the letter in person. But at the same time, I pray his presence hasn't tainted the place that's brought me so much peace.

Sebastian calls a short time later from the BA airport and then again after he's landed and made his way through immigration. He's phoned the vet, as he promised he would, and since Poco is ready to come home, he mentions he'll pick him up on the way. I don't say anything about Logan yet. I want to do that in person.

After the call, I change out of jeans into flowy pants and a V-neck sweater. When the two finally arrive, Poco bolts through the door first, giving me the cold shoulder. It seems obvious that he's blaming me entirely for the induced vomiting.

My partner, on the other hand, drops his bag, takes me in his arms, and kisses me hungrily. Though I feel a tingle of desire the moment his lips press against mine, it's also relief that rushes through me. Maybe before long, last night will seem like nothing more than a strange aberration.

Bas steps back finally, sliding his hands down my arms until his fingers are entwined with mine. He smiles.

"If you've worn this fetching sweater to remind me of what I've been missing, it was totally unnecessary," he says. "By the way, my parents send their love. They said I'm not allowed to come home again unless you agree to come, too."

"Oh, that's so sweet of them," I say. "You can tell them it's a deal."

"Good. I'm dying to catch up, but I'd like to take a quick shower first."

"Do you want lunch when you're done? There's a plate for you in the fridge."

"Maybe later. For now, I'll probably just have some maté."

"Let me fix it for you," I say, smiling. As Sebastian heads to the bedroom, Poco trots after him. "And can you please have a talk with your dog and ask him to let me off the hook?"

He glances over his shoulder at me, chuckling. "I'll do my best, but you know how stubborn he is."

In the kitchen I heat up the water and use it to make the maté, a caffeine-intense herbal beverage that some Argentines and Uruguayans drink all day long. Since I've never acquired a taste, I make black tea for myself. It's cooler today than it was yesterday, so I carry a tray with our drinks to the coffee table in the great room instead of the galería.

Minutes later, Sebastian reappears, his graying-black hair still tousled and damp from the shower. He plops down beside me and stretches his long, slim legs out on the coffee table. The house feels *right* again.

"I assume no news is good news," he says. "Other than what happened to our four-legged roommate."

I'd planned to wait a little bit before bringing up Logan, giving Bas time to decompress from his trip and fill me in more about his visit, but with a question that straightforward, it wouldn't be fair to wait.

Plus, a weird guilt has begun to seep its way through me. There wasn't a single moment last night or this morning when I noticed even a stir of emotion for Logan again, and yet I can't get rid of a slightly tawdry feeling, like I've drunkenly kissed another man behind Sebastian's back.

"Well, actually, there *is* something," I say.

And then I walk him through it—Logan's arrival and the news he shared. Bas's face remains neutral as I speak, but I sense the muscles of his body tensing. Which catches me off guard. I'd somehow pictured him taking the situation more in stride.

"Wow" is all he says when I've finished. "You had no idea he was coming?"

"No, none at all," I say. "Bas, I would have told you if I had."

"Of course. It's just such a surprise, him turning up that way. It must have been very strange for you."

"Yes," I say, feeling my defensiveness recede. "And to be honest, I'm still really rattled by it."

Sebastian narrows his eyes. "Do you think he figured out I was going to be away?"

Another question that throws me slightly for a loop.

"Sweetheart, I never mentioned to anyone you were going to BA, so, *no*, he hadn't a clue you were gone—unless he flew a drone over the property in advance."

He reaches over and gives my hand a squeeze. "I'm sorry to be focusing on the wrong thing, it's just such a shock . . . the business with Ruck. How are you feeling about it?"

This is more the Bas I know. Curious about my reaction to something before even getting all the details.

"Still slightly sick to my stomach," I say. "I've always prayed I'd die without ever hearing his name again."

"Do you think what he said might be true?"

I shake my head. "No, definitely not. The information about the two other missing women *is* true—the police have already unearthed their remains. But the part about Melanie has to be a lie."

"Because . . . ?"

"Because all the evidence says he did it!"

"And he was found guilty, of course."

"Well . . . not specifically for Melanie's death."

"What do you mean?" he asks.

I've shared bits and pieces about the story with Sebastian—you don't start a new relationship and leave out the fact that your daughter was brutally murdered—but I've also stuck with a decision I made from the start not to do a big information dump. Beyond despising the idea of rehashing everything, I worried it would be both a burden to him and weirdly toxic to our relationship. He was better off not knowing every detail, especially the more gruesome ones.

And yet we can't be talking about this now without me offering more. I take a quick sip of tea before continuing.

"He was tried in Plattsburgh, New York, a city about two and a half hours north of where Mel went to school, for the rape and murder of two college students—Sailor Abbott and Amanda Kline. Sailor went missing in early September, right after the school term started, and her body was discovered by hunters in a wooded area a few weeks later. Though the police had DNA from the semen, it didn't match anyone in their system. But they got incredibly lucky with the next murder in the area—in early November. A cop spotted Ruck on the road and thought he looked suspicious, so he decided to tail him for a while and caught him trying to dispose of Amanda's body in the woods along the road. She'd been killed the same way Sailor had, and the police matched Ruck's DNA to Sailor's body."

"How does Melanie fit into this time frame?" Bas asks, his brow furrowed.

"He murdered her in between—in mid-October—when he'd gone to stay with his sister in Cartersville, supposedly to help her pack up her house but probably looking for a fresh killing field. The police had no real suspects initially, though Mel's ex-boyfriend was on their radar for a while. But after Amanda was killed, one of the state police in the

Cartersville area got wind of the cases up north and connected all the dots. We ended up attending parts of the trial."

Bas's expression darkens even more. "Oh, Bree," he says. "It pains me so much to think of you going through this . . . So why was he brought to trial for the two Plattsburgh murders but not for Melanie's?"

I let out an anxious breath, wishing I could table the whole thing, but I'm already in knee-deep.

"The local prosecutor we dealt with felt it was better not to rock the boat. It appeared Ruck tried to assault Mel sexually but wasn't successful, so there was no DNA or, for that matter, any other forensic evidence linking him to the crime. The prosecutor was worried that with only circumstantial evidence, she wouldn't get a conviction, and that might muddy things."

"But the police were positive he'd done it?"

"Completely. Ruck's cell phone proved he was in the area when Mel died, though he'd been smart enough to leave it at his sister's house that night."

I take a few seconds to steel myself.

"Plus," I add, "the MO was the same. Mel was first struck in the head with a heavy object, the same way the other girls were. And the pattern marks on her neck indicated that she'd been repeatedly strangled with the same type of ligature used on the others. A dog leash."

Bas winces. "God, Bree, I'm so sorry. But it sounds like there's little room for doubt that Ruck was the guy."

"Exactly, and yet the New York State Police are looking at the files again, and who knows what will happen from there."

He scoots closer and wraps an arm around me. "Please, how can I help?"

"You already have, just by listening," I say.

He looks off, clearly thinking, and then returns his gaze to me.

"But you're still worried, I can tell. You think that the cops will decide Ruck didn't do it."

With that simple statement of his, something lets go in me. That's exactly what's worrying me, and whatever dread I've felt since Logan's visit isn't going to dissipate simply because he's ridden off in his rental car.

"Yes. And even though I know Ruck did it, if the cops start having doubts about their original theory, those seeds of doubt will soon end up with me. The little bit of closure I've had will be eaten alive. And I'll spend the rest of my life wondering, never knowing for sure."

Sebastian nods and takes a few seconds before speaking again.

"You know what I think, though? I think that the seeds of doubt are already with you."

He's right.

"I can't let them take hold in me, Bas," I say. "I can't."

"What if you call the lawyer yourself?" he asks. "Maybe he has some information that he didn't put in the letter. It could help clarify things, even bring you peace of mind."

The idea of hearing Schmidt's voice again nauseates me, but Bas is right. I need to do it.

And I need to do it now.

Chapter 5

"Thank you," I say, and give his hand a squeeze. "I want to hear more about your dad and your staff meeting, but let me try to reach this lawyer first."

As we rise from the couch, I remind Bas that there's lunch for him in the fridge, but he says he first wants to check something with Jorge. He seems slightly distracted, and I'm left wondering if it's because of the grisly details I shared or the fact that I've kept so much to myself all this time. Or both.

I make my way to my office, a lovely space at the back of the house originally designed as an extra guest bedroom. The two windows look out onto the back of the property, and from here I can see Maitena and Jorge's half dozen cows grazing on the grass.

I grab my phone, tug Schmidt's letter from under the pile of books where I left it, and settle into the old leather armchair. After taking a deep breath, I call the cell number listed on the letter. The call goes straight to voicemail, so I leave a message, asking him to call as soon as possible today.

My gaze drifts to the small bookcase next to the desk and the two framed photographs of Melanie perched on top of it.

One is from the last year of her life, when she was home briefly during the summer, a picture taken clandestinely by me while she was reading in an armchair, her long brunette hair piled on her head in a messy topknot. Though most people who saw her would have pegged her as the "creative" type, she was also strikingly pretty, which in high school had probably kept her from being marginalized.

The other photograph is of Mel at ten. She beams at the camera, holding up a copy of *A Wrinkle in Time*, which we'd just finished reading together.

"Mom, I want to be *Meg*," she'd exclaimed. "More than anything."

Once, during the months after she died, as I wept alone in our loft, I stupidly wondered what it would be like if Mel were only traveling through a tesseract and eventually found her way back to us.

Seconds later, as I'm about to return to the great room, Schmidt calls.

"I know you spoke to Logan," I tell him after a perfunctory hello, "but I wanted the chance to talk to you as well."

"Of course, not a problem," he says. "I have to jump on another call in . . . in ten minutes or so, but I'm free to chat until then."

I snicker to myself over his word choice. *Chat.* Is that really how he'd describe a discussion about Calvin Ruck?

Plus, hearing his voice again has rocked me more than I expected. Despite how many years have passed, it's so familiar—both the slightly distinctive cadence and the forced deep tone, his clear attempt to disguise a slightly higher-than-normal pitch. I used to wonder why he'd chosen to be a litigator since it meant working so hard each time he opened his mouth in court.

"Needless to say, I've read your letter," I say. "Are there any updates I should be aware of?"

"Not really from my end, though as you probably heard, the police in Ohio and Pennsylvania have recovered the remains of the two other women Ruck claimed he killed. And I'm sure your husband told you that Ruck passed away not long after I met with him."

"He told me, yes." I'm about to correct the *husband* mistake but catch myself. Why should I advertise the extent of my losses to Schmidt, of all people?

"From what I hear, a distant relative arranged to have the body cremated," he adds.

If only Ruck had been alive for that experience. But he was never going to get his due, even with two consecutive life sentences.

"And what about Ruck's claim regarding my daughter?" I say. "What are your thoughts on that?"

"Gosh, I know it's probably thrown everything into a horrible tailspin for you and your husband, but I've come to assume it's true."

"*Really?* You don't think he was just pulling your leg?"

Silence.

"I did initially," he says after a few beats. "He always seemed to get off on messing with people's heads, especially the cops'. But based on the veracity of what he divulged about the two missing women, and the fact that he finally copped to the Plattsburgh murders, I'd say he probably *wasn't* pulling my leg—or anyone else's."

"Oh, so he summoned you purely to clear his conscience," I say with as much sarcasm as I can manage. "He wanted to confess his sins and also give a heads-up that Mel's killer was never apprehended."

I hear him clear his throat.

"I don't believe Calvin Ruck had a conscience. No, in my opinion, this was all about ego."

I feel my frustration mounting.

"What are you talking about?"

"I hate putting it this way—especially to you—but Ruck seemed to have a horrifying pride in what he'd done. In his handiwork, if you will. He wanted credit where it was due and not where it wasn't."

I can't stay on a minute longer.

"Thank you for your time," I say. "Good day."

I end the call without giving him a chance to say goodbye. My hands are trembling, not only from talking so much about Ruck but also from the last thing Schmidt said, that Ruck wouldn't want credit for an atrocity that wasn't his own.

So what am I supposed to do with all this? Just bide my time at the chacra as things unfold—even un*ravel*—over five thousand miles north?

I force myself from the armchair, take a seat at the desk, and open my laptop. I promised Logan I'd select some of Mel's poems for the program, and I decide to do it now and take my mind off the call with Schmidt.

I don't have a lot of her work, just one short story, a ten-minute play, and about twenty haikus, several of which were published in the campus literary magazine, *The Muse*, which Mel became editor of during her sophomore year. Logan and I found printouts of the others in a file on her desk—in the off-campus apartment where she was living at the time of her death.

I know all the haikus by heart and, as crazy as it sounds, the play, too. I've reread the poems countless times and *studied* them, not only in the hope of understanding the full meaning of her words but also understanding Mel as well. I only wish there were more.

Because the thing that I've never shared with Sebastian—and that Logan was always decent enough not to draw attention to—is that Mel and I weren't close when she died. In fact, we weren't close during big chunks of her life.

As much as it hurts to admit that to myself, it's been better to face the truth than let it stalk me during the middle of the night.

Mel had been a difficult baby, crying for hours at a time the way colicky babies do for no apparent reason. Though her pediatrician assured us it would probably pass by the six-week mark, it lasted far longer.

The situation was made worse by my low-grade postpartum depression. I wanted so desperately to be a good mother, and my failure to comfort her left me glum and exhausted. I seemed so klutzy at mothering in general, awkward at handling both her and the endless equipment that came with the job (grade for collapsing a stroller easily: D; grade for strapping on a snuggly: C+; grade for using a breast pump: C-). Once, when she was a few weeks old, I took her to the park, holding her for a while in my arms. As I was struggling to place her back in the stroller, a drunken derelict sitting on another bench yelled out, "Hold her *neck* up." Even he knew what to do better than I did.

The clouds finally lifted when she was about four months. Her colic abated, and I began to find her staring at me in utter fascination with those lovely blue-green eyes, the same shade as Logan's and so much more arresting than my pale-blue ones. At last, we were deliriously in love. And I felt a million times more competent.

But around the age of three, things went to hell again. She developed, of all things, a phobia of buttons. Known as koumpounophobia, it's extremely rare, and, like my childhood fear of the dark, there's not always a clear reason.

The child psychologist we consulted suggested she might have become fearful of swallowing one or worried they were germy, but, regardless, she insisted on wearing only pants and skirts with elasticized waists, pullover tops, and jackets with zippers. She even refused to look at picture books in which buttons were drawn on the characters' clothing (yes to *Goodnight Moon* because you can't see the buttons on the bunny's pajamas, but "No, no, no!" to *Corduroy* because the darn bear was actually *searching* for a button). Her preschool teachers had to work around it, and playdates were loaded with land mines.

That's not to say she couldn't be wonderfully affectionate, but there were other times when she acted sullen and disinterested. I only made it worse by pushing and prodding—"Sweetheart, come sit with Mommy" or "Look what Mommy has for you." The therapist I saw encouraged me to back off a little, and I tried, but it did little good.

And then, when she was around seven, she grew less agitated and seemed to fall in love with me again. She'd become a voracious reader by that point, but also adored being read to, and we spent hours on the couch or in bed devouring children's novels as well as poetry, both the kind of poems that kids her age found fun—like "Paul Revere's Ride"—and more sophisticated fare.

I loved seeing how curious certain poems made her. After we'd read Robert Frost's "Birches" for the first time, she'd wanted to know if *I* had been a swinger of birches as a girl, and did I dream of going back to be one again, like the poet did. ("No, we never had birches in our yard," I told her, "but I so wish we had."). She'd also asked why Frost said life could feel too much like a "pathless wood."

I giddily thought this was it, that we'd found our groove as mother and daughter, but that period was over in five or so years. The teen years arrived—*erupted*, really—and next to them, the button-bashing phase seemed like a breeze. Logan wasn't spared, but I got the brunt of it, with her finding fault over the simplest things I said and did. Once, when I told her, "Have a good day," she responded with, "*Never* tell me what to do."

Things finally started to improve slightly during her sophomore year at Carter, perhaps because she was coming into her own. She was more civil to me suddenly, and when she was home for breaks, she made Logan and me laugh with her wry observations about both campus life and the world at large. She was editing the campus literary magazine, just as I'd done in college, and once or twice, she asked for my opinion. At moments here and there, she even seemed to appreciate me again.

But then, before I could begin to relish the change, she was gone.

Sitting quietly at the desk, I copy four of the haikus and paste them into a fresh document. Then I compose a short email to Logan:

> Not sure how many you have room for in the program, but if it's only one, please let it be this one:
>
> Will you welcome me?
> As I leave a pathless wood
> Returning to birch.

I don't explain why to him, but there's a specific reason for my request. Maybe I've been grasping at straws all these years, but since the haiku—one of those we found on her desk—has a clear reference to the Frost poem Mel and I read so many times together, I've told myself that in the last days of her life, she was hoping for us to really connect like we had when she was a child.

A soft knock at the door tears me from my thoughts.

"Come in," I call out.

I twist around in the desk chair as Sebastian enters the room. He's wearing his brown suede jacket with the sherpa collar and lining, and his cheeks are ruddy from the wind. Though Bas has an MBA and sees himself as both book lover and businessman, he really enjoys working on the property—mowing, doing repairs, tending the vegetable garden, even helping Jorge with his cows and the goats that he and Maitena keep for making cheese to sell.

"You've been outside all this time?" I ask.

"Yeah, walking around with Poco, trying to figure out what he ate out there, but so far, no clue." He smiles. "Though we had a heart-to-heart, and he's assured me he's done blaming you for the stomach purge."

I smile back. "Good, because he's breaking my heart . . . What are you up to now?"

"I thought I'd make a fire and do some paperwork on the couch. Want to join me?"

"Love to."

"Were you able to reach the lawyer?"

I let out a gust of air. "Yeah, just a minute ago."

"And?"

Lifting my head, I raise my eyes to the white plaster ceiling, with its beautiful old wooden beams. I try to gather the thoughts that have been swimming in the back of my mind since Schmidt uttered that grim explanation—about Ruck wanting credit where it was due and not where it wasn't. An explanation that has the horrible ring of truth. It feels suddenly as if I'm standing on a frozen lake and have just heard the faint crack of ice beneath my feet.

"Those seeds of doubt," I say, meeting his eyes again. "They're even bigger now. Because the lawyer doesn't believe Ruck killed Melanie."

"Oh, Bree," he says. "This must be awful for you."

All I can do is nod.

"What will happen from here, do you think?"

"I don't know." I rise from the chair and walk toward the window, staring out without really seeing. "It's possible that when the detective compares all the files, he'll decide Ruck *was* just fucking with his lawyer, and then it's back to case closed. But if things don't sit right with him, I suppose he might reopen the investigation."

"Will Logan keep you informed, at least?"

I spin around.

"Yes, but I can't count on him to play middleman. I need to find out myself what the cops are thinking and make sure this whole thing doesn't go off the rails."

"You're going to call them?"

"No, not call them," I say, feeling a swell of anxiety. Because a decision that's been taking shape since I spoke to Schmidt is now fully formed. "I've got to go back to Cartersville—as soon as possible."

Chapter 6

For a few seconds a weird silence hangs between us, and we stand there awkwardly, like we're ex-lovers who've bumped into each other on a subway platform and don't know which words should follow *hello*.

"That makes sense," Bas finally says. "But would it be best to wait a few days and see how things play out?"

I shake my head. "If I wait, they might decide things without me having any input."

"Right . . ." He looks straight at me, and I see real concern in his dark-brown eyes. "Why don't I go with you, Bree? I can work as easily from the US as I can from here."

His offer is immensely gratifying, especially since he doesn't appear to dread the idea, and yet there are several cons to it.

"That's wonderful of you, Bas, but no, it's too much to ask. The airfare to New York is insane, as you know, and it will be even higher booking at the last minute. I think it's best if I go alone, take care of what needs to be done, and then get out of there as fast as I can."

What I don't say is that I can't bear the thought of dragging him into the gruesome past even more than I've already done this afternoon. And at the end of the day, it'll be better if I'm on my own, able to focus totally on what's at hand.

"You sure?" he asks. "The money doesn't matter to me."

"Thank you, sweetheart, but, yes, I'm sure."

"If you change your mind, even at the last minute, just let me know."

"Will do." I step toward him, and we hug each other tightly. He smells like fresh air and the outdoors.

For a while I read on the couch with Sebastian, trying to find comfort in his presence and the crackle of the fire he's started, but after an hour I grow restless and retreat to my office. Seated at my desk, I book a Sunday-night flight from Montevideo to New York's JFK, with a two-hour layover in São Paulo, the fare as pricey as I expected.

I also reserve a seat on an eleven-o'clock train Monday from Penn Station north to Albany-Rensselaer, and from there it will be a twenty-five-minute cab or Uber ride northwest to Cartersville. With any luck, I won't be completely ragged by the time I show up.

Once I'm done planning the trip, I email Logan the itinerary, saying that I'm coming to the reception next Thursday after all and will arrive a few days early in order to be included in the meeting with Detective Halligan. I also make it clear that, though he's welcome to introduce me at the reception, I don't want to make any remarks.

"Thank you, Bree, that's great," he writes back soon after. "I've just texted Halligan."

I assume that's the end of the thread, but a minute later he writes saying there's an issue he needs to raise. When it seemed like I wouldn't be attending the reception, he'd invited his girlfriend, Lisa, and she's looking forward to it, especially since she helped with some of the paperwork for the scholarships. Is that a problem for me?

I certainly don't love the idea. Not because I'd ever feel jealous—as the other night reinforced for me, my desire for my ex-husband burned off long ago—but being around his girlfriend is bound to be slightly awkward. Still, I'm in a solid, happy relationship of my own, and it seems unfair to make Logan disinvite her.

And at least I have a glimmer of what to expect. I met Lisa once years ago when she briefly worked at his company.

"No, not a problem," I respond.

Before I have time to research hotels, Logan writes yet again to say he's booked me into the Cartersville Arms, a charming inn that I never managed to snag a room at when we visited Mel, and where Logan will be staying as well. I feel a pinch of annoyance—how typical of him to be all in charge. But at least this saves me the effort of searching for a place, and it probably means he'll be picking up the tab, which I won't argue with.

While I'm still at my desk, I take a few minutes to write to the college president, Maya Williams, letting her know I'll be attending the event. When Mel died, she did everything possible to be of help to us, and I'm grateful even now.

For dinner, Sebastian opens a bottle of Tannat—the terrific red wine you find in Uruguay—and I finally get him to elaborate about his visit home. Though it's so good to have him back, and he makes me chuckle with more stories about the dating life of the newly single Manuel, there's a slight stiltedness between us. It's like Logan's still in the house somewhere, casting a pall.

Maybe, I think, Bas is concerned about how much time I'll be forced to spend with my ex. As the meal winds down, I bring up the fact that Lisa will be coming to Cartersville, too, and I sense him relaxing a little.

"You've met her, right?" he says. "What's she like?"

"I didn't meet her long enough to get a real sense, but I know from Logan that she's divorced, no kids, works in the hotel business now. I think she's about forty-five."

"Were they involved when they worked together?"

"No, not then. She left the company a few years before Logan and I broke up, and from what he told me, they ran into each other about a year and a half ago."

Bas presses a hand against his cheek, thinking. "Is there anyone at the reception who can be a kind of wingman for you? Isn't that what you Americans call it?"

"Ah yes, a wingman, that's what I need." My friend Ellie would make the perfect one, and I'm sure she'd be willing to take the train from the city and spend a night upstate with me, but I already know she'll be in the Caribbean next week with her husband on a desperately needed vacation. "Maybe I can use Maya, the college president, that way. She was always very supportive."

I glance across the room, at the fire still going strong in the graystone hearth. In three days, I'll be gone from here, and the thought already fills me with trepidation.

And yet I haven't once second-guessed my decision. Because nothing about this place, including Sebastian, will be able to soothe me anymore if the current situation about Ruck isn't resolved.

"I haven't even asked about your return," Bas says. "I take it you're flying back Friday night?"

I hesitate a few seconds before answering, though I'm not sure why.

"I haven't booked a flight home yet. Logan's arranging for us to meet with the state police before the reception, but there might be ground to cover after that, and I want to keep my plans open for now."

"Makes sense," he says, nodding. But I feel a bit of awkwardness return. Does he have some crazy fear I won't be coming back?

I think that again as we make love later. Since we've been together just two and half years, and much of the first year involved seeing each other only a handful of days a month, sex with Bas still feels excitingly new and erotic, but tonight he brings a different kind of urgency to bed—with how he touches me, pulls me to him, moves inside me.

I do my best to match his urgency with my own. I don't want him worried about my trip and what it means for us.

On Sunday, as Bas drives me to Carrasco, the airport on the outskirts of Montevideo, I rack my brain for some final way to reassure him without coming on too strong or sounding like I'm protesting too much.

"Would you mind watering my herbs when I'm gone?" I ask. "Maitena tends to overwater, so I'd much prefer to have you do it."

"Of course."

"And thank you for being so understanding this week. I know I've seemed preoccupied at times, and anxious, too."

"That's to be expected, Bree. Just promise you'll let me know if there's anything I can do, okay?"

With one hand on the wheel, he reaches over with the other and cups it tenderly around the back of my head.

"For sure," I say. "I miss you already."

And then the airport appears up ahead, the bright interior lights highlighting the wing shape of its iconic white roof. My stomach churns at the sight of it.

The trip north, at least, ends up being wrinkle-free. Since I've booked a business-class ticket, it makes it easier for me to sleep on the second flight, the leg that's nine-plus hours long. As soon as I'm through immigration and customs and have collected my bag, I spot the driver from the car service I've hired, holding an iPad with my name on it.

Still, by the time I finally arrive at Penn Station, I'm frayed around the edges. The train, fortunately, is on time, and I manage to grab a window seat on the west side of the first car I enter, sagging with exhaustion as soon as I'm settled. I use a facial wipe to remove the grungy traces of yesterday's makeup and take a few bites of the sandwich I bought at the station. Ten minutes later, the train starts lumbering along the tracks. I text Sebastian, who I spoke to from JFK, to let him know I'm now on my final leg and will update him again later.

The first minutes of the journey are underground, through the dank, graffiti-covered tunnels beneath the station. But soon enough we're pulling out of the city, and the Hudson River appears on my left, silvery gray and undaunted. I finally relax a little, slightly hypnotized by the way the river water ripples from the wind.

But when the train departs Rhinebeck, New York, an hour and a half later and the conductor announces, "Hudson'll be next," my body begins humming with anxiety—because my stop is soon after that. I check my phone. Logan still hasn't responded to my most recent text, asking for details about our meeting with the state police. Since I've come all this way, it had damn well better happen.

Just as I start to stuff the phone back into my purse, it pings with a text from him.

We're all set with Halligan. Will fill you in when I see you.

Okay, I should be at the inn by 3.

Finally, the conductor announces that we're approaching Albany-Rensselaer. After hauling my bag down from the overhead rack, I rock my way up the aisle to the end of the car and join the crowd of departing passengers.

I feel jittery, even weirdly fearful, and it doesn't help when I step off the train and get my first taste of the local weather. It's about sixty degrees, with a slight bite to the breeze. Though Melanie was murdered in mid-October, the weather is eerily reminiscent of that time. *Lovely*, I think. *Just the fucking welcome I need.*

Before crossing over the track to reach the station house, I fumble for my phone, desperate to order an Uber. To my shock, I hear a man call my name. I lift my head, searching ahead of me.

"Bree," he calls again. "Bree, over here."

Glancing farther to the right, I see Logan standing by the door of the station with one hand raised in greeting. Of *course* he'd show up without telling me.

I offer a tepid wave in return and flick my eyes to the left and right of him, making sure before taking a step that Lisa isn't here, too. Thank God, he's been smart enough not to make her part of the welcome wagon. As soon as I reach him, he leans toward me, obviously planning to kiss my cheek, but I step back a little, adjusting the strap of my purse, so that he can't follow through.

"You didn't have to do this," I say.

"Happy to. I would have let you know, but I was afraid you'd tell me not to."

"Maybe," I say, smiling wanly.

"Plus, I figured you must be fried by this point, and it might help to see a friendly face."

Friendly face. Is that what he considers himself to me? What's he going to do next—suggest he, Lisa, and I meet for cocktails this week? And yet, I can't deny that it's good not to be facing this moment alone.

He takes my roller bag from me and leads me across the parking lot. He's in what I came to know as his typical work outfit: nice jeans, a blue-and-white-striped dress shirt—perfectly pressed—and a navy blazer. His hair is slicked back a little, unlike when I saw him in Uruguay. Logan is at heart a power player, and maybe he feels that's the role he needs to step into this week.

"So, when's the meeting?" I ask as soon as we're in his car. Yup, a black BMW, always his vehicle of choice.

"That's another reason I came to pick you up," he says, firing up the engine. "Halligan can meet today, so once I saw your train was on time, I suggested thirty minutes from now. You okay with that?"

"Sure," I say, though I grumble internally. I'm grungy and sweaty and wearing the same underwear that I put on yesterday morning. But I can't let that get in the way.

"I could ask him to postpone it until tomorrow or at least until later today, when you've had time to freshen up at the inn."

"Really, I'm fine."

I give Logan a minute to maneuver out of the parking lot before lobbing my next question at him.

"So, what's he going to cover today, do you have any idea?"

"I don't know the full agenda, but he mentioned he'd talked to law enforcement in Pennsylvania and Ohio, so that'll be part of it."

Logan is speaking matter-of-factly enough, but even after all these years, I can detect the undertone of worry in his voice.

"Did something he said concern you?"

"Not something he said. It was *how* he said it. I got the feeling that whatever he has to report, we're not going to like it."

Chapter 7

"Not like it how?" I demand. I've been here ten minutes, and I already hate how things are going.

"I don't know. We'll just have to wait till we get there."

I take a couple of long deep breaths, the kind that are supposed to calm you but have never really worked for me.

We're quiet for the next few minutes as Logan zigzags along the charmless streets of Rensselaer. We reach the highway, and as soon as he's merged into traffic, he clears his throat and briefly glances over at me.

"There's something else I need to talk to you about," he says. "Maya is hosting a thank-you dinner for us at the president's house tomorrow night. Nothing fancy, she assured me, and only about a dozen people, including a few English professors and the head of donor relations. Of course, if you aren't up for it, I'm sure she'd understand."

"You're just mentioning this now, Logan?" I say, not bothering to keep the annoyance out of my voice. I've packed only one fancy dress, for the reception on Thursday. Beyond that, I don't need him looking out for me, wondering if I can handle something.

"I didn't know myself until late yesterday. She had a prior event on her schedule, but once she heard you were coming, she decided to cancel it so she could do this instead."

The idea of being there has zero appeal—it's going to be tough enough to be at the reception. But not attending would be rude, especially after Maya's gone to the trouble. And if the cops reopen the investigation, we might need her support.

"I'd like to go."

"I'll let her office know . . . By the way, I haven't breathed a word yet to Maya about what's going on with the police. If and when there's something more definitive, I'll bring her up to speed."

"Do you think it's started to leak out?"

"Not yet, apparently, but Halligan said a reporter has been snooping around."

"That's not necessarily a bad thing, right?" I say. "If it's out in the open, the police will probably be less tempted to sit on things."

"Exactly."

After flipping down the visor, I dig a tube of stick foundation from my purse along with blush and lipstick. It's not about glamming myself up for the cops but just looking pulled together. What I always told myself in the past was that the more presentable you look in discussions with the authorities, the more seriously they take you. I guess the jury is out on whether that did any good.

I'm just swiping on lipstick when I catch myself. During our marriage I fixed my face in front of Logan countless times—using visor mirrors in a pinch and even restaurant cutlery on occasion—but it's the kind of familiar behavior that's ceased to be appropriate. I'm not Logan's wife, and I'm not even his friend. I can't make him understand that if I ignore boundaries myself.

With the makeup back in my purse, I stare out the window. Based on my mental calculation, state police headquarters is a twenty-five-minute drive from here, and though I've never come at it from this direction, the terrain is vaguely familiar. We're off the highway now and on a regular road, passing clapboard houses, their yards still muddy from the winter; shabby bars; gas stations; and local businesses with garish signs in red, blue, and black. Within seconds I realize my eyes are too heavy to keep open a second more, and I feel my head loll toward the window.

When I stir awake, I see we're pulling into a large parking lot in front of a one-story brick building I don't recognize.

"Wait," I say, "where are we?"

"Oh right, you wouldn't know. They built a new headquarters a few years ago, about a mile from the other one."

Good, I think. I won't have to sit in one of the same airless interview rooms I was trapped in before, forced to relive my past in the exact setting. Now, if only Cartersville and Carter College could be transformed into places unrecognizable to me.

We emerge from the car and cross the lot side by side, though I'm dragging a little and sense that Logan is itching to move faster. The only person in the lobby when we enter is a middle-aged female receptionist. As we approach the glass window she's sitting behind, she raises her head from some paperwork, trains her gaze at Logan, and offers a polite smile.

"Logan Chase and Bree Winter for Detective Halligan," he says. "We're a little early for our appointment, but hopefully he can see us as soon as possible."

He's all Logan Chase in Charge right now, more the Logan I remember than the subdued version who showed up at my door in the dark last week.

"Please have a seat," the woman says, "and I'll let him know you're here."

We do as she says, settling into two straight-backed chairs in the silent windowless room. About five minutes later, the double doors in front of us swing open, and a man in a brown suit heads in our direction, his lace-up shoes squeaking a little on the artificial-tile floor. It's Halligan, obviously, but I'm surprised by how unfamiliar he looks to me. I guess since Caputo was the lead detective originally, my attention was focused mostly on him back then, the only man who mattered in my mind.

"Logan, Bree, thanks for coming in," Halligan says as we rise and step forward. He shakes my hand, then Logan's.

Had he called us by our first names before? Perhaps toward the end of our experience with him.

"Thanks for being flexible about the meeting time," Logan says. "Bree's barely off the plane from South America, but like me, she's very happy you can see us now."

"Let's get started, then."

Halligan uses a fob to click open the doors he came through and leads us down a long corridor to a small, nondescript interview room. He motions for us to sit on the side of the table nearest the door, across from a spot where there's already a stuffed manila folder. After asking whether we'd like water, which we both decline, he takes his seat.

Inside my purse are a small pad and pen, two things I tend to carry out of habit as an editor, and I briefly wonder if I should fish them out and take notes. But no, I can't do that, can't have the words that will surface today jostling around in my purse. I'll just have to listen carefully.

There's something I *will* do today, however, as well as during the days ahead, and that's assert myself. Eight years ago, I was so distraught and needy that I tended to go with the horrible flow, rarely challenging what we were told. One of the therapists I later saw told me that though "fight, flight, and freeze" are the stress responses we hear the most about, there's a fourth one called *fawn*. It's when you end up over-agreeing with those around you and/or trying to cope by being way too helpful or solicitous.

I was a fawner back then, but I have no intention of being one now.

"First let me start by saying how much I empathize with both of you," Halligan says. "This is an upsetting turn of events for all of us."

He smiles sympathetically. Though I think he's heavier than he used to be, and the mustache might be new, he's beginning to seem more familiar—the light-brown eyes, Roman nose, and faint acne scars along his cheeks. He had a kind of hyper, eager-beaver manner back then, which I'd sensed reflected a desire to look good to his boss, Caputo, but he's clearly gained confidence in the ensuing years and seems at home in his skin. Good. That's what we need.

"We appreciate that," Logan tells him. "And we're eager to hear whatever you've learned."

"It's been a busy week and a half," Halligan says, opening the folder while moving his gaze back and forth between us. "I've spoken multiple times to investigators in both Pennsylvania and Ohio and also touched base with one of the detectives we dealt with in Plattsburgh. And I've gone back over our own files as well."

Please, I think, *just tell us.*

"And?" Logan says as if reading my thoughts.

"Why don't I lay out what I learned, and then we can discuss the possible implications. What you need to bear in mind is that we're working with a lot more information now that there are two additional cases in the mix."

There's an ominous undertone to his words. *More information.* If it were more information in our favor, he'd probably be saying so upfront. I squeeze my hands into fists in my lap, urging myself again not to get ahead of things.

"Based on the directions Ruck gave," Halligan continues, "the police in both states had little trouble finding the remains of the two college students he killed. The body of Jessica Lombardo, the Ohio girl, was buried under leaves and dirt in some thick woods about two miles from the highway, and the girl from Pennsylvania, Rachel Mullen, was also found in a wooded area."

He pauses and plucks two pieces of paper from his folder and then, after turning them around, slides them across the table toward us. They are photocopies of the "Missing" poster created for each girl a decade ago. I wince at the sight of the photos on them. Jessica is brunette and Rachel, very blond. They're both pretty and friendly looking and seem full of life. Ready to take on the world.

"They were each killed in the same way," Halligan continues. "Struck on the back of the head with some kind of blunt object and then strangled."

"Jesus," Logan exclaims. "They were able to tell that after all this time?"

"Yes, with the help of both a pathologist and a forensic anthropologist, who examined the skeletal remains. In each instance there was a small linear fracture in the skull from the blow, as well as a fracture of the hyoid bone in the throat, caused by strangulation. Since the skull fracture in each case was not catastrophic and probably didn't result in the crushing of any brain tissue, it indicates that the victims must have been struck first, probably to incapacitate them, and strangled to death afterward."

I get a taste of bile in my throat and wish I'd accepted the offer for water.

"So, Ruck had the same MO right from the start," I say.

Halligan nods. "Yes, it appears that way."

"Can they tell what type of ligature was used?" Logan asks. "I mean, was it a dog leash?"

When I glance his way, I see that his face has gone slightly gray. Underneath that confident demeanor, he must be as distressed as I am to be covering this ground again.

Halligan shakes his head. "Since there was no tissue remaining in either case, it was impossible to make that determination."

"But there's no reason to think it *wasn't* a leash?" Logan says.

"That's right."

"So even without the leash marks, there are strong consistencies among all five crimes," he says.

Crinkles form in Halligan's forehead. "Yes and no. There are a couple of similarities among the two newer cases and the two in Plattsburgh that aren't there in Melanie's case."

Okay, here it comes, just what I was dreading. Out of the corner of my eye, I see Logan shift anxiously in his seat.

"The first has to do with the location of the bodies," Halligan continues. "What we've learned in law enforcement over many years is that some serial sexual murderers take pains to conceal the bodies of their victims in a so-called organized way, and others simply leave them at the crime scene, and they stick with one approach or another, rarely varying it. As I'm sure you recall, Sailor Abbott's body was discovered in a wooded area a few days after she disappeared. And Ruck was apprehended hiding Amanda Kline's body in woods north of Plattsburgh. But there appeared to be no attempt to dispose of Melanie's body."

"That never bothered you eight years ago," I say and quickly warn myself to tone it down. The goal here is to be less fawning, not hostile.

"And it wasn't a concern for good reason," Logan says. "It always seemed that Ruck got spooked somehow that night and didn't finish what he set out to do."

"Yes, that's still a possible scenario," Halligan says. "But I want us to factor it in now that we have something else to consider."

"Well, let's hear it," Logan says. He's letting his agitation show, but I can hardly blame him.

Halligan turns over the page he's been glancing at and picks up the sheet underneath it. "As I mentioned a minute ago, forensic anthropologists were brought in to examine the remains in both Ohio and Pennsylvania. In the end, a forensic odontologist was also consulted."

"An *odontologist*?" Logan says.

"It's a specially trained dentist that police sometimes rely on during an investigation. They can help identify a deceased person from dental work when the body is badly decomposed, and in certain cases, they're asked to examine bite marks on victims. What they found in each of these two new cases is a bite mark on the victims' right index finger."

The bile is back, nearly making me gag.

"A *bite* mark?" Logan exclaims. "They think the fucking bastard *bit* them?"

"Yes. It might have been in a frenzy, but since it was on the same finger in each case, we're thinking it could be some kind of signature. As we touched on in the past, serial murderers often leave those."

"But couldn't those marks have been made by animals?" I say. "The bodies were in the woods for years."

"From what the odontologist concluded, the marks were from human teeth," Halligan explains. "So, as soon as I heard this, I requested a fresh look at the Plattsburgh autopsy report and photos. And lo and behold, there were similar bite marks."

We stare at him, now waiting for the other shoe to drop.

"Then we took another look at Melanie's file," he adds. "There were no bite wounds on any of her fingers."

Chapter 8

The winter I was a freshman in college, burning the candle at both ends so I could make the dean's list but also help edit the literary magazine and play intramural volleyball, I developed a case of bronchitis so bad that it landed me the infirmary for four days straight. On the second night I was there, alone in a room for two, I found myself suddenly floating above the bed and staring at my body from a place just beneath the ceiling. The girl I was looking at—*me*—was face down in her pajamas with one leg dangling over the side of the mattress.

And then seconds later, the whole bizarre thing ended. I read later that out-of-body experiences aren't uncommon when you're young and/or ill, though at the time the episode so alarmed me that I told no one about it and just prayed there'd never be a second time.

But right now, here in the police station, it feels like it's happening again. I'm staring down from someplace above, watching Logan's stricken face and hearing Detective Halligan talk about bones and teeth and bite marks in terms of our vibrant, talented daughter, the girl who wrote about birches and will never set eyes on one again.

And then I'm dropping back into my chair with a thud I can almost hear.

"Wait, can you go back a sec," I say, interrupting a question Logan has begun to ask. "Why didn't they notice the bite marks on Amanda and Sailor at the time?"

"They *were* noticed in one instance, but thought to be a defensive wound, not a signature left by the killer. But it's now clear the marks we see in the autopsy photos of both women are almost identical to the ones on the two other victims. And as I said, there was nothing like that on any of Melanie's fingers."

"But as Logan just mentioned," I say, "it always looked like Ruck had been interrupted in Cartersville—by a noise or some person coming along." I take a breath, knowing what I'm about to say next. "That's why Mel was never raped."

Halligan nods. "Yes, that might be what happened. But I wanted you to be aware of where things stand at this point. There are four cases with a couple of similarities that are missing in Melanie's case. I think we need to at least consider that Ruck might have been telling his lawyer the truth."

I look off, shaking my head in frustration. Ruck must be laughing in his grave at the sight of Logan and me right now, the two of us sitting here with hapless, bewildered expressions. This is exactly what he wanted, isn't it? To throw us into a nightmarish tailspin. But it's not going to do me any good to lose my cool.

"Please don't get me wrong," I say, returning my gaze to Halligan. "We appreciate the effort you've put into this. But can we please step back for a second and make sure that despite the discrepancies, we're not losing sight of what's most important—the similarities that *do* exist. All the victims were pretty, long-haired college students who were first struck in the head and then strangled. Doesn't that say a huge amount?"

"That definitely adds up to something," Halligan concedes. "But in police work, discrepancies can be just as significant, and we shouldn't ignore them."

This time I can't help myself—I let out a groan of frustration. Halligan doesn't want to commit one way or the other, and we're just stuck, suspended in time.

"So, what's the plan, then?" Logan says. "Are you going to reopen the case?"

"For starters, I've made arrangements to speak to a behavioral analyst with the FBI—someone who does profiling—and get her opinion on how significant the discrepancies are," Halligan says. "Then we'll take it from there."

He glances at his watch. "I hate to rush you out of here, but there's another meeting I need to attend. I'll get back to you as soon as I've learned anything from the analyst."

And then suddenly we're being ushered out of the room and down the long hall to the lobby.

"Are you okay?" Logan says as soon as we're in the car.

"Barely. I can't believe this."

"Me either. That we had to sit there forced to wonder if Ruck isn't to blame because there were no fucking bite marks on Mel's hand."

"And now everything's up in the air again. There might even be a new investigation."

Logan swivels in his seat to get a better look at me. "But if Ruck *didn't* do it, don't we want to know that?"

"Of course I'd want to know," I snap. "How can you possibly think otherwise? But I abhor the idea of starting all over again, wondering who really did it and why—and whether he'll ever be caught. Frankly, I'm not sure I'd survive not knowing."

I sound, I realize, like a whiny, overtired toddler, and I've left Logan speechless.

"I'm sorry," I say. "I shouldn't have bitten your head off. I'm just exhausted from the trip."

"Don't worry about it." He reaches out to touch my shoulder, but I shrug out of his grasp.

"Please, can we just get to the inn?" I say. "I'm too exhausted to talk anymore."

He nods and fires up the engine, exits the parking lot. For the rest of the drive, he keeps his eyes on the road, and I lean against the window, staring out but barely seeing what flashes by me. When we pull into the parking lot of the inn, it takes me a few seconds to realize we're finally here. I'm only a few blocks from campus now, I realize, and though I'm not looking forward to being back there, I've already steeled myself for that experience.

The place I won't be going near is Pebble Creek Park. Fortunately, it's a mile and a half away in the opposite direction from the college.

I shove myself out of the front seat and walk back to the trunk, where Logan's now removing my bags. He hands me the tote I brought but takes the roller bag himself.

"Where's Lisa at the moment?" I ask, hoping not to make the day any worse with an encounter. I've accepted she has a right to be here, but she's going to be a sad reminder of all that's been lost for me.

"Still in the city. She's driving up tomorrow morning."

We reach the front and enter the wood-paneled lobby, where the brass light scones have already been turned on for the evening. There's just one person at the small reception desk, an older woman with bright-white hair, now finishing a phone call. After disconnecting, she smiles and wishes us good afternoon.

"Shelly, this is Bree Winter," Logan says. "I reconfirmed her reservation yesterday."

I don't know how much more of Logan Chase in Charge I can tolerate, but as I'm about to insert myself into the exchange, I realize what's going on. He wants to make sure there's no confusion about me and Lisa, that I'm being positioned as a friend, with separate accommodations.

"Oh yes, we've been expecting you, Ms. Winter," the woman says with friendly efficiency.

After I've registered, she explains that breakfast is the only meal served in the dining room, but small plates of food can be ordered through room service.

I reach out for the roller bag and grab the handle.

"You sure you don't need any help?" Logan asks as we make our way to the elevator.

"None, thank you," I say, hopefully signaling that I prefer to be left to my own devices when we're not dealing with the cops or the college. It's possible he was going to suggest we grab an early dinner together, but one meal with him this month seems like more than enough. In fact, it probably would have been better to opt for another hotel, where we'd have less of a chance for interaction. Right now, I'd happily trade this lovely inn for a tedious, historically insignificant room at the nearest Embassy Suites.

As we step into the elevator, I'm glad to see Logan press the button for the fourth floor. I'm on three.

"Please text me the details about the dinner tomorrow night," I say as I disembark, barely looking at him. "And let me know if you hear anything at all from Halligan."

"Will do."

I regret my tone and attitude as soon as the elevator door closes, and I start to trudge down the hall, dragging the roller bag behind me. Though I don't want shoulder squeezes and bellhop service from Logan, he's only trying to be helpful. Plus, it's essential we stay in sync this week—so the cops see us as a united front.

At a glance, my room seems charming, but I give myself little time to take it in. After hoisting my bag onto the luggage rack, I hang up the dress, skirts, and two blouses I've brought with me, pee, then collapse onto the bed. I'm so dead tired that when I fall asleep, it feels like I'm blacking out.

For a few long seconds after I wake, I have no memory of where I am, though I can tell from the light outside that it must be dusk. My head is throbbing, like someone's tried to crush it with a car tire. Stretching out an arm, I pat around next to me, searching, I guess, for Sebastian.

Then, with a pang, I remember: *Cartersville*. And I'm alone. I know it's best that I made the trip on my own, but right now I wish Bas was stirring awake beside me, reaching out to stroke my face.

I force myself up onto an elbow and fumble until I've found the switch on the bedside lamp. The room, once I finally absorb it, is indeed charming. The wallpaper, floor-length curtains, bed runner, and shams have been done in a pretty light-green and white toile. There's a desk of dark wood against one wall and a stuffed armchair, also in the toile, by the window. I see why people love this inn—at least people whose daughters haven't been murdered not far from here.

I check my watch. It's a few minutes after six. I've slept for over an hour, which I pray doesn't mean I'll have trouble falling asleep tonight. After firing up the shower and stripping off my clothes, I search around the top of the credenza for the menu of small plates the woman at reception referred to. Part of the reason for my headache, I assume, is that I haven't eaten in hours.

It turns out there aren't many options, so I settle on the plate of Brie, grapes, and olives. I call down to reception to ask about having my order sent up in fifteen minutes. I'm pretty sure it's Shelly on the other end of the line.

"I'd be glad to do that, but you're also welcome to enjoy it in the parlor," she tells me. "It's not a busy week for us, and you'll probably have the room to yourself."

"Great, I'll eat there, then," I say. "And can I please get a glass of red wine as well?"

"Yes, we have an honesty bar in the parlor. Help yourself to whatever you like and simply sign the book."

Once I've showered, I dress quickly in fresh jeans and a navy turtleneck sweater, partially dry my hair, and pull it still damp into a short ponytail. As soon as I enter the empty parlor, Shelly comes up from behind me with the plate of food, utensils, and a basket of bread and crackers, which she sets on a coffee table. Next, I turn my attention to the built-in bar. There's a bottle of Bordeaux already opened, and after signing the log, I pour myself a glass.

Finally, I settle on the couch with my meal. Between bites of bread and cheese, I text Sebastian—who's an hour ahead of me—telling him I'm at the hotel, miss him already, and will call tomorrow morning when I'm not so drained. He's probably sitting by the fire right now, reading or working on his laptop. This is the first time I've ever been away from the chacra without him for more than a couple of hours. Does it feel as weird—and lonely—for him as it does for me?

Next, I email Jeffrey Handler, a former professor of Melanie's who's also chairman of the English department—as well as a published poet—to confirm our appointment for tomorrow morning. As I was looking through Mel's writing the other day and wishing yet again I had more of it, I wondered if there was any chance I could access additional poems or stories—old classwork of hers—through the school, something I hadn't thought to do during the years my brain was so addled. Recently an old friend I'm still in a bit of contact with mentioned that the college her youngest child attends stores student classwork on an archive service called Blackboard, and after checking online, I discovered that Carter College uses that, too, and probably even did when Mel was there.

I've just finished the email when my phone pings with a return text from Sebastian.

> Missing you, my love. Stay strong + call if you need me, no matter when.

I could call him *now* actually. But despite the glass of wine I've drunk and how eager I am to hear his voice, I'm still too churned up for conversation tonight, for going over the ground that was covered today with Halligan and the horrible fact that the truth might now be up for grabs.

Tomorrow will be better, when I have my bearings back.

And then what happens from there? If the cops end up with serious doubts about Ruck, it will not only crush me emotionally, but it's bound to also shape-shift my relationship with Sebastian. How's Bas going to react when he meets a different version of me, someone tortured by uncertainty and perhaps even slightly unglued by it?

In one sense, I'm being silly. When you're in relationship, you're supposed to share the bad stuff that happens and let the other person have your back. But as the demise of my former marriage made clear, bad stuff shared can wreck things rather than make them better. I can't let that happen to Sebastian and me.

And then suddenly a new thought strikes me. I'm making this all about *me*. I don't want to have doubts about Ruck because they'll eat away at me, undermining my lovely new life in Uruguay and my relationship with Bas.

I need to think of Mel, however—and about getting justice for her. Which means I have to at least do what Halligan suggested: consider the inconsistencies that turned up. I flew over five thousand miles hoping to reassure myself of Ruck's guilt, but David Schmidt's instincts could be right after all. His chilling words ring in my ears again: Ruck wanted credit only for his own evil handiwork, not for someone else's.

And if Ruck didn't murder Mel, it means someone else did.

The wood floor creaks, and when I glance up, I see Logan standing in the doorway of the parlor. He's wearing a suede jacket over jeans, and since his cheeks are flushed, I assume he's returning rather than leaving. He looks far more tired than he did earlier, as if a whole day and night have passed since I saw him, and he's been up the entire time.

"Good, you got something to eat," he says. He offers a wan smile. "Did you opt for the balsamic-glazed prosciutto and melon or your almost-namesake cheese and fruit?"

"The cheese plate," I say—though what I'm thinking is: *Stop acting concerned about my well-being, about how heavy my bag might be, or how tired or hungry I am. That's not your business anymore.* "Did you go out?"

"Yeah, I thought I'd check out this new farm-to-table restaurant in town—because that's a trend that isn't going anywhere—though by the time I got there, I didn't have much appetite." He takes a few steps into the room, coming closer to me. "That meeting with Halligan really rattled me."

"Which way are you leaning now?" I ask. Maybe this isn't the best time or place for this conversation, but I realize now that I can't put it off.

He massages the back of his neck, drops his arm, then, after a beat, points his chin toward the armchair across from me. "Mind?" he asks.

Good, he's picked up my cues about boundaries and doesn't just assume he can sit.

"No, go ahead," I say.

He closes the gap to the chair and drops down. "It's hard to know what to think when Halligan doesn't seem to have a firm idea himself. What about you? Are you still convinced Ruck was lying?"

I let out a pent-up sigh. "No."

Logan's eyes widen in surprise. "What made you change your mind?"

"I realized I wasn't being fair to Mel. I can't stand the thought of living in a no-man's-land of uncertainty, but I don't want to put blinders on, either. And if I—or both of us—resist the idea that Ruck didn't kill her, it might discourage the cops from doing anything else."

He nods. "Right, that's what I've been worried about, too. So, what do you propose we do?"

"Put pressure on Halligan."

"Pressure to keep his foot on the gas?"

"More than that. Pressure to start looking for the real killer."

Chapter 9

"Just to be clear," I add, "I'm not convinced Ruck was telling the truth. But I want Halligan to know I'm now seriously considering that possibility—and I want to see what he does about it besides talking to some kind of profiler."

Logan starts to say something, then swivels around in his chair, obviously checking to confirm that we still have the room to ourselves. And we do.

"I'm totally in line with you," he says, turning back around but lowering his voice.

"Meaning you think the killer could still be out there?"

"Yeah, possibly. And what's the worst that could happen if we press for a new investigation? The cops either do enough digging to prove that Ruck really *was* guilty, or they learn it was someone else."

I bet Logan's been thinking this way since we left police headquarters but was tiptoeing around with me, trying to sense where my head was at.

"Since you've had most of the contact with Halligan, can you let him know where we stand?" I ask.

"Yup, first thing tomorrow."

Fatigue is starting to creep up on me again, but there's a question I need to ask so that it won't be throbbing in my head all night like a toothache.

"Do you think we should have pushed harder years ago?" My voice catches as I say it. "And not been so quick to believe it was Ruck once we heard about him?"

Logan shakes his head. "Honestly, no. The MO was the same as the two Plattsburgh cases, and he'd been right here in town when Mel died."

"But it could all be a coincidence, right? A killer who just happened to operate the way Ruck did?"

"If it turns out he didn't do it, then coincidence would be the first explanation . . . Or maybe what you suggested when I was in Uruguay—a copycat. I don't think it's likely, but it might be time to consider that, too."

He clearly misunderstood me last week.

"I brought up the word *copycat* because I wondered if *you* were thinking that way, not because I was. I'm still not. As you said, only Sailor was dead by the time Mel was killed, and no one was talking about that case yet. How would a killer have known what to copy?"

"Right, of course. It's too far-fetched."

I've been letting my gaze bounce around a bit, but now I look directly into Logan's eyes. Though his expression gives nothing away, I'm sure he's just jumped to the same thought I have.

"Do you think it was someone Mel knew?" I ask.

He steeples his hands and presses them against his lips, taps a few times, then drops them into his lap.

"You mean like Jack?" he says.

I nod. It makes sense for Jack Lawler's name to cross our minds right now. He was Melanie's boyfriend at the time, or rather, her ex because, as she'd told us without explanation, they'd split soon after the start of the school year. The police talked to him more than once, and he soon became grist for the fast-churning campus rumor mill.

Logan and I felt torn about him at the time. We knew that, statistically, male exes kill their former girlfriends and wives in not-small numbers, but that's mostly when they're enraged over being dumped, and Jack made it clear to us and others that he was the one who'd broken things off. Plus, he had a decent—though not airtight—alibi for the night of the murder. He'd been on campus, he said, and someone confirmed seeing him fairly close to the window of time when Mel must have been killed.

And then, of course, it all became a moot point when Ruck was arrested in Plattsburgh several weeks later. Jack receded into the background for us, not much more than a blip in Mel's short life.

"Yes, Jack," I say. "His name is bound to surface again, right?"

"I would assume so, though if they reopen this thing, they're also going to be looking at guys with records around here. Sexual predators, Peeping Toms . . ."

In other words, more compelling suspects. Besides his apparent lack of motive, Jack, the self-possessed, slightly broody aspiring actor, hadn't seemed up to such a brutal act of violence.

Though how can you ever be sure of what someone is capable of? Perhaps Jack had suddenly wanted Mel back, but she refused to take him.

Or there'd been someone else with a hatred for our enchanting daughter. We should have asked more questions then.

"I wonder what happened to Jack," I say.

"He's in New York, waiting tables and still trying to make it as an actor."

I pull back in surprise. "How do you—?"

"I spoke to him. He heard about the reception somehow and decided to come."

"*What?*" I exclaim, not only taken aback but annoyed as well. "You're only telling me this now, as I'm bringing up his name?"

"All my focus has been on the meeting today, and he only confirmed late last night. I told him the event was really something for the press and college faculty and staff, not friends and former classmates, but he pushed, so I agreed. I mean, the guy had a few tough weeks back then, everyone whispering behind his back before the cops zeroed in on Ruck."

I sigh, letting my irritation dissipate. "But how do you feel now about him coming—in light of what we've heard today?"

"I think it's a good thing. How he reacts will be telling—and I'll let Halligan know he'll be in the vicinity."

"Okay." I'm not looking forward to setting eyes on Jack again, but Logan's right. Best to keep possible enemies close.

I drain the last of my wine and set the empty glass down. "I think I'm going to read on my phone down here for a little while. It's good for us to be talking about all this, but I'm spent on that front right now."

"Right, right," Logan says, catching the hint and standing up. "Good night, then."

"By the way," I say before he departs, "how did the program for the reception turn out?"

"Very nice. I used all four poems you sent and put the one about birch trees on the front along with Mel's photo."

After he exits the parlor, I read for only a short time, then I leave myself, making my way to the room. While stripping off my clothes, I check the time on the bedside clock. There's a call to the West Coast I've decided to make, but I'll wait until tomorrow—when I've had a chance to think through what to say.

Before crawling between the covers, I turn the bathroom light on and leave the door slightly ajar so there's light streaming into the room. Perhaps with me away, Bas will leave our own bathroom light off tonight. Unexpectedly, desire stirs in me and I find myself longing for his touch.

I sleep fitfully, waking every couple of hours. When the alarm goes off at six thirty, I fight the urge to tap the snooze button and instead force myself out of bed. I'm exhausted still, with despair creeping around the edges, but mostly I feel stuck in this weird state of limbo. Waiting for what Halligan will come back with. Waiting for the reception to happen and then be over. Waiting to fly home.

At least the meeting with Professor Handler will give me something to do.

After dressing, I head down to the dining room for coffee and an omelet. Though there are guests at several other tables, there's no sign of my ex, which I guess is to be expected. Logan, or at least the Logan I once knew, isn't a big breakfast person. Which is good because I need some time away from him.

As soon as I'm back in my room, I call Sebastian. He answers on the first ring.

"Ah, there you are," he says. "I've been dying to talk to you."

"Same here, sweetheart," I reply. A sense of calm comes over me just from hearing his voice.

"Tell me what's happening."

I do a short recap of the meeting with Halligan, sparing him the gory details about stuff like bite marks and crushed brain tissue, and instead focusing on the takeaway: the detective in charge wants us to consider that Ruck wasn't the killer, and that's what we're doing, at least until we know more. I try not to let my angst color the call.

"Wow, it's just what you were worried about," he says. "Are you okay, Bree?"

"Doing my best."

"When do you expect to hear back from this detective?"

"He didn't say, but hopefully we'll learn something more today or tomorrow. How are things there?"

"Quiet. Lonely without you. The guy I talked to about doing a lap pool next spring came by and took some more measurements. And you'll be happy to hear I'm minding your herb pots with complete devotion. It got chilly last night, so I think it might be time to move the basil indoors."

"Good idea. Speaking of basil, maybe I'll try to smuggle in a few balls of buffalo mozzarella on my return flight."

I've yet to locate any in Uruguay, and the kind made from cow's milk there is really bland.

"I wouldn't chance it, cariño," Bas says with a laugh. "Those K9 units might be trained to sniff out cheese along with cash and cocaine . . . Oh shoot, Jorge is honking the horn of his truck. We're headed out to do some errands."

"No problem."

"Let's talk later, though. Love you so much, cariño."

"Love you, too, Bas."

I hang up thinking how close his voice sounded, and yet he also seems oceans away. If I'm lucky, we'll soon hear something firm from Halligan, and I really can fly home on Friday.

It's too early to start out for my meeting with Handler, so I sit for a while, sipping the extra coffee I brought upstairs in a paper cup. I think suddenly of the way my mother loved to relax with her coffee early each morning, resting the mug on the padded arm of the chair in the corner of our pretty kitchen outside Philadelphia. She was gathering her thoughts for the day, she used to say, and as a girl I imagined her scooting them together in a pile like I did with my toys.

There have been countless times since Mel's death when I've wondered achingly what it would be like to have my loving parents around to lean on. My mom was supportive and helpful during Mel's colic phase and the worst years of the button phobia, assuring me it would all get better one day. But my parents died three years apart when I was in my thirties. As much as I've longed for them in the years since, I've been forever grateful that they weren't alive to see what happened to their only grandchild, and to watch how my life fell apart afterward: the broken marriage, the smashed dream of being a star in book publishing, the ever-shrinking circle of friends, to say nothing of the deep depression that enveloped me for close to four years.

Finally, it's time to head to campus, only a few short blocks away. I grab my trench coat and slip out the side entrance of the inn. The first half of the walk goes well enough, but then suddenly the spire of the old campus chapel slides into view, and my heart squeezes.

Part of my anguish comes from being back in a place that Melanie loved and thrived in, that inspired her both intellectually and creatively, a place she never left because she died before graduating. Maybe, I think ruefully, if I walk around long enough, I will bump into her ghost here.

But my distress is also due to my own complicated relationship with the school. It's a beautiful place, a right-out-of-a-movie campus featuring two-hundred-year-old ivy-covered brick buildings set around a perfectly landscaped quad, and though a bunch of modern structures have been added to the campus over time, for the most part, they're both boldly designed and attractive, energizing the environment rather than undermining it. When Mel decided to go here, I fantasized about the moments we'd spend together when Logan and I visited.

I should have known better. During parents' weekend the first autumn, she bristled at several comments I made, slipped out of my grasp when I took her arm—as if mortified by the idea of us touching in public—and widened her eyes disapprovingly at the pencil skirt and silk blouse I wore for the welcoming lunch on the quad. "Mom," she blurted out, "they said *casual*, for God's sake."

Fortunately, parents' weekend was something mostly freshmen and their parents took part in, so there was no reason to attend another. I did drive upstate with Logan in the spring of freshman year and twice when Mel was a sophomore to see her perform in plays, and though she was less dismissive of me by then, it was hard to erase that very first weekend from my memory.

I enter the college through the eastern gate. Spring hasn't fully arrived, and yet the campus looks stunning. The grass on the quad is a bright green, and there are daffodils in the border gardens, shimmying from the breeze. Students are everywhere: dashing down pathways, huddled in clusters, and, despite the slight nip in the air, tossing Frisbees to one another on the quad.

I easily find the humanities building. Though it's far quieter inside than out, I pick up the sound of voices and even laughter from behind classroom doors. Checking the directory on the wall, I see that Handler's office is on the second floor, and it turns out to be at the very end of the hall, beyond a small anteroom with a desk for an assistant, presently unoccupied. Before knocking at his door, I shrug out of my trench coat and hang it on one of the hooks along the wall.

There's no verbal reply to my knock, though I can hear Handler shuffling papers inside and then scooting a desk chair around. At least thirty seconds pass. I've just knocked again when he finally swings the door open.

"Ms. Winter, how nice to meet you," he says formally, extending a hand and offering a careful smile.

I've set eyes on him in person only once before, and that was from a distance at the campus memorial for Mel, though I was already familiar with what he looked like from the photo on one of his poetry collections, which I bought after Mel took her first class with him. He's in his early to mid-sixties now, I'd say. Average weight and about five ten, so only a few inches taller than I am. He has a large, uniquely shaped nose and a high forehead, with his dark-brown hair cut close on the sides, and a tiny bit high on top.

Not classically handsome at all, but still, he's an attractive man in his own distinct way.

"Call me Bree, please," I say. "And thanks for seeing me today. I'm sure this is a busy period for you."

"Well, we're in the last stretch, closing in on exams, but I'm more than happy to make the time." He swings an arm out behind him. "Come in, won't you? And please excuse the clutter. English departments are still a long way from paperless."

He's not being facetious. There are stacks of papers on almost every surface and plenty of books, too. Overall, though, the office is a nice one, with a fetching view of the quad from the window and a large fern in the corner.

I follow him into the room, surprised a little by his choice of wardrobe. I guess in the back of my mind I was expecting something along the lines of a cardigan with elbow patches over a rumpled button-down, but he's in a spiffy navy blazer with windowpane checks over a crisp lavender shirt.

We sit.

"I hear you've traveled all the way from Paraguay," he says. "My goodness, that's a long trip."

"Uruguay, actually, though in the same part of the world."

"Well, it's good of you to come. As you'll hear me say in my remarks Thursday night, we are incredibly grateful to you and Mr. Chase for your very generous gifts."

Since Logan's been insistent about my name being attached to everything, I don't correct him.

"Well, we're grateful for all the school has planned in response. The reception, the outreach to high school students about the scholarships, everything."

He inches a hand across the desk and straightens a pencil.

"It's the least we can do," he says "Melanie, as you're well aware, was a wonderful student and writer. Shakespeare advised that we give sorrow words, which unfortunately is far easier said than done, but let me say that her loss was keenly felt here."

Though his tone has been nothing but polite so far, he seems haughty to me—taking his time to answer the door, dropping the quote from *Macbeth*, the way he keeps his chin slightly elevated.

And there's something else, I realize, something odd. From the moment I've arrived, he's trained his gaze at a spot in the middle of my forehead instead of looking me directly in the eye.

Chapter 10

Am I making him uncomfortable? Perhaps he fears I've come hoping for a pity party about a girl he probably can't even picture anymore.

"I appreciate you saying that," I tell him. "And I won't use up much of your time. I know Melanie studied creative writing with you, and I was hoping you could help me get my hands on her old schoolwork. I already have some of her poems and a couple of longer works, but it occurred to me I might be able to access more through the school."

Handler looks off, tapping his fist to his mouth in thought, then returns his gaze to me—or at least to my forehead. If I didn't know better, I'd think a giant boil had erupted there since I left the inn this morning.

"You mean, do I have copies of the literary magazine from back then?" he asks. "I don't, unfortunately, but surely the library does. I'd be glad to speak to someone and see if there are extras—or at the very least have them photocopy pages for you."

I smile politely. "Thank you, but I already have copies of *The Muse* from the time Mel was here. I'm talking about anything from, let's say, the poetry workshops you taught. I know the college uses Blackboard, and I thought that some of her writing assignments might still be archived online."

For a few seconds his face goes blank, expressionless, like he's been turned to stone by an ancient curse.

"Ah yes, of course," he says finally. "Let me have my assistant investigate and see what we can find . . . Was there anything else I could be of help with?"

"No, that's all, and thank you. See you Thursday night."

"As a matter of fact, you'll see me again today. My wife and I are attending the dinner at President Williams's house in your honor."

"Oh great. See you tonight, then."

He offers a second handshake before I depart.

It's not until I'm outside, feeling the chill in the air, that I realize I've stupidly left my coat behind. I return to the building and make my back to the second floor. As I reach the anteroom, I see that Handler's door is half open now, and I hear the murmur of someone's voice coming from his office. A woman's voice. Almost without thinking, I step closer and peek through the doorway.

Handler is sitting at his desk, and the woman is standing right next to him, rather than on the other side of the desk. She's so close, in fact, that if she reached out a little, she could easily touch the tip of his nose. And she must be a student because she's young, with her hair in a long braid and a backpack slung over her shoulder.

Hearing my footsteps, they both glance over and spot me. Handler's face is a blank, but the girl steps back a foot, appearing flustered.

I grab my coat and hurry off.

A couple of blocks from campus, a coffee shop appears on my right, and I slip inside, taking a seat at a table by the window and ordering a cup of chamomile tea. I'm feeling unsettled, I realize, by my experience with Handler, especially the part involving the young woman by his desk.

Taking a sip of tea, I try to look at the situation from his vantage point. He's forced into an uncomfortable meeting with the mother of a murdered student, so how can I blame him for seeming ill at ease? As for the student, I know kids that age can sometimes act entitled and overly familiar. Maybe the girl was pushing for a higher grade on a paper and inadvertently violated his personal space.

Mel, I know, thought highly of Handler. In her view, he was a talented poet and mesmerizing to listen to, and though he could be demanding in class, he apparently treated students with respect. On warm days he sometimes held class in his backyard, and once or twice his wife had even joined the group. She is, or at least was, an artist of some kind, and she'd contributed thoughtful comments on the similarities between art and poetry.

Mel hadn't told *me* this, of course. I'd overheard her sharing it with Logan.

I chase Handler from my thoughts, finish my tea, and walk briskly back to the inn. It's time to make the phone call to the West Coast, which I need to do from the privacy of my room.

I'm still not in the mood to see Logan, but he's, of course, right there in the lobby when I arrive, standing in line at the desk behind a woman whose long hair has been colored in a blond ombre style. At her feet is a Louis Vuitton duffel bag the size of a wolfhound. She's busy asking Shelly—in a voice too loud for the space—how soon she can get several of the small plates sent to the room.

As I close the door behind me, it makes a thud, and Logan turns around.

"Bree," he says, a little too loudly himself. "There you are."

"I've been at the college. Has something happened?"

"Nothing significant, but I spoke to Halligan, and I wanted to update you."

The semi-blonde has spun around, too, as if we've piqued her curiosity. She's in her mid-forties, I'd guess, and doesn't exactly read as some college student's mom, so she's probably in town for another reason.

Logan crosses his arms, looking suddenly awkward, and takes a step closer to me.

"First, though," he says, "let me introduce you to Lisa."

My lips part in surprise. This woman is *not* Lisa—or at least the person I met years ago. Unless she's decided to color her raven hair and has somehow shaved off several inches of height.

"Bree, hello," she says from the reception desk, and flashes a too-wide smile. "Give me a moment and I'll be right with you."

Clearly, I've been confused all this time, assuming some other woman who once worked for Logan—and whose name started with an *L*—had reentered his life as his latest girlfriend. I take a breath, trying to center myself and manage a smile, but by the time I do, she's already redirected her attention back to Shelly.

I don't want to seem like a bitch, but I also have no intention of standing around the lobby waiting for her to put in a food order. I move past Logan into the parlor, and he follows right behind me. He knows this is slightly uncomfortable, and since he's Logan, the master finesser, I assume he'll make every attempt to smooth things over.

"Sorry this is all happening in public," he says, keeping his voice low.

"Not a problem."

"I did text you this morning and ask you to call me." His tone is apologetic, not accusatory. "I was going to let you know Lisa was here."

"I *said* it's not a problem, Logan. What happened with Halligan?"

"I told him which way we were leaning, and though he seemed receptive, he was noncommittal. Said he's still waiting to hear back from the analyst."

"Did you tell him about Jack?" I ask, dropping my own voice now.

"Yup, and I let him know he'd be in the area this week and worth talking to. All he said to that was *thanks*."

A sense of dismay begins to creep over me.

"Like they're not interested in taking another look at him?" I ask.

Logan shakes his head. "More like he's not going to tell us one way or the other. I think he was being more candid than usual yesterday, and going forward, we're probably going to be on a need-to-know ba—"

"Sorry for the delay." It's Lisa, striding from the lobby in a stylish beige coat and high brown boots, with the Louis Vuitton bag hooked over her left arm. I'm surprised she doesn't have it handcuffed to her wrist.

I warn myself to stop the snide inner critique of her, and more importantly not to be rude. I swivel fully in her direction. Now that I'm closer, I see that her skin is nearly wrinkle-free.

"We were just catching up," Logan overexplains.

"Of course," Lisa says. She thrusts a hand out to me. "Bree, how nice to finally meet you."

I'm still disconcerted by the sight of her. Not only because she isn't the woman I dug from my memory bank, but she's also so different from what I consider to be Logan's type. From what I knew of the women he dated before me, he seemed to favor fairly laid-back, natural-seeming females, a category I thought I fell into myself. Was he always secretly yearning for someone super chic, a woman who wore pricey designer clothes and whose lips were artificially buoyant enough to save her if she found herself shipwrecked on the high seas one day?

I accept the handshake and almost wince at the strength of her grip. It feels like she's trying to crack a lobster claw.

"Thank you, nice to meet you, too," I reply.

"My God, you must be *exhausted*."

"I'm okay, thanks."

"But Logan told me how long the trip is door to door. Like almost twenty-four hours, right?"

"I've made a bunch of trips back and forth, so I'm pretty used to it."

"Well, that's good, then." She rakes a manicured hand through her hair. "I'm hopeless on overnight flights myself. You're in that ridiculously narrow flat bed with people moving up and down the aisle, and I'm lucky if I get an hour's sleep."

"How was your drive from the city?" I say, deciding I need to lob at least one question her way.

"Easy-peasy, thank goodness. As I guess you know, we're in Tribeca, so I just hopped on the West Side Highway and headed north."

Relax, Lisa. There's nothing left between Logan and me, so you don't need to get all territorial.

I'm about to extricate myself from this cringe-worthy encounter, but she ends up making the first move.

"I should go up and get settled," she says, turning to Logan. "And I ordered us a few snacks. They're going to send them up momentarily."

"Right, right," Logan says. "I'll join you in a minute." Though he doesn't look flustered, I know that he is.

"Okay," she says after a brief hesitation. "See you shortly."

She strides away, her two-toned hair swinging behind her.

"Thanks for being gracious about this," Logan says quietly after we've heard the elevator ascend.

I shrug. Part of me resents Logan for creating this situation—couldn't he have just given Lisa a pair of fucking diamond earrings to show his gratitude for her help on the scholarships—but I also feel sorry for him. The dinner tonight and the reception Thursday are a culmination of his yearslong plan to pay tribute to our daughter, to make sure her name lives on, and instead of simply relishing the experience, he's got to navigate having both his ex-wife and current girlfriend on-site with him.

"What we *should* be focusing on right now is Halligan," I tell him. "Making sure he talks to Jack when he's here and also starts thinking about other suspects."

"Absolutely. By the way, I also texted you the details for the dinner tonight. Will you need a lift?"

You mean: Do I want to ride over with you and Lisa?

"No, thanks. And Maya isn't expecting me to say anything tonight, is she?"

Logan shakes his head. "Not unless you want to. I can speak for both of us if you like."

"Yes, please . . . See you later, then."

I take the stairs to my floor, and after peeling off my coat, I sit in the armchair for a couple of minutes, decompressing. Being around Lisa would be far more tolerable if she weren't so irritating.

Finally, I dig my phone from my purse, scroll through my contacts, and tap the number for Harry Kronish. He was one of Melanie's two apartment mates the year she died, and as far as I know, he's still living in San Francisco. He'd been out of town at his family home the Friday night of the murder—her other roommate, Jennifer Choi, had been away as well—but he'd rushed back as soon as he heard the news.

Once the police went through everything in the apartment, Harry joined Logan and me in packing up Mel's belongings, and he also helped us track down extra copies of *The Muse*, which he'd worked on, too. He even wrote to us a few times in the years right afterward. Since last night I've had time to consider what I want to say to Harry, and I'm just hoping that the old number I have for him is still one he uses.

The phone rings and rings, not even going to voicemail. I'm about to hang up when a man answers, though—to my dismay—not one who sounds like the Harry I remember.

"Hello?" he asks, his tone wary.

I tell him who I'm looking for and inquire if this is the right number.

"Yup, but it's a landline, not a cell. And he's at work right now."

I give my name and ask if he'd mind providing Harry's cell number, adding that he used to share an apartment with my daughter.

"Why don't you give me *your* number, and I'll have him get in touch."

I do, half expecting that I might never hear back, but twenty minutes later, Harry calls me.

"Bree, *hi*," he says. "My partner just gave me your message."

His voice sounds deeper, more mature than I remember, and I realize that the image I have of him in my mind—the dark spiky hair, the oversize greatcoat—is probably all wrong now, too.

"Thanks so much for calling back, Harry."

"I'm just happy you got through to me. Though I've had this landline ever since I moved here, I'm finally about to get rid of it."

"How lucky for me, then. Tell me what you're up to these days."

"Still loving the Bay Area. As you might have surmised, I've got a boyfriend with the social skills of a stapler—but otherwise he's a great guy, ridiculously brilliant—and I handle branding and social media for a big apparel company here. Which means I didn't end up becoming the fabulous writer of my dreams, but it's a fun job."

"I'm so glad to hear that, Harry."

And I mean it. I remember him as a warm, funny person who I once imagined being in Mel's life forever.

"What about *you*?" he asks. "I sense something's going on."

"It is. I'm in Cartersville now, and, confidentially, the cops have some doubts now about Melanie's case. They're wondering if someone other than Ruck murdered her."

"What? Oh my God. Do—do they have a new suspect?"

"Not yet. It's possible the police will reach out to you at some point, but in the meantime, I wondered if anyone comes to mind."

"You mean, could it have been someone she *knew*?" he asks.

"There's no suggestion of that right now, but it has to be considered."

While I'm speaking, I fish quickly in my purse for my pen and notepad.

"Wow, off the top of my head, I can't think of anyone," Harry says. "As you know, Mel didn't suffer fools, but people liked her. And though she sometimes got irritated by some of the slackers on the literary magazine or maybe a castmate in one of the plays she did, it never seemed like a major deal."

"What about her personal relationships? Were you ever aware of any conflict?"

"Uh, not that I remember, but, of course, it's been a while. Are you wondering about the romantic front, too?"

As far as Logan and I were aware, there'd been no one since Jack, and we guessed she was still smarting from the breakup, but who knows, maybe something had begun to percolate.

"Right, the romantic front, too."

"There was nothing full-blown as far as I know, but I had the sense she'd started seeing someone new. And that she might have been smitten."

The hairs on the back of my neck have shot up. "We weren't aware of that," I say. "Did you mention this to the police?"

"Yeah, and I figured they'd look into it, but I assumed they lost interest in that angle once they made the arrest."

"She never said a name?"

"No."

"But what made you think there *was* someone?"

"She was walking around with a certain look on her face, like the cat that ate the canary. At first, I thought it was all because of the weather. It had been cold and rainy during the first half of October, and then suddenly there was this beautiful stretch of Indian summer, which put everyone in a good mood. But I finally suspected it was more than that with her. I asked her something like, 'You don't have a new squeeze, do you?' and she laughed and said, 'My lips are sealed.'"

I take a deep breath, jotting down some of his words. I know my daughter was a mystery to me, but it always hurts to be reminded of that.

"So this was right before she died."

"Yeah."

"She must have been over Jack finally," I say.

"Oh, she was *long* over him."

"She wasn't heartbroken anymore?"

"God, no, she was never heartbroken over Jack. Mel dumped *him*, though I know he let everyone think it was the other way around."

Chapter 11

I gasp but hope Harry hasn't heard. I can't let on that I'm suspicious of Jack. After all, there's never been any evidence linking him to the crime.

"Do you think the cops knew that?" I ask.

"You mean that *Mel* ended it? I'm pretty sure I told them when they asked about her love life, and Jen Choi might have, too, but parts of those awful days are such a blur, I don't remember for certain."

"That's understandable, Harry . . . Why did Mel break it off, do you know?" I'm trying to sound casual despite how fast my pulse is racing.

"I think she just lost interest. I remember her saying that once you got beyond the fantastic hair, there wasn't much there. God, remember that hair?"

Yeah, I remember the hair. Thick and shaggy, and the color of burnished gold. I remember the rest, too. When you looked at Jack's features one by one, there was nothing remarkable about any of them—in fact, his eyes were on the smallish side and his jaw too square—but beauty kismet had arranged them together in a truly arresting way. And they were only enhanced by his broody manner and the slightly petulant curl of his lips.

He had the lead role in several campus plays, including one Mel was cast in during the fall of sophomore year. I only learned of the relationship when Logan leaned over to me during the first act and whispered, "The main guy? He and Mel are an item apparently." During intermission he explained that he'd wormed the information out of her when they'd been discussing our plans to drive up from the city for the performance.

I ended up meeting Jack only twice: briefly after that first play, when Mel introduced us outside the theater, and then again the following May, after another campus play they both had roles in. To my shock, she invited him to join us when we went out for coffee later.

"Was he upset about getting dumped?" I ask Harry, still careful with my tone.

"At first, I guess. She said he sulked for a while and badgered her to get back together. But Jack had one of those egos that never lets you categorize yourself in a loser role. According to Mel, he was sure he'd leave college and become the next Robert Pattinson."

I let out a gust of air, processing all I've just learned. *Jack* was the one who'd been kicked to the curb. And though he might have seemed only sulky to Mel, it's possible her decision infuriated him.

"Why are you asking so much about Jack?" Harry asks. "Are you thinking *he* could have done it?"

"Oh no, just putting a few things in perspective. Thank you for all your help, Harry. And it was good to hear your voice again."

"Let me know if there's anything I can do—you've got my cell number now. And just so you know, I think of Mel so often. I really miss her."

"That means a lot, Harry."

We wish each other a warm goodbye. I immediately send Logan a text, telling him what I've learned and asking that he update Halligan.

It's after one o'clock by now, and though I'm not very hungry, I need to eat. I put my coat on again, and since I can't think of another option—and I've had my fill of Brie and grapes—I return on foot to the coffee shop I stopped at earlier. Without bothering to look at the menu, I order a Cobb salad and an iced tea.

Twice while I'm eating, I check to see if Logan's responded to my text about Jack. Based on what Harry said, there's a chance the cops never knew that Mel, not Jack, broke off the relationship, and they need to hear this as soon as possible.

There's no reply, though. I try calling next, but I reach only voicemail and leave a message for him to phone back as soon as possible. I feel even more in limbo than I did when I woke up this morning.

As I leave the restaurant, I decide to walk for a while, hoping the activity will subdue some of my agitation. Turning right isn't an option because that will take me south, to the area where Mel and Harry had their apartment junior year. So, I make a left.

Before long I'm walking parallel to the college, and after about six or seven blocks, I reach the corner of Lennox Road, which, from what I recall, is the street that runs along the northern boundary of campus. I keep going. By now I'm in an affluent-looking residential area I vaguely remember driving through years ago. Some of the houses are perfectly preserved Victorians in white, yellow, or gray with gabled roofs, decorative woodwork, and wraparound porches; others are smaller and simpler but well tended. Though the tree branches are still bare, there's forsythia blooming wildly in many of the yards, a promise of warmer days ahead.

I turn right onto Oak Street and walk for a couple more blocks. It's been good to stretch my legs, but when I reach the next intersection, I realize I'm too antsy to continue, too eager to track down Logan and see why he's not responding. As I turn around, ready to head back, I glance up absentmindedly at the street sign above my head to the right: "Birch St."

How odd to see that word at this moment, with Mel's haiku top of mind for me.

I stare at the sign a minute more, my curiosity stirred. Is it possible that Mel sometimes took walks in this area, too, walks that gave her time to reflect and conjure up lines of poetry? What if the *birch* she refers to in her haiku is simply a reference to a street she sometimes wandered down and has nothing to do with the Frost poem we read together and loved so much? The thought crushes me a little.

I start to walk again, faster this time, and once I reach the inn, I nearly race to my room. I grab my laptop and open the file with Mel's poems, scrolling down to the haiku I want.

> Will you welcome me?
> As I leave a pathless wood
> Returning to birch.

The words *pathless wood* are a clear reference to the Frost poem, so her haiku *must* be about the two of us somehow, not the street. Maybe the street sign was just the universe calling out to me.

I kick off my shoes and lay down on the freshly made bed. Despite how wired I still feel, I somehow drift off to sleep.

My phone rings, waking me, and when I grab it from the bedside table, I see Bas's name on the screen.

"Hi, is everything okay?" I ask groggily. It takes me a second to remember that it's not the middle of the night.

"Yes, I just wanted to check in once more today," he says. "I hated cutting you off like that earlier."

"No worries," I say, propping myself up on an elbow. "It's so good to hear your voice again. To say nothing of that sexy accent."

"Ah, let me pour that on a little more, then . . . Have you heard anything else from the police?"

"Not yet. The detective says he's planning to talk to a profiler—you know the term, right?"

"Yes, of course."

"And then he's going to circle back to us—so until then, we're in a holding pattern. In other news, Logan's girlfriend arrived today."

"So, what's she like?"

"Very glam. Very talky. Hates the too-skinny beds in first-class air travel. I can't tell you more without sounding like a total bitch."

Sebastian chuckles. "Please, go ahead. I could use some amusement."

As I struggle into a full sitting position, I notice the time on the clock.

"Oh gosh, it's later than I realized," I tell him. "I need to dress for a dinner at the college president's house."

"Call me tomorrow morning, then, okay? I want to hear how it goes."

"Yes, yes, for sure. Love you."

"Love you, too, cariño."

For the second time, I feel a twinge of regret over not letting Bas come with me. How much easier tonight would be if I wasn't going to be the odd woman out, if I knew I could come back to this room after a night of awkward small talk and awful reminders and fall asleep with my head in the crook of his arm.

As I'm setting the phone down, I spot a text from Logan that came in while I was sleeping and somehow managed not to wake me.

> I've let Halligan know Jack wasn't the one who broke it off. See you in a while. Sorry not to respond earlier.

I wash my face, apply some makeup, and then peruse the clothes I've hung in the closet. Since I'm saving the dress I've packed for the reception, my only option for tonight is a pencil-style black gabardine skirt; a cream-colored silk blouse; and sort of dressy, short black boots.

After I'm ready, I head downstairs and order an Uber. Yes, I'm running late, but at least that will cut down on the amount of predinner mingling I'll be stuck doing.

The president's house is right inside the eastern gate of the college, and once the car drops me off, I've got only a short walk. Though I'm familiar with the house, a stately gray stucco structure with a white portico, I've never been inside. As I start up the front steps, I can see bright lights burning and a few people moving around.

The door is answered by a slim, fortysomething Asian woman, who smiles broadly as she ushers me inside.

"Bree, welcome," she says. "I'm Eileen Zhao, head of donor relations. It's so nice to finally meet you."

"Likewise," I say. "Logan's mentioned how much he's enjoyed working with you."

The entrance hall is large and gracious, with a wide red-carpeted staircase leading to the second floor. Before I have time to survey more of my surroundings, a waiter appears, asking for my coat, and another shows up with a tray of wine and sparkling water. I decline the invitation for a drink.

"Maya is eager to see you, so why don't we go inside," Eileen says.

She gestures with her arm for me to precede her into the parlor. It's an impressive room with pale-yellow walls, antique furniture cushioned in various yellow fabrics, and walls lined with oil portraits and landscapes. About a half dozen or so people are gathered inside, including Maya, who notices me right away and heads in my direction. There's no immediate sign of Logan, but seconds later I spot him and Lisa in the adjacent conservatory, speaking to Jeffrey Handler and a woman I assume must be his wife.

"Oh, Bree, it's wonderful to see you," Maya says, clasping my hand. Eileen recedes discreetly into the background. "I know you were undecided about attending the reception, which I don't blame you for, but we're very glad you changed your mind."

"Thank you, Maya, and thank you for this tonight."

Maya is tall, close to six feet, with dark-brown skin, nearly black eyes, and slightly wavy black hair cut to just beneath her chin. Other than a few ribbons of gray in her hair, she hardly seems to have changed since I saw her last. And though she's dressed without pretension tonight in pants and a dark-orange blouse, she exudes, as always, college president.

"Uruguay is agreeing with you, Bree. You look very well."

"That's nice of you to say. I'll give some of the credit to the *papas fritas* and Tannat wine."

At first glance you might think a woman with Maya's formidable presence could be intimidating, but as I discovered when I met her, she's warm and generous of heart. I remembered thinking once that if I'd met her under different circumstances, we might have become friends.

"I hear you chatted with Jeffrey today, and you've just said hello to Eileen, so let me have you meet some others before we head in for dinner."

In a bit of blur, I'm introduced to two English professors, the dean of faculty, the head of financial aid, a guy from media relations named Chip, and someone's spouse. Before there's a chance for any small talk, Maya cocks her chin toward someone across the way, and the next thing I know, Eileen and the waiter are gently herding people toward the table in the room ahead of us.

Logan and Lisa, I notice, enter the dining room through a door from the conservatory, so there's no immediate contact with them. She's decided on all white for this event, a sheath dress topped by a three-quarter-length matching jacket, like she mistakenly thinks we're here to salute the suffragettes.

Stop being bitchy, I tell myself. After this week I'll never set eyes on Lisa again, so why let her get under my skin?

As I make my way into the dining room, Handler and his wife come through the parlor from the conservatory and approach me.

"Hello again," he says, his gaze still favoring the middle of my forehead. "Bree, this is my wife, Alison."

She's striking, ethereal almost, with long, wavy light-brown hair, almond-shaped hazel eyes, and a delicate-looking face. The long-sleeved black velvet dress she's wearing is old-fashioned in style but charming on her.

"What a terrible loss you've experienced," she says, shaking my hand. "Though I don't have children myself, I can only imagine how horrible your daughter's death has been for you."

Her voice is soft and silky, as ethereal as she is, and yet she's also surprisingly direct, something unexpected but appreciated. I've had so little patience for some of the strange euphemisms and platitudes people have offered over the years.

"Thank you, Alison," I say. "Are you still painting? I remember hearing you're an artist."

"Yes, still an artist," she says. "I'm fortunate to be able to do that full time."

Her pale skin is slightly weathered from the sun, and it takes a minute to realize she's probably considerably younger than her husband.

I nod to Handler and his wife and begin moving down the long mahogany table, searching for my name card. Maya reappears at my side, clasps my elbow, and leads me to the place on the left of hers at the head of the table. The man standing on the other side of me quickly reintroduces himself as Chip Conway, the associate director of media relations. He's around thirty, I guess, and the only guy in the room who's wearing a tie with his jacket.

Lisa and Logan are on the opposite side of the table, and thankfully, at the far end. I sense Logan working hard to catch my eye, and I finally meet his gaze, offering him a small smile. *There*, I'm trying.

After we're settled and wine is poured, Maya leans forward in her seat and gently taps her water glass with a knife.

"Thank you all for coming," she says once the room is quiet, "and a warm welcome to our guests of honor, Bree Winter and Logan Chase. Thursday night will be our chance to properly thank you for your wonderful gifts to Carter College—both the scholarships and the new *Muse* office—and also celebrate your remarkable daughter, Melanie. But I thought it would be nice for some of us to meet in a more intimate setting beforehand. Bree, Logan, we couldn't be more grateful."

I smile and add a nod of appreciation. To my surprise, there's a prick of tears in my eyes, and I fight to prevent them from spilling. I've had years to perfect the ability not to choke up in public, so I'm not sure why that's happening now. Needy for a distraction, I lift my dinner roll off the small plate it's resting on and discreetly start to butter it.

Out of the corner of my eye, I see Logan lean forward, clearly ready to speak, and I turn my head in his direction.

"Thank you, Maya, we're very honored to be guests tonight in this lovely home," he says. To the untrained ear, he sounds utterly charming, someone very used to being on his feet in public, but I can hear a faint tension in his voice, like he's fighting to keep his own emotions under control. "On behalf of Bree and myself, I want to say how much we appreciate both this dinner and the upcoming reception. Mel *flourished* at Carter, and we're incredibly happy to have her remembered here."

Murmurs of appreciation follow, and then to my complete shock, Lisa opens her mouth to speak.

"In case we haven't met yet, I'm Lisa," she says, exuding confidence and smiling as best as she can with a face pumped with filler. "And I'd like to take just a second to thank you, too—for everything you're doing and for including me in the events this week. Sadly, I never had the chance to meet Melanie, but I've heard so much about her from Logan, and in so many ways, I feel like I know her. It's wonderful to see her honored like this."

It takes everything in my power not to fly down the length of the table and stab her in the throat with my butter knife.

Chapter 12

I look away and stare into the middle distance, wiping all expression from my face. But inside I'm seething, anger lacing through me like a brush fire. How dare she usurp this moment for herself? How dare she speak about *Me*? And how dare Logan let her do it?

"Before we begin our meal, I'd like Professor Handler to give us an update on the new *Muse* office," Maya announces quickly as if on a rescue mission. "It should be finished within a matter of weeks."

Handler doesn't miss a beat. The office, he explains, is in the same location it's been in for years, the basement of the humanities building, but instead of simply being a large room, it's been expanded and designed to be like the office of an actual literary magazine, with workstations, a meeting room, two podcast studios, and a comfy conversation pit where editors can brainstorm or just hang with their laptops and read submissions.

Everyone nods enthusiastically, and Logan mentions he was at the site Monday morning and thinks it looks fantastic. There's an awkward moment of silence, but then, almost miraculously, two waiters enter the room, serving a beet and goat cheese salad, and guests begin speaking among themselves.

Chip directs his attention to me. He's a nice-looking guy, with light-blue eyes, a clean-shaven face, and conservatively cut brown hair, the kind of style you'd see on an upstate politician.

I force myself to smile and focus on him instead of my fury.

"So, you've had quite the trip," he says. "How far is Uruguay, anyway? It's near Brazil, right?"

"Yes, just south of Brazil, about five and a half thousand miles from here. What about you? Do you live in Cartersville?"

"A couple of towns over. It's a bit of a hike each morning, but I enjoy the drive." He flashes a grin. "And I get in plenty of audiobooks that way."

"How long have you been working at Carter?"

"Since I got out of school. In fact, I'm a Carter College graduate."

"Ahh. You must have liked the school a lot, then."

He cocks his head. "It was hard not to. And Maya is making it better every year."

"That's wonderful to hear."

There's something overly smooth about his manner, like he's reluctant to slip out of his PR guy role. Which means he not only looks like a politician but sounds like one, too.

Our brief exchange is interrupted by Maya asking the head of financial aid to talk about the impact she expects the scholarships to have. While the woman fills us in, I pick at my salad and let my gaze crawl down the table toward Logan. He's obviously been expecting it because he's staring right in my direction. He looks *pained*, his face pinched in remorse. Is it possible he had no idea Lisa was going to vomit her thoughts all over the table tonight?

For a few brief seconds, I feel pained, too, seeing how stricken he seems, but when I finally glance away, I remind myself where I've seen that look before. Not when Mel was murdered. Raw grief did something else altogether to his face, contorting it to the point where he was barely recognizable.

No, that face showed itself a year later, not long after the trial, when I told him I knew he was cheating. He was at least man enough to cop to it.

Knowing Logan, he probably spent days wondering how he'd given himself away, but it was actually the woman—his company's brand manager—who ended up tipping me off. It was at a party he and his partner were hosting to celebrate a new restaurant acquisition. In hindsight I realized he hadn't specifically invited me, but I'd attended many of his events and went that night to show my support and prove I was trying to engage with the world again. He was standing next to her when I walked into the room, taking a sip from a glass of wine. After he set it down on a table, she picked up the glass and took a sip herself.

As soon as she'd swallowed, she'd cocked her head, smiled, and said something I couldn't hear, maybe just "Nice" or "Not bad." But that's all it took for me to realize they were lovers. You don't sample your boss's drink unless you're also fucking him.

I'm torn from my thoughts by the mention of my own name. Jerking a little in my chair, I focus my attention quickly back on the present. The head of financial aid seems to be wrapping up her remarks and is thanking Logan and me again for our gifts.

The salad plates are whisked away, and the main course is served. Maya asks me a little about Uruguay, but before long a waiter interrupts, discreetly mentioning that she has a phone call, and she excuses herself. As soon as she's gone, I sense Handler's attention on me from across the table.

"Are you acclimatizing to the weather here?" he asks.

"Fortunately, I haven't had to. It's the same temperature in Uruguay right now. As we're transitioning into spring here, they're heading into fall."

It's only when the words are out of my mouth that I realize what I've said, categorizing myself as someone who lives *here*, not there. Is that what being gone two days has done to me?

"Well, that's not so bad, then," Handler says.

Alison leans toward her husband so that she's even more in my line of vision. "Did you know Charles Darwin spent time in Uruguay when he was traveling the coastline of South America?" she says. "One of the skulls he found there was from a giant species of mammals with a head almost as big as an elephant's."

"Really?" I say. "I read he was in Uruguay for many weeks, but I don't know much about his time there."

"People think everything crystalized for him in the Galapagos, but he—"

"Darling, excuse me for cutting you off," Handler says, touching her shoulder, "but while I have the chance, I want to give Bree some information I promised her."

"Of course," she says with a pleasant smile.

"Were you able to find Mel's classwork?" I ask eagerly.

He shakes his head, lips pinched together. "I'm afraid not. Unfortunately, class material is only archived on Blackboard for five years, and then it's automatically deleted."

The news deflates me like I've had all the air sucked out of me and there's nothing left on the chair but my blouse and skirt.

"And there's no way to retrieve it?" I say, not disguising my frustration.

"Not that I'm aware of. But I've saved some student writing in my files at home, and I'll look through them tomorrow to see if there's anything of Mel's."

"Terrific. That would mean so much to me."

"And though I know you have copies of *The Muse* from your daughter's time here, I had the library pull a few extra copies for you. There'll be at the front desk there tomorrow or I can have someone drop them off at your hotel."

"I'd be happy to pick them up," I say, grateful he made the effort. Perhaps he's not as haughty as I pegged him to be.

Maya returns to her seat just as the key lime tart is served and seems eager to engage again, but I'm desperate now for a few moments alone. I inquire where the restroom is, and depart using the door not far from me, rather than the one at Logan's end of the table.

In the mirror, I find that my cheeks are so red they look ready to blister. I run a paper towel under cold water and dab at them, but it does little good. Thank God the dinner can't go on much longer.

When I open the door, I discover Logan standing right there, clearly waiting for me. Why am I surprised?

"I'm really sorry," he says, keeping his voice low. He's still wearing his guy-in-the-doghouse expression.

"How *could* you?" I demand.

"Bree, you know me—so you know I wouldn't have planned or okayed anything like that."

"I *know* you, Logan? As we both came to see, that wasn't the case at all."

"Come on," he says, looking agitated now. "I was a profound jerk, but let's not rewrite a nearly twenty-year marriage. You *do* know me, and you know I didn't have a fucking clue she was going to say something."

I exhale, trying to defuse my anger a little.

"Okay, so you weren't aware she was going to toast our dead daughter, a person she never met, but events this week are bound to be emotionally fraught, and you brought someone with no clue how to act under the circumstances. For a guy who's legendary at reading a room, you picked a girlfriend who's an utter failure at it."

All the emotion drains from his face, so it's impossible to tell his reaction.

"Look, I meant what I told you," he says gently after a few beats. "I'm truly sorry. But I just didn't feel I could handle this week alone."

For the second time tonight, I feel a twinge of pain on his behalf. This whole experience is as crushing for him as it is for me.

"Okay, apology accepted. But she'd better not open her mouth Thursday night."

"Understood. I'll speak to her, of course."

"And please leave the dinner ahead of me tonight so the three of us aren't bunched together at the front door."

"Yup . . . Why don't you go back in first? I need to use the restroom anyway."

I stroll back to the table, and though I half expect to find people staring at me with their eyebrows raised, wondering why the ex-spouses have sneaked out of the room at around the same time, they seem oblivious. Some of them are even caught up in the early stages of departure, laying their napkins on the table, scooting their chairs back. Though the grandfather clock hasn't even struck nine yet, people seem eager to be on their way, and I can hardly blame them. A night like tonight couldn't have been much fun for anyone.

I refuse to look directly at Lisa, but I glimpse her out of the corner of my eye, and she's sitting up stick straight, obviously on alert. *She* certainly noticed that both Logan and I had left the table. He appears moments later, and after saying something in her ear, she rises from her chair.

I give the two of them a chance to skirt behind me so they can offer their thanks to Maya. When I'm sure they're gone, I lean toward Maya and express my own gratitude.

"I know this can't have been easy for you, Bree," she says, her voice not much above a whisper. "But I so appreciate you coming,"

"Thank you, Maya. It was lovely of you to do."

As I wait in the hall for my coat, I suddenly find myself next to Alison Handler.

"I enjoyed hearing about the fossil Darwin found in Uruguay," I say. "You don't paint fossils, do you?"

She chuckles a little. "Not as of now, but maybe one day, because they fascinate me."

"So, what does your work tend to feature?"

"I paint dreams," she says.

Her answer startles me a little, and I'm momentarily at a loss for words.

"How intriguing," I say finally. "And do you still find time to talk to students about the connection between art and poetry? Melanie mentioned you did that during her years here, and she really enjoyed it."

Alison hesitates as if she isn't sure at first what I'm speaking about.

"Oh right . . . And it was my pleasure to do that. As Plutarch said, 'Painting is silent poetry, and poetry is painting that speaks.' But sadly, I don't have the time to participate anymore."

"That's a shame. But well put, Plutarch."

"Would you be interested in seeing some of my paintings?" she asks, cocking her head slightly. "You could come by my studio this week."

In another life I might say yes, curious to see her dreams put to paintings. Not now, though.

"Unfortunately I'm only here for a couple of days, so I doubt I'll have the chance."

As Handler joins his wife, a waiter hands me my coat, and I quickly slip into it, eager to leave.

"Are you staying nearby?" Handler asks me.

"At the Cartersville Arms."

"I hope someone has arranged a ride back for you tonight."

"I'm actually going to walk." It's a white lie, but if they find out I'm planning to order a car, they might insist on driving me.

"Don't be silly. Let us give you a lift."

"Thank you, but it's only a few blocks from here, and I don't want to put you to any trouble."

"It's no trouble," Alison interjects. "We live just over on Birch Street."

Chapter 13

For a split second, I have this odd sense that I'm being teased, that she somehow knows the word *birch* has been on my mind and she's playfully riffing off it. But then I realize how absurd that thought is.

"Do you know the street?" Alison asks, obviously confused by my furrowed brow.

"Vaguely," I say. "I appreciate the offer, but I'm fine getting back on my own tonight. After that wonderful meal, I could use the walk."

I flick my gaze back to Handler. His eyes read curious, too, but there's a tight set to his mouth.

"Good night," I add, and hurry from the house.

Once I reach the campus gate, I lean, bone weary, against the stone pillar, trying to process what I've just heard. Jeffrey Handler lives on Birch Street. Meaning there's a chance Mel's haiku was about *him* and the backyard classes he held there. I'd already worried today it might have nothing to do with me, but this seems to be partial proof.

I push off from the pillar and dig for my phone. To my dismay, an Uber is going to take seventeen minutes to arrive, and when I try a local cab company next, I reach only voicemail. I'm too mentally exhausted to wait, so I decide to walk after all. It's early still, and I'll be near campus much of the way.

Before I've gone a block, though, I'm struck by how dark the street is. There are streetlamps, of course, but since the stores on the opposite side from me are closed, and so are the administrative buildings at this end of campus, there's little additional light.

And there's absolutely no one else around. This, I realize, is the quiet, small-town darkness Mel found soothing but, in the end, doomed her.

As my body floods with dread, I slow my pace, trying to decide what to do. The street seems even more forbidding up ahead, but when I check behind me, I see that section is empty as well. I try Uber again, but now the app says the wait will be twenty minutes.

Just keep going, I tell myself. Though there are heels on my boots, I begin to jog along the sidewalk, looking, I'm sure, like a woman fleeing from zombies or werewolves in a horror film.

A car approaches from behind me, but instead of zooming past, I sense it slowing. I shoot a glance to the left. Though I can barely make out the driver, it looks like he's turned his head and is studying me.

Shit. Is it just a concerned citizen or some kind of bad actor? The irony of me possibly being in danger in Cartersville makes me want to scream. I keep jogging, eyes straight ahead now, but the car is still crawling along beside me. I jab my hand in my purse again, wondering if I should call 911.

"Ms. Winter?" a male voice calls out.

I stop dead in my tracks and glance again toward the car. The driver, a male, is leaning across the front seat with the passenger-side window lowered. It takes me a moment, but then I recognize the PR guy I sat next to at dinner. I feel a simultaneous surge of relief and embarrassment.

"Oh, hi," I call back.

"Are you headed to the Cartersville Arms?"

"Yes, exactly."

"Why don't I give you a lift. It's in my general direction."

"Oh, that would be great." A second later I'm sliding into the passenger seat.

"Is everything okay?" he asks once we're on our way. "You seemed to be running."

"Everything's fine, thanks." The car smells vaguely like take-out food, and there are crinkly wrappers near my feet, a funny contrast to his crisp dress shirt, striped tie, and classic navy blazer. "I thought a walk would be nice, but it's later than I realized, and I'm supposed to do a Zoom call tonight with someone in Uruguay."

"How fortuitous, then," he says, oblivious to the lie, it seems. "And actually, I'm glad I spotted you for another reason. There's an issue I wanted to discuss, but I didn't feel comfortable raising it at the table tonight."

"Yes?" I say, my body tensing again.

"A piece went up on the Albany *Times Union* website first thing this morning—and I assume it will be in the print edition tomorrow. It says Calvin Ruck has recently been linked to two additional murders, each out of state. I'd no sooner read it when the same reporter called our office and said he'd heard the police might be reopening your daughter's case."

The news catches me off guard, but it's not a total shock. Halligan told Logan that a reporter had been snooping around.

"Was it a guess on his part, or did he have specific details?" I ask, then brace myself for the response.

"He might have been fishing, but it sounded like he was working with some kind of tip."

"What did you tell him?"

"That I didn't have any information myself, and beyond that, I wasn't the right person to ask."

"That's a perfect response, Chip," I say, finally summoning his name in my mind.

He makes a left with his eyes on the road, but as soon as he's brought the wheel back, he glances over at me. "Is it true, though? Are they reopening the case?"

This is the last thing I want to be discussing now, on top of everything else I've had to contend with tonight.

"I'm not at liberty to share anything at the moment, but I appreciate the heads-up. Will you let us know if you get any other calls like that?"

"Sure thing," he says. "And I hope you'll reconsider about sharing. It would be good for the college to be in the loop, and of course we'd be discreet."

He makes another turn, and I spot the inn just ahead.

"If there's anything to share down the road," I say, "I'll definitely let Maya know."

He pulls up to the front of the inn and puts the car in park.

"And if there's any way I can be of assistance," he says, "call me day or night."

He reaches into his jacket pocket and passes me his business card.

"Thank you, Chip."

As soon as I'm in my room, I tug off my boots and sink onto the bed. My feet ache—it's been over a year since I've stuffed them into anything with heels—and beyond that my body is humming with nervous anxiety, though it's hard to pinpoint the main contributor. Lisa's awful little tribute? The discovery that Mel's schoolwork has been erased from the cybersphere and there's no chance of ever seeing other poems or stories of hers.

Or the fact that Handler lives on Birch Street?

I suspect a hot bath might help, but once I've pushed off the bed, I find myself drifting over to the desk. I plop into the chair and open my laptop.

If Mel's haiku really was a reference to Birch Street—and sadly not to reading poems with me—perhaps Handler was a bigger influence on her than Logan and I recognized. Spending time in his presence—not mine—might have been what she longed for when life to her felt too much like a pathless wood.

I google the college website and click my way to a bio for Professor Jeffrey Handler. He did his undergraduate work, it says, at Bates College in Maine, which, like Carter, is a small, prestigious liberal arts school, and he earned both his master's and PhD from Princeton. Under "Publications" are the five volumes of poetry he's written, as well as a dozen or more academic articles. It appears he's been at the college for over fifteen years, but there's no mention of where he was previously.

Then, out of curiosity, I search online for "Alison Handler, artist." A link to her website pops up immediately.

As it turns out, she does paint dreams—just not very nice ones. Though the paintings are done in pretty, gauzy colors, every image is downright creepy. In one of the four on the home page, there's a horse standing on a dining chair and staring across a small table at a young woman eating from a plate piled with wax lips. In another, a baby about nine months old sits on a blanket with one of his chubby arms stretched outward. As I peer closely at the image, I notice he's holding a bunch of tiny teeth in the palm of his hand.

These must be some of her newer pieces, so I take a minute to scroll through what's featured under "Work" in the nav bar, wondering how her style has evolved. But these paintings are just as disturbing. In one, a woman in a sleeveless white dress is lying prone on a trapeze-like platform with her right arm dangling over the side. There are three silver zippers running from her wrist to her elbow. Do they represent a series of injuries?

At the bottom of the page is a contact link for Alison as well as the address for her studio—"57b Birch St." It must be in a section of their house with its own entrance, or in a separate building on the property.

I check the bio page next. It's brief, stating only that she grew up in Boston, graduated from Oberlin College, and has an MFA in studio art from the State University of New York at Albany, which is about twenty-five miles southeast of Cartersville. The bio also lists some art shows she's been featured in and provides a link to an article from a local publication that's a roundup of young artists from the region. Published five years ago, it gives her age then as thirty-four.

My best guess is that Handler is in his early sixties, which means Alison is over twenty years his junior.

With my curiosity further piqued, I search next for a wedding announcement and soon find it. They married in Boston sixteen years ago. The announcement gives Handler's job then as professor of English at Colby College in Maine and Alison's simply as artist.

How did they meet? I wonder. *In New England somewhere, when he was at Colby and she, perhaps, had moved back to the Boston area?*

I go to the Amazon site and click one by one on the five poetry books he's published, swiping through each "Look Inside" sample until I reach the bio in the back. The three most recent collections list him as a professor at Carter. He wrote his second volume, I see, while teaching at Colby.

It's the bio in the very first collection that makes me bite my lip in surprise. These poems were published twenty-five years ago when Handler was an associate professor at Oberlin College. That must be where he eventually met Alison.

I'm about to close the link but catch myself and instead scroll back to the dedication page.

It reads: *To my wife, Dalia.*

So, he was married to someone else while at Oberlin—at least initially. Until, perhaps, he met and fell for Alison. Whoa . . . was she a student in one of his classes, and he began seeing her clandestinely?

I'm whisked back to the awkward moment I witnessed this morning in Handler's office, the female student standing too deep into his personal space.

Does Jeffrey Handler have a taste for younger women, particularly college girls? What . . . what if Mel wrote about returning to birch not because the backyard classes were inspirational for her but because Handler was the new man she was smitten with?

The thought chills me, and yet right now, at least, I don't have a shred of proof that I'm right.

I strip off my clothes and open the taps on the tub, but as the hot water begins to steam the room, I realize I'm now too wired to soak in a bath. I throw on my jeans, along with a sweater and loafers, and take the elevator to the first floor. Currently, there's no one manning the front desk.

I cross the hall to the parlor. At first glance it appears empty again, but as I approach the bar, I catch movement out of the corner of my eye and jerk in surprise. Turning, I see that it's Logan, reclining in one of the wingback chairs and holding a snifter filled with an amber-hued liquid.

"Oh," I blurt out.

"Hello," he says quietly, not faking any cheer. It looks like he's practically melted into the chair, with one leg stretched out across the bloodred ottoman.

My eyes dart to the chair across from him, checking for another presence, but fortunately, he's alone. I wonder if Lisa is sulking in the room after being told she should have kept her mouth shut.

"What are you doing here?" I ask.

"Having a brandy, trying to drive terms like *forensic odontologist* out of my head . . . Shall I pour you one, too?"

"No, I just want sparkling water," I say, continuing to the bar. "I'm not much of a brandy drinker anyway."

I hear him chuckle behind me, and turning back around, I see him take a long swallow of his drink.

"What's so funny?" I ask.

"You not remembering the winter that we lived in Nolita. Our apartment was always freezing, so after dinner we sometimes used to go to that little bar on the next block and have a brandy."

I tug a cobalt-blue bottle of sparkling water from the small fridge and allow my memory to scramble, trying to find its way back to Nolita. I certainly remember the apartment, the first we rented together as a couple, which was hopelessly drafty from November until April. I recall the little bistro as well, and the two of us scurrying there in our black down coats. Then, as the water fizzes in my glass, I see myself *inside* the bistro, with a brandy snifter in my hand.

"I remember now," I say. I return with my glass to the seating area and lower myself into the chair across from Logan. "There was a fireplace, wasn't there? And then one night we went, and the bistro was closed, right? Closed for good. Without any warning."

Logan snickers but in a conspiratorial way. "Oh, there were warnings."

"Such as?"

"I'd been in the restaurant business long enough to know that shrinking portion sizes was a harbinger of bad things ahead."

"I must have missed that," I say, and a second later I feel a swell of sadness. There's an analogy to our marriage somewhere in this discussion, isn't there? Me clueless that our life together wasn't what I thought it was—until I saw that smug, entitled young woman take a sip from his glass of wine.

"No, no, you noticed," he says. "You complained that each time you ordered the fried calamari, there were fewer and fewer in the basket."

"I'll have to take your word for that," I say, and the most I can manage is a wan smile.

He studies me without comment, his eyes slightly narrowed and the crease between his eyes even deeper. It's time to extricate myself before things turn truly morose.

"I should let you get back to your brandy," I say rising, "but since you're here, I'll share what I was going to put in a text first thing tomorrow. That guy in communications, Chip? He ended up giving me a ride back tonight and mentioned there was a post this morning on the Albany paper website about Ruck's two other murders. And the reporter called him asking if Mel's case might be reopened."

Logan nods. "Halligan was right, then. But as we agreed, it's not necessarily a bad thing if a story comes out. It could increase the pressure on the cops to do more. I trust you didn't offer him any info."

"None. If we become convinced the police accused the wrong person, then yes, we need to inform the school, but right now there's no reason to share everything that's going on . . . Well, good night."

"Good night. And about tomorrow—shall we meet down here?"

I pause, confused. "For what?"

"The meeting with Halligan. Didn't you get my text?"

"What? No." I use my free hand to extricate my phone from the back pocket of my jeans. As soon as I tap the screen, I spot it, sent just as I was rushing into the inn.

Halligan wants to see us tomorrow at one. Let's meet downstairs at 12:15.

My heart jumps. "Is there news?"

"Sounds like it. He says there's someone important he wants the two of us to hear from, and it's got to happen tomorrow."

Chapter 14

"Do you think it's the behavioral analyst?" I ask. "I didn't realize he was talking to someone in the area."

"There's an FBI office in Albany, so it could be a profiler from there," Logan says. "Or maybe someone higher up in the state police just wants to meet with us and throw in their two cents."

"He didn't drop any hints?"

"Nope. Before I could press, he said he had to take another call."

"Do you—" I start to ask him to make a guess, to speculate, but catch myself.

Speculating is one of the things that nearly undid me during the original investigation—the constant, exhaustive wondering, feeling certain of something at one moment but not the next. It became addictive back then, and I can't let myself get caught up in that again.

"What?" Logan asks.

"Nothing. See you at twelve fifteen."

As I turn to leave, I hear Logan shift in the chair, and instinctively I glance back. He's staring at me again, but now with a wistful expression.

"You really didn't remember drinking brandy with me at that little bistro?" he says.

I hesitate briefly, considering how to respond.

"Not at first, but, as I said, I sort of do now."

"Only sort of?"

I shrug, feeling a prick of irritation. "To be honest, Logan, those kinds of experiences are never fresh in my mind."

"Because?"

God, does he really want me to answer that? My first instinct is to simply blame my memory lapse on exhaustion, but I'm still bristling enough from Lisa's comments at dinner that I override my better instincts.

"Because once I start with a thought like that, I'm suddenly white-water rafting forward in time, landing somewhere I never imagined or wanted to be. You and me *over*. *Divorced.* Living on separate continents. So why go trolling through memories that will only take me someplace heart-wrenching in the end?"

He glances off briefly, clearly mulling over my response, and then looks back at me, his eyes nearly boring into mine.

"I didn't end it, Bree," he says bluntly. "You did. I asked for forgiveness and the chance to start again."

I glance behind me, double-checking that there's still no one in the lobby who could overhear.

"Forgiveness wasn't the issue, Logan. I *did* forgive you. You found your own way to deal with the pain. But your personal grief-relief strategy didn't just leave me lower than I thought I could go, it meant I could never trust you again, so how was I—"

Quit while you're ahead, I think, and then scoff at myself because this isn't some game I want to win at.

"There's really nothing more to add," I continue. "We've been over this ground before. Good night."

"Night."

As soon as I'm in my room, I regret how harsh I sounded. Before I left Uruguay, I'd assured myself that my instinct to punish Logan had long been quelled—inviting him to stay at the chacra was proof of that, after all—and that I'd be able to stunt any resentment that reared its head this week. Well, I've been here only a day and a half and already failed at that. Logan, on the other hand, has been nothing but gracious and solicitous with me.

I'm fifty-three years old, and it's time to stop acting like a Taylor Swift song.

Assuming he's still in the parlor and not in bed with Lisa yet, I grab my phone and text him.

> I'm sorry about laying on the guilt that way. I appreciate everything you're doing.

Three little dots pulse for a minute, then disappear, like someone slipping out of a room without warning. But a minute later the reply comes.

> Thanks. I know how hard this must be for you. See you tomorrow.

Chances are he wasn't troubled by my comments anyway. He seems to be taking me in stride this week, letting my irritation and anger roll off his back. If the past is, in the words of the author L. P. Hartley, "a foreign country," I've become that both literally and figuratively for Logan.

Against my will, I picture him in my mind, taking the last swallow of brandy and preparing to head upstairs to his room. Perhaps he's eager for some makeup sex with Lisa. Logan was great at makeup sex—any kind of sex, for that matter—his people skills extending perfectly into the bedroom. He derived pleasure not only from satisfying his own coital needs but also making sure my hair was standing on end by the time we rolled onto our backs.

With Bas, I never sense his ego in bed with us, just his passion and generosity.

Though I'm even more desperate now for a bath, I'm too exhausted to bother. I drain the tub, quickly get ready for bed, and slip under the soft white duvet. I'm out within minutes.

By eight thirty the next morning, I'm on my way to campus again, this time to pick up the copies of *The Muse* that Handler put aside for me at the library. It's something to do at least.

I try to let the walk relax me. It's breezy today but a little warmer than yesterday, and the sun keeps threatening to burn through the film of pale-gray clouds. And yet for a reason I can't define, I notice a brand-new hum of anxiety inside me, like the churr of an insect. Maybe it's due to the meeting ahead with Halligan and the mystery guest he refused to identify.

By the time I near the library, it's nine o'clock, and I place a call to Maya's office. I'm not expecting to reach her directly, but I want to leave a message with her assistant, thanking her again for last night. To my surprise, I'm put through as soon as I identify myself.

"Bree, good morning," she says warmly.

"Maya, hi. I won't keep you, but I just wanted to say how much I appreciate the dinner you gave last night."

"It was my pleasure. And you had a chance to speak with Chip, I know. He tells me he's expecting some nice pickup about the scholarships."

"That's terrific . . . And, oh, speaking of Chip, he mentioned that a reporter had called about Mel's case, asking if it might be reopened. Confidentially, the police are reviewing certain details again, but for the time being, Logan and I need to keep this development under wraps. I hope you understand."

"Of course. If there are details relevant to what we do in terms of campus security, we'd want to be informed, but how much you tell us otherwise is up to you."

"Chip seemed to think it was important for the college to be in the loop."

"He was probably just being extra diligent. And, of course, the situation resonates for him personally."

"What do you mean?" I say, confused.

"He was a student at the same time as Melanie, in the English department, too. And I believe he also worked on *The Muse* when she was editor."

Chip said he'd gone to Carter but never what year. On the one hand, it's odd he didn't mention being familiar with Mel, but by now I'm used to people tiptoeing around the topic, reluctant to even mention her name.

We end the call just as I reach the library, with me telling Maya I'll see her tomorrow night. Once I'm inside the building, I approach a twentysomething redheaded woman at the front desk and explain my purpose there. She smiles pleasantly and, after rifling under the counter, hands me a small shopping bag with the Carter College logo. Back outside, I quickly check through the bag. There are four old issues of *The Muse*, each of which I already have. Still, it's nice to now own extra copies.

Handler has also promised to check through his files at home, and if I'm lucky, he'll find some work of Mel's I've never laid eyes on.

I start to retrace my steps across the quad. Students are dashing, clustering, chatting together, half of them in Carter College hoodies. I don't think Mel ever owned one of those. She might have loved her time here, but she wasn't a rah-rah kind of girl and rarely dressed like other kids I remember seeing. Instead of jeans and hoodies, she favored flowy pants and skirts (all still without buttons if possible), paired with black T-shirts and chunky boots.

I'm halfway to the other side of the quad when I jerk to a stop. To my shock, Jack Lawler is sitting on a cement bench just yards ahead of me. The shaggy hair is gone—he's now sporting a crew cut with a bit longer growth on top that he's obviously spiked with product—but I recognize the face and the lanky frame. His long legs are spread out in front of him, and he's talking with an older man in a quilted vest, probably a professor.

I quickly pivot, hurry toward a maple tree near the center of the quad, and then duck behind it. I lean my head out just enough to have a view.

The two men are speaking animatedly, and I watch Jack flash a smile and nod in agreement. At a glance, he looks less broody, more outgoing than he used to be, and even less like the kind of guy who could have flown into a murderous rage over being dumped.

But who knows? He lied about the breakup after all, and that might have been less out of embarrassment than a need for no one to guess how furious he was. Jack, more than anyone, would have been aware of Mel's rituals, how she liked to walk to the park in the evening and sit quietly by the creek, away from the commotion on campus. Maybe he showed up there that Friday night in the hope of convincing her to be a couple again, and when she rebuffed him, he lost control. He could have hurried back to campus, making sure to show his face.

But then where would he have gotten his hands on a dog leash so quickly? If he *is* the killer, he must have intended right from the start to murder her and make it look like an attempted rape.

And it would also mean that everything about Mel's murder *is* coincidental, that the method he chose just happened to be like Ruck's. Unless, of course, he somehow learned details about Sailor Abbott's death and copied them. Though her murder hadn't been reported locally, he might have had friends or family in Plattsburgh who'd told him about it. That's something that needs to be investigated.

My phone rings from inside my purse. *Bas*, it turns out.

"Good morning, cariño," he says. "Everything okay?"

"Oh, sweetheart," I say with a twinge of guilt. I'd promised to reach out first thing today. "I'm sorry not to have called yet, but I had to run an errand on campus this morning."

"Not to worry. Tell me how last night went."

I sneak one more peek at Jack and his companion, then turn and begin walking across the quad again.

"Dinner was tough," I say. "Trying to be social when that's the last thing in the world I felt like. And here's the worst part. Lisa decided she needed to make some comments about Mel, who she never met in her life."

"That's terrible. What did you do?"

"There wasn't really anything I *could* do at the moment, other than let the steam come out of my ears, though I warned Logan later not to let it happen again."

"Good. And what about the police? Any word yet?"

"The detective wants us to meet with him and someone else today, though he won't say who. I'm praying it's the person he asked for some profiling help."

"Well, that will give you some answers, right?"

"I hope so—and that this expert says Ruck must have done it, and I can pack up and come home. God, I miss you."

"Same here, cariño. Poco is starting to look sorry for me."

"Tell him I'll be back very soon."

When we're done, I'm surprised to find myself slightly disconcerted. I've given a couple of brief updates to Bas since I've been here, but I realize I've left out so much: the bite marks on the other victims and what they could imply about Mel's case; the reignited concerns about Jack; my unease regarding Handler and the weirdness about him living on Birch Street, which would, of course, mean telling him about the haiku, something I've never brought up. I still seem afraid of swamping our relationship with details from the heartbreaking past.

But is that the only reason I've kept him so much in the dark about Mel's murder and its full impact on me? Maybe . . . maybe deep down I'm also reluctant to reveal certain parts of myself—like the mother clinging to a haiku because she's desperate to know her daughter loved her and the woman so distraught about the murder that she let her life unspool for years. Because what would that suggest about who I really am and how I'd handle what fate might throw our way one day?

But a shrink might argue it's unfair, even duplicitous, of me not to share. And unfair not to expect more of Bas.

I meet Logan as planned in the lobby. His hair is slightly damp, suggesting he's showered only a short while ago.

"So, guess who I spotted on campus today?" I say as soon as we drive off, winding our way through the streets of Cartersville. "Jack."

"Yeah, he texted me this morning to say he came up a day early. He's meeting with a friend and a couple of his old professors."

"And he felt the need to let you know?"

"That's because he also wants to have a drink with me, which I agreed to." Logan raises a hand from the steering wheel in a "Hold on" gesture as if expecting me to object. "Look, I certainly don't relish a one-on-one with the guy, but I want to see him up close with his guard down."

"Okay, that makes sense. And maybe he'll explain why he's coming to the reception."

"What do you mean?"

"It just seems weird to me. I could see him coming back for some kind of remembrance service, but why a reception about a couple of scholarships? It's like he's got a hidden agenda."

"Yeah, maybe," Logan says, lightly nodding his head.

We're on the highway now, driving through a sprawl of stores, fast-food restaurants, and town-house communities. I leave Logan to his thoughts, and I stay with mine.

It's been strange being in a car with him again after all this time. During our marriage, we kept a car in the city, partly for traveling to Cape Cod with Mel during the summers, but the two of us also took a fair amount of road trips on weekends before she was born and during the time she was at Carter. We drove all over New England together—Logan so at home behind the wheel—and sometimes places farther afield, like Virginia, the Carolinas, and Georgia.

Conversation came easily to us on those trips, but sometimes we said nothing at all, at ease in the silence. Once, after pulling into the parking lot of our hotel in Savannah and checking the time, I realized we hadn't spoken to each other for hours. Yet we'd felt in sync the whole time, and when we made love later in a room infused with the scent of jasmine, all that silence beforehand had seemed like its own kind of foreplay, making sex even more erotic.

I shake my head a little, chasing the image away.

"What?" he asks, obviously noticing the movement.

"Nothing. Just nervous tension."

Finally, the state police building appears ahead. Logan finds a spot for the car, and then we stride together across the parking lot. It's even breezier now than it was earlier, and a plastic bag scurries just ahead of us as if trying to beat us to the door. Logan smiles grimly at me.

"You okay?" he asks.

"I guess so," I lie. I hate not knowing what's coming. "You?"

"Hanging in there, too, but eager to get this the hell over with."

Only moments after we check in, a gray-uniformed trooper appears and leads us to an interview room across the hall from the one we were in on Monday. Halligan is seated at the far side of the table with two women, one to his left and the other next to her at the end of the table.

Nothing about either of them suggests they are higher-ups here, as Logan said we might expect. The woman seated at the head is mid-fiftyish with dark-brown hair in a slightly dated flip, and though she's dressed like someone in a professional role, her outfit doesn't shout "law enforcement." The other woman is much younger, probably not even thirty yet. She's heavyset with long dark-blond hair and a pretty face, and she's wearing a mint-colored blouse with rows of pin tucks. Her eyes, gray or blue, are wide with something close to panic.

My first thought: we've mistakenly been escorted into a meeting Halligan is holding prior to the one he has scheduled with us.

That can't be the case, however, because the trooper is now closing the door behind us, and Halligan is rising and nodding hello. And then he's making introductions, giving the older woman's name as Hilary Brown, and the younger's as Riley Reynolds. I'm now hopelessly confused.

"Thanks for coming on such short notice," Halligan says, gesturing for us to take seats across from him and Riley. "Ms. Reynolds requested this meeting because she has something important she wants to share with you. Ms. Brown is her attorney."

"Wait," Logan says, pressing a hand to his forehead, "I thought we were getting some kind of update."

"This *is* an update of sorts. Let me turn it over to Ms. Reynolds."

The young woman nods and folds one hand over the other on the table. Her fingernails, I notice, have been bitten to the quick.

"I saw the story online yesterday morning about your daughter's case and how police might be questioning some things," she says, her voice trembling a little, "and I knew I finally had to come forward. That it was time, you know, after all these years."

I seem to have sucked the panic from Riley Reynolds's eyes into my own body because my heart is hammering, and I feel sweat blooming on my palms. What in God's name is going on?

"Okay." Logan says it politely, as if he's got all the patience in the world, but I can sense how flummoxed he is. "We're happy to listen."

"I went to Carter College at the same time as Melanie," she says. "My sophomore year, I was raped and almost killed." She glances down at the table and then back at Logan and me. "It—it was two nights after your daughter died. And the man who hurt me . . . it was Calvin Ruck."

Chapter 15

My lips part in astonishment, but other than that, I'm frozen in place. It takes a few seconds to grasp what she's said, and even then, it's almost too slippery to hold on to.

Next to me, Logan shifts in his seat, clearly stunned as well.

"I'm sorry I never told anyone when it happened," Riley continues, her eyes now brimming with tears. "I was an English major, like Melanie, and I even knew her from a class, and I should have come forward right away. But my parents, they're evangelical Christians. They think that sex before marriage, no matter *how* it happens, is wrong, and I knew that if I told them I'd been raped, they would never treat me the same way after that."

What she's just shared is wretched and heartbreaking, but I'm still struggling to make total sense of it.

"And this happened in Cartersville?" Logan asks, his voice still gentle.

"Yes, in Mohegan Park," she says. "I was on the field hockey team at Carter, and I used to train by running there after dinner."

"Mohegan is about a mile and a half north of Pebble Creek Park," Halligan interjects. "But along the same creek."

So, we're talking about a place very close to where Mel was killed. Only two nights later. This could shift everything we've been thinking since first talking to Halligan—if her attacker is who she says he is.

"Thank you so much for sharing this, Riley," I say. My own voice, I realize, is wobbly, too. "And I'm sorry this terrible thing happened to you. Can you just tell us how you know for sure it was Calvin Ruck?"

"I recognized him from the picture in the paper after he was arrested."

"And it was definitely that Sunday?" I ask. If it was later than that, it couldn't have been Ruck because cell data showed he was back in Plattsburgh by Monday evening.

Her eyes flicker nervously for a moment. This is obviously agonizing for her to relive.

"Yes, I'm positive," she says. "Like I said, I'm so sorry to have waited until now. After it happened, I kept telling myself I needed to come forward, but once he was arrested, it didn't seem necessary anymore. The news said there was plenty of evidence against him."

Riley blinks away a few tears, and her attorney passes a tissue, which she uses to dab at her eyes.

She's clearly hurting badly. There's that fearful, almost haunted look in her eyes—blue, I realize now—and her shoulders have the defeated slope of someone who's suffered for years. But something feels funny to me.

"So, you must have gotten a good look at him," Logan says.

"Yes. It was dark, but I saw him . . . I *talked* to him."

"Riley," Halligan says, "can you please share some of the details about that night, starting from the beginning? I know Bree and Logan would appreciate any information you're able to pass along."

Riley glances quickly at Hilary Brown, who nods encouragement.

"Like I mentioned," she says, "I was running in the park and this man stopped me. He had a dog leash in his hand, and he said his dog had run off and he wondered if I'd seen her."

My heart pitches forward. Eight years ago, the police theorized that Ruck might have used the leash not only as a murder weapon but also as a way to approach potential victims in an unthreatening manner, claiming to be looking for a lost pet.

"After I told him I'd keep an eye out for the dog," she adds, "I started to run again, and out of nowhere I felt this crushing pain on the back of my head. He'd hit me with something hard, something metal, I think, that he must have had in his backpack. I fell, and . . . oh God, he dragged me off the path, onto one of the picnic tables under the trees, and that's when he raped me. And while he was doing it, he—"

She lowers her face into her hands, breathing hard, and then, after a few seconds, looks up again. "He wrapped something around my neck—the leash, I think—and pulled it so tight that I passed out, and after, I guess, only a few seconds, he loosened it until I came to, and then he did it all over again."

For a second, I worry I'm going to wail in anguish. The story is not only horrifying but also Mel's story, too: a blow to the head, being strangled repeatedly . . .

Riley herself is gasping for air at this point.

"Do you need a short break, Riley?" Halligan asks.

"No, no, I'm okay," she says after taking a longer breath.

"And then somehow, thank goodness, you got away," I say.

"It was just *luck*. I kicked at him and managed to hit his testicles, and when he bent over, I had enough time to slide off the table and run. My shorts were still below my knees so I could barely move, and he was never very far behind me, calling me a fucking bitch.

"When I got to the edge of the creek, I could tell he was about to catch me, so I just threw myself in. The water was moving really fast, and I ended up being carried away by the current."

She takes another breath and exhales a ragged gust. "I thought I was going to drown. My shorts were still down, but I managed to get them back up, and the leash off me, too, and somehow, I kept my head above water. Then finally, maybe a mile away, I was able to paddle to the shore and scramble up. I was sure he was going to come after me, but there was no sign of him. My phone was gone—I think in the creek—but I got to a road and flagged down a driver. It was this older woman, who dropped me back at my apartment."

The attorney lays her hand supportively over Riley's. For a few moments the room is completely silent.

"Thank you, Riley," Halligan says. "That must have been very hard, but I know how grateful Melanie's parents must be."

"We *are*," Logan assures her. "And if you don't mind, I have one more question. First, please know that I'm not blaming you in any way, but I'm curious. Hadn't you heard that a girl from the college had been murdered in an area park that weekend?"

Exactly. How could she have had the nerve to go running by herself?

Riley clears her throat. "Yes, but people said the cops were talking to Melanie's ex-boyfriend and he probably did it. That he wanted to get back together and was mad because she didn't want to."

Her shoulders sag even more, and she brushes fresh tears from her eyes.

"If that's all, I think it's finally time to give Riley a break," the attorney announces.

"Please, Riley, I have a question, too," I say, "and then I swear we'll let you go. Are we the only ones who know all this?"

Because I'm bothered by something I can't put my finger on and I could use corroboration. I'd settle for anything, even an eight-year-old diary entry of hers.

Riley shakes her head. "No, my fiancé knows about it. I told him when we started to get serious. And my gynecologist knows now, too."

"What about the woman who drove you home that Sunday night?" I say.

And then, oddly, her eyes flicker again.

"I never got her name," she replies. "And all I told her was that I'd been running along the creek and accidentally stumbled in."

"And you didn't speak to anyone else back then? A school friend, a relative other than your par—"

"I believe that's enough," the lawyer interjects.

"No, that's all right," Riley says. "There *was* someone, yes."

"Okay," I say expectantly, and squeeze my hands together, warning myself not to pounce.

"Her name's Morgan Kroll, and she was a teaching assistant for the Carter English department. I went by there the next morning and ended up telling her everything."

Halligan has a pad and pen in front of him, but he's not writing anything, which makes me think he's already been given this information.

"She really wanted me to go to the police," Riley adds, "but I told her I couldn't, and I pleaded with her not to say anything. A few weeks later I decided to drop out of school. All my parents knew was that I was having a mental health crisis, and even *that* pissed them off."

The room goes briefly still again. And then Halligan is rising, signaling we are indeed finally done. He tells the two women that he wants to see us out, but that he'll be back momentarily. I thank Riley for her honesty, and so does Logan, and then we both rise from the table.

As tragic as the story is, I should be relieved by it. But there's an even bigger pit in my stomach than the one I arrived with.

Chapter 16

Halligan escorts us from the interview room and pushes open the door to the still-empty lobby. "Thank you for coming at such short notice," he says. "And let's keep this under wraps for now."

"Of course," Logan tells him. "But we'd love to hear your take on it."

"I'd say what we've heard is critical information. If her story checks out and she's correct about Ruck, it puts him not simply in the area that week but a short distance from Pebble Creek Park and on the prowl for potential victims . . . I'll follow up with you when I know more, okay?"

"Can you just tell me," I say. "Did Riley ever get to go back to college for a degree?"

"No, that wasn't in the cards for her. But she's the manager of a small insurance agency in Buffalo, and I sense she's worked hard to put her life back together."

We nod sober goodbyes and depart. As we cross the parking lot toward the car, Logan lightly clasps my arm, a gesture of support, and I'm too unsettled right now to shrug it off.

"So, what do you think?" he asks as soon as he's navigated the car out of the parking lot.

"You first," I tell him.

"Well, as Halligan suggested, it seems to confirm that Ruck was on a killing spree in Cartersville, making it easier to assume that Mel was one of his victims—and that he was lying his ass off when he told David Schmidt he didn't do it. I'm pissed, though. What happened to

Riley Reynolds is horrific, but Christ, if she'd reported the crime at the time, the police here wouldn't have spent nearly a month spinning their wheels—and Amanda Kline might still be alive."

"I know." The truth of that has just started sinking in for me.

"Your turn now."

"Okay . . . I'm having trouble with her story."

He jerks his head so he's got me in his line of sight. "You think she's wrong about Ruck?"

"Maybe. All I know is that something felt off to me." And then, right there in the car, I put my finger on why. "She looked away a couple of times as she was sharing information—like she was being evasive."

Logan's in profile now, but I see his brows shoot up in surprise. "Wait, are you saying she *lied* to us?"

I shrug, at a loss. "At certain moments, it seemed that way. Remember that time Mel's senior year in high school, when you and I went out of town one Saturday night, and her friend Hadley was going to stay over, and we came back to find Mel had broken her foot? She told us this whole saga about how she and Hadley were moving the couch and it slipped out of their hands. But there was something evasive about her, and it turned out she'd thrown a party that night, and someone had dropped a case of beer on her foot. That's what today felt like—though I can't imagine *why* Riley would lie."

"A desperate need for attention?"

"That would be pretty darn desperate."

I glance out the window. We're on the highway now, and I let the cars and signs all fuzz together, losing myself in the blur. Another memory suddenly stirs.

"What if she's having some kind of mental health crisis?" I say. "Years ago, I edited a book on false memories—it was around the time when there was all that backlash about people claiming things about their parents that weren't true—and I remember the author, a shrink, saying that people who suffered from PTSD or depression sometimes created false memories after they became exposed to certain information, like a news story."

"Meaning she might *believe* it happened to her even if it didn't."

"Right. Let's say something horrible occurred when she was in college, so devastating that she felt the need to drop out of school, and she's never really dealt with the trauma. Then she sees that Mel's case might be reopened, and from there she reads up on the trial and what the women experienced, and she starts imagining she's a victim of the same kind of crime."

"We should run that by Halligan."

I appreciate Logan hearing me out, keeping an open mind, but at the same time I know I'm grasping at straws.

"Of course, maybe I just read Riley the wrong way. I—I was in a bit of state, hearing all those horrible details and thinking about Mel."

"I know, me too," he says grimly. "And Riley might have seemed evasive only out of shame or embarrassment. On the other hand, that doesn't mean you should totally dismiss what you're feeling, Bree. Who knows, maybe you've got some kind of mother's intuition going on right now, and you need to pay attention to it."

I press a hand to my cheek, caught off guard by the comment. I'm not sure how to reply.

"Hmm" is all I manage.

"At least Halligan sounds like he plans to check out her story."

"Right. And I think I would be fine if I just had some kind of corroboration."

I rest my head back against the seat, letting my eyes close.

Part of me yearns to call Bas right now, to be comforted by the sound of his voice and to ask for his help clearing up my confusion. But I'm not about to let Logan eavesdrop on a conversation with my partner.

"Would you like to be dropped someplace or just back at the inn?" Logan asks.

When I open my eyes, I see we're already in Cartersville.

"The inn, thanks . . . What are you up to today?"

"Gonna make some calls from my room. Try to catch up on work."

"Is Lisa going to mind being stuck in the room?"

I don't know why I'm asking that. She could be stuck in a fucking mine shaft for all I care.

"I decided it was best if Lisa went back to New York," he replies, his voice low. "She left early this morning."

Wow. I was pretty sure Logan was going to lay into her, but I never expected that he'd send her packing.

"Oh . . . Is it going to be hard for you, being here on your own?"

"I thought so at first, but it's better this way. Besides, it's tough for an outsider to know how to handle any of this."

Yeah, we're in a club that few people have the eligibility to join. Beyond that, I'm delighted I won't have to interact with her again.

As we enter the inn, Logan says he'll let me know as soon as he hears from Halligan. Back in my room, I take a seat at the desk. I'm troubled, I realize, not only by the encounter with Riley but also by something Logan said: his comment about my "mother's intuition."

Was that just Logan—in a caring but misguided way—rewriting history for my benefit? Surely he knows that, if asked, Mel would have sworn I didn't have an ounce of intuition in her regard. Yeah, I could smell a lie about a broken foot, but she found me clueless when it came to knowing who she was, or what she really longed for in life, or understanding the quirks that defined her. She reminded me of that not only with sighs and eye rolls but also occasional comments she made, like the snidely delivered, "Mom, you'll never get it, so don't waste your time trying."

No, there can't be a dormant reserve of mother's intuition at work here. But there's *something*, and it's making me still question the veracity of Riley's story.

I search Amazon on my laptop until I find the book I mentioned to Logan, purchase the Kindle edition, and spend the next thirty minutes skimming through the early chapters. The concept is pretty much as I remembered. People who have been severely traumatized sometimes come to believe, erroneously, that an entirely different trauma has befallen them, triggered by exposure to that information. But it's *rare*.

Next, I pull up a map of Cartersville and study the positions of both Pebble Creek Park and Mohegan. As Halligan mentioned, they border the same creek, not all that far apart. At the sight of Pebble Creek Park outlined on the map, my chest tightens and a sob catches in my throat.

I stumble up from the desk and plop down on the end of the freshly made bed. A friend told me years ago that she sometimes "channels" her late mother and pretends they're in conversation, with her mother offering pearls of wisdom. Though I tried that kind of exercise after my own mom died heartbreakingly young, it felt hopelessly fake to me. Sometimes, though, I reflect on some of the advice she offered me when she was alive.

It was always based on solid common sense, along with a keen awareness of my tendency, mainly when I was younger, to want to accept certain things at face value. Once, when I was in my twenties and having trouble deciding whether to accept a position I was being offered at another book publishing company, she told me, "It sounds like you don't have all the facts yet, honey." And once I got them, I decided to pass on the offer.

Okay, what I need now, I realize, are more facts. I return to the desk and do a Google search for Morgan Kroll, the teaching assistant that Riley reportedly broke down in front of. A surprising number of women with that name turn up, but I soon zero in on one who must be her: an associate professor of English and creative writing at Hudson River Community College, a school within an hour's drive of here. That seems like the kind of job someone in her role would have aimed for.

I study the college website photo of Morgan, taken in too bright light. The confident-looking, faintly smiling woman I see is probably in her early to mid-thirties, which would fit, too. Her wavy black hair is cut to just below her chin, and she has a longish face with brown eyes and thick, perfectly groomed eyebrows. Not a beautiful woman but a very arresting-looking one.

Since Halligan is going to try to verify Riley's testimony, that effort will surely include talking to Professor Kroll. But I don't feel like waiting any longer.

I dial the number for the college, and within moments, Kroll's line is ringing and then goes to voicemail.

I've acted rashly, without planning in advance what my message should be, but rather than hang up, I end up blurting out my name and saying that I'm the mother of Melanie Chase, who died while attending Carter College. I ask if she would have a few minutes to speak to me about her time at Carter, if she had indeed worked there.

"I could really use your help," I say at the end. It's a clumsy add to my request, but I don't want her to think I'm planning to throw any blame her way.

As soon as I hang up, I'm second-guessing myself. Did I reveal too much in my message—or not enough?

But twenty-five minutes later, my phone rings, and I see with a jolt that it's her.

"Thanks so much for calling back," I say. "Are you the Morgan Kroll who once worked at Carter College?"

"Yes, that's me," she replies.

I exhale the breath I've been holding. "I'd like to ask you a few questions about something that happened while you were at Carter. Would you be open to that?"

A few beats of silence follow.

"All right," she says at last. "I've actually been expecting your call."

Chapter 17

This seems like more than I could have hoped for. I've not only tracked Morgan Kroll down but she's also willing to talk.

"You're familiar with a former Carter student named Riley Reynolds?" I ask.

"Yes, I know who she is."

"And she—"

"Excuse me for cutting you off," Kroll says crisply, "but I didn't mean I could speak right this second. I need to leave for an appointment, and to be honest, I'd prefer to do this in person."

"I'm in Cartersville, so just tell me when," I say, antsy to speed up the process. "I could come to your location anytime tomorrow."

"That won't work, I'm afraid, because my schedule tomorrow is packed. Let me think . . . My appointment today—it's in Barrow, which is probably only thirty, thirty-five, minutes from Cartersville. Could you meet me there at, uh, let's say five o'clock, after I'm done? There's a little diner in town called Bea's. Kind of a throwback place."

"I can absolutely meet you there," I say. "And I trust it's not a problem if Melanie's father comes along?"

Logan will want to hear this, and beyond that, I need a ride.

The line goes quiet for a couple of seconds. "Can it please just be two of us," she says. "I've been dragged into something I never saw coming, and I'd like to keep this as simple as possible."

Dragged into something. So maybe she won't be backing up Riley's story.

"Okay," I say. "I'll see you at five. And thank you."

I check the time: three thirty. Since I'm being forced to go alone, I need to nail down a ride, and after brief consideration, I decide a taxi is a better option than Uber because it will allow me to handle logistics with an actual human. Though my call to Cartersville Taxi went to voicemail last night, within seconds now I'm talking to the gruff-voiced owner, Craig. I arrange for a round trip to Barrow that will get me there fifteen minutes early, just to be on the safe side, and I let him know that I'll need the taxi to wait for as much as forty-five minutes.

Craig, wearing a green satin New York Jets jacket, arrives exactly when promised, and we reach Bea's Diner even sooner than I anticipated. It turns out to be truly old-fashioned, a place with a Formica-topped counter, chrome stools, and red vinyl booths.

It's only about a quarter full, so I help myself to a booth, the last in the row and with a window looking out to the parking lot. When the waitress strolls over, I order a tuna sandwich and a sparkling water since I realize I haven't eaten a bite since breakfast.

"You mind club soda, hon?" she asks. "'Cause that's the only kind of bubbly water we got."

"That's fine, thank you."

As hungry as I am, I'm also jittery, and in the end, I manage to consume only half the sandwich and a couple of the chips scattered on the edge of the plate.

A few more customers show up, but not Morgan. It's now four minutes after five. What if she blows me off, deciding that a meeting with me is more trouble than she wants to take on?

And then suddenly there she is, pushing open the glass door. Before I have a chance to signal to her, I see her gaze race down the row of booths, and once it lights on me, she lifts her chin in acknowledgment. I'm the only woman sitting by herself.

Several heads turn as she strides the length of the diner in my direction. She's tall and slightly short waisted, so that her legs seem to go on forever, and she's dressed in a striking outfit: a black collared shirt, very slim black pants, stylish short black boots, and a tan sweater coat. As she gets closer, I see that, as in her photo, the only makeup she seems to be wearing is dark-red lipstick.

"Morgan Kroll," she says, sliding onto the seat across from me. She lifts a small black cross-body bag over her head, sets it on the seat, and shrugs off the sweater coat so that it's bunched behind her. "Though I guess I've made that clear by plopping down in your booth."

I offer a small smile, the best I can muster by this point in a punishing day. "Bree Winter. Thank you again for agreeing to see me."

"You're the one who should be thanked for coming to sad little Barrow. My acupuncturist relocated to this town, and it's the only reason I ever come here."

"Do I have it right—that you teach English and creative writing at Hudson River Community College?"

"Correct." She tugs her mouth over in a small smirk. "The Harvard of riverside community colleges."

The waitress saunters back, pad in hand, and asks if Morgan would like something to eat or drink.

"No," she replies tersely. "Nothing for me."

Clearly, her plan is to say what she has to say and be done with it. But that's just fine. All I want is the truth from her.

"How did you know I'd be contacting you?" I ask.

"Riley Reynolds called me yesterday to say she was about to speak to the police, and then a detective got ahold of me several hours ago. I figured you or your husband might be next."

"So, you've given a statement to the police?"

"Briefly on the phone, but I'm going in tomorrow to do it officially. So, tell me what you need from me."

She's polite but no-nonsense. Maybe it's a style she's honed dealing with impatient Gen Z students and their helicopter parents.

"We met with Riley today at police headquarters," I say. "I'm wondering if you can confirm a harrowing story she shared with us—or refute it if that's what's called for."

Morgan briefly presses her dark-red lips together. "The police said I shouldn't be discussing this, but since you're in the loop anyway, I don't see any harm in telling you."

My body fizzes uncomfortably with anticipation.

"Which is it, then?" I say.

She levels her gaze at me. "If you're asking if Riley Reynolds was brutally raped and almost killed, then the answer is yes."

I slowly exhale, a breath I seem to have held since I left Cartersville.

"And she told you this eight years ago, on a Monday morning?" I ask.

Morgan nods, her expression grim. "Yes, and I saw the evidence—these awful bruises she had on her neck from where she'd been strangled. She was wearing a turtleneck, but she pulled it down for me to see."

So, the attack really happened. I feel awful about doubting Riley's story.

"Did she share anything about the circumstances?"

She nods again. "Some. She said she'd been running in the park the night before, which she had every right to do, of course, so I'm not *blaming* her. I was a jock in college myself, so I know the kind of dedication that's called for. But it wasn't the smartest thing to be doing after dark."

"Especially after another girl had been murdered two nights before."

Morgan shifts a little in her seat and crosses her arms in front of her on the Formica table. She's fit-looking, like she's probably still an athlete or likes to work out. As the shirtsleeve hikes up her right arm, I spot a small tattoo on the back of her wrist, several Asian symbols.

"True," she says. "But she said the rumor going around was that a boyfriend was responsible, and so she didn't think she was in any danger . . . It goes without saying that I'm sorry about your daughter. I read about it at the time, of course."

She delivers the condolence matter-of-factly, like she's apologizing for a minor oversight, but that's all right. I'm not here for sympathy.

"Thank you. Just so I'm clear, I take it you knew Riley from the classroom. Is that why she came to you?"

"The classroom?" she asks, her brow wrinkling.

"Weren't you a teaching assistant at Carter?"

She shakes her head. "She might have assumed that, but I had no direct involvement with the college. I was getting an MFA from SUNY Albany that year, studying creative writing with a focus on poetry, and I had a part-time job helping Jeffrey Handler with his latest collection. He paid me to type and organize his notes and do a little bit of research. I mostly worked remotely, though occasionally I needed to stop by his office."

I stare at her blankly for a moment, confused. "So, if you were rarely there, how did she get to know you?"

"*Know* me? I'd never met her before. I was leaving something for Handler early that morning, and she walked into the department. No one was around except me, and she said she was hoping to talk to the department assistant about getting extensions or to drop out without penalty, and before I could explain I didn't even work there, she started shaking violently. I got her to sit, calmed her down a little, and then she blurted out what happened—the rape, almost dying, jumping into the creek."

"She's lucky you were there—someone to share the horror with."

"Yeah, she said she'd been all alone for the rest of the night, going out of her mind. By the way, I hope she explained that I tried like crazy to convince her to call nine-one-one or let me drive her to an ER. But she refused and swore me to secrecy."

"Yes, she told us. You must have felt in a terrible bind."

"That's putting it mildly." She picks up the saltshaker and absentmindedly draws a couple of circles on the table with the bottom of it. "She made clear she'd kill herself if anyone else found out, so I didn't dare go to the police. It turned out she'd lost her phone in the creek, but she was planning to get a new one right away, so I took down her number and called her over the next couple of weeks. She knew by then she wasn't pregnant, thank God, but I still couldn't talk her into going to the cops. And then, all of a sudden, Calvin Ruck was arrested, and she convinced herself there was no need to come forward."

"How sure was she that he was the guy?"

"*Very.*"

It seems that every detail Riley shared with Logan and me was the truth. So where did my unease spring from?

"Is something the matter?" Morgan asks, and I realize I'm frowning.

"No, I guess I'm just feeling a tad guilty. When Riley spoke to us, I found myself struggling to accept everything."

"Why's that, do you think?"

I shrug. "She seemed evasive at times, but I guess it was just torturous for her to describe the experience . . . I suppose I'm also distressed by how long she waited to tell the police. If I put myself in her shoes, I can understand her reluctance years ago, but it would have made a big difference if she'd come forward in real time."

"And now it's too late to do anything with the information, right? I just read online that this man Ruck died in prison, so he can't be prosecuted for additional crimes."

"Right" is all I say. I'm not comfortable offering her any more than that.

Morgan checks her watch. "I should get going. I promised to pick up my partner, and I don't want to keep her waiting."

"Before you leave, can I ask a quick question on an entirely different subject? I assume your college uses Blackboard or a similar system. I was hoping to find some of my daughter's writing assignments on the Blackboard system that Carter uses, but I was told classwork is deleted after five years. Do you think there's any chance it's still in the cloud somewhere?"

"I doubt it. We use a similar system at HRCC, and far as I know, once material is deleted, it's gone for good."

"Damn."

"But wait," she says, stuffing an arm into the sleeve of her coat. "There's a digital archive at Carter specifically for creative work that students might want to upload there. Handler started it himself to encourage kids to think about possibly publishing one day, and I assume it's still active. Perhaps your daughter opted in with some of her work."

Okay, this is interesting. But why hadn't Handler himself mentioned it?

"Great, I'll look into it," I say.

Morgan is clearly eager to split, but I can't resist lobbing one more question now that a certain name is on the table. "What was your impression of Handler back then?"

She pauses what she's doing, letting the coat sag behind her again, and her lips curl infinitesimally in displeasure.

"The acclaimed Jeffrey Handler?" she says. "Well, the *students* seemed to be in awe of him."

"Not you?"

"If you don't mind, I'd prefer not to discuss him. It was a long time ago."

So, not a fan at all.

"Well, thank you again for your time. It's been a huge help."

She resumes putting on her sweater coat and loops her bag over her head.

"You're welcome, and I'm sorry for being a bit brusque earlier," she says. For the first time since we've sat down, there's a trace of warmth in her voice. "It's just that I've been worried that if this stuff about Riley gets out, my failure to alert the police myself could blow back on me professionally somehow. But if I can be of more help, let me know."

It's not what I've been expecting from her—leaving a door open.

"That's very kind of you," I say.

I wish her goodbye and watch her move in long strides toward the exit. As soon as she's gone, I extract my phone and tap Logan's number. I'm not sure how he'll feel about me going around Halligan, but I need to share what I've learned about Riley—that she was telling the truth after all. When the call goes to voicemail, I leave a message asking him to get in touch as soon as possible.

I should be relieved. Halligan now has important new information to take into consideration, and Logan and I don't have to add *duped* to the list of crap we've been through this week.

Instead, my body is practically humming with unease again. I do my best to interpret the sensation, but it's like trying to eavesdrop on an ominous-sounding conversation from another room and not making out a single word.

Chapter 18

The waitress drifts over, smiling pleasantly.

"You all set, hon?" she asks.

I glance at my watch. I've still got a little time left on the clock with Craig.

"Actually, I'd love a cup of tea," I say.

Once she saunters off, I return to my disquiet, trying to make sense of it. Maybe doubting Riley gave me something to focus on besides the ghastly details she shared, and now that I've got good reason to accept her story, those awful images are fighting their way back into my head. And they're taunting me about Mel, telling me, "See, this is the living hell your daughter was forced to endure as well."

But there's something else at work now, too, and I'm pretty sure its name is Jeffrey Handler.

Morgan clearly disliked the man, and since she hasn't let go of that sentiment with time, the issue was probably bigger than him being gruff or demanding as a boss. Maybe he failed to credit her for the research she did, a "crime" that plenty of academics apparently have been guilty of.

Or maybe the answer is hiding right there in the snide comment she made: "Well, *students* were in total awe of him." It's possible Morgan sensed something inappropriate between Handler and one of the students, a variation of the scene I saw yesterday. He might have even come on to *her*.

And then there's her revelation about the archive for creative work. Why wouldn't Handler at least have mentioned it to me? It could almost make me think he doesn't want me to see Mel's writing.

Somehow, I need to learn more about Handler and his relationship with Mel.

The waitress sets the tea down in front of me, and as she does, I think instantly of Bas, who's probably having a cup of maté at the kitchen table. I realize I promised to update him after the meeting with Halligan, so I quickly make the call.

This time, I decide, I'm going to share more and better loop him in to what's happening here. Luckily, the nearest diners are three booths away.

"Sorry I didn't call earlier," I tell him, "but things have been crazy since the meeting."

"So, how did it go? I've been on pins and needles." His voice sounds huskier than normal, and I wonder if he was dozing when I called.

"It was a total shock," I say. "Turns out, there's a victim we never knew about."

"I thought there were two?"

"What?" I ask, confused.

"I thought there were two new victims: one in Ohio and one in another state . . . Pennsylvania."

"Right, but this is someone else entirely, a survivor who we met today. She says she was attacked by Ruck the same week as Melanie, very close to Pebble Creek Park. Which gives us a reason to think what he told his lawyer about Mel really *was* a lie."

"Pebble Creek Park is . . . ?"

"The name of the park Mel was murdered in."

"Right, of course. My God, this is a shock."

"I know. And it's all happening so fast."

"Which way are you leaning now, about Ruck?"

I want to describe the meetings with Riley and Morgan and share some of the odd qualms I've had—*still* sort of have—but a party of two has entered the diner and is making a beeline in this direction, perhaps headed for the next booth.

"Let me tell you more when I'm not out in public, okay?"

"Of course. But are you all right, Bree? This must be so stressful."

"Yeah, I'm just hoping that the detective makes some kind of ruling soon and I can definitely head back by the end of the week."

"Have you been able to avoid Lisa at least?"

"Ah—yes, fortunately," I say with a twinge of guilt. But I don't want to worry him unnecessarily.

"Good. Please take care, okay?"

"Same here, sweetheart . . . Wait, do you have a cold, Bas?"

"I seem to be coming down with something, but I hope if I go to bed early tonight, I can shake it."

"I wish I could be tucking you in."

"Same here. Love you, cariño."

"Love you, too."

The call ends, leaving me weirdly deflated—and feeling disconnected from Bas, and not simply because of the distance in miles. Though I was determined to share more with him, those old reservations clearly flared up again, helping me light on a new reason to hold back. It makes sense that I can talk about all this with Logan—Melanie was his daughter, too—but I have to find a way to address it with Bas as well.

The taxi trip back to Cartersville seems to take longer than the one here, and I grow twitchier with each mile. I try Logan once more, but I still get only voicemail.

"Slight change of plans, Craig," I announce as we reach the outskirts of town. "Can you drop me at Oak and Birch Streets instead of the inn?"

While we've been traveling, I've decided to get a look at Handler's home, maybe even grab a glimpse of the legendary backyard. I can't imagine it will unlock any mysteries, but it's a place to start.

"Got a house number?" he asks.

"No, just the corner is fine."

As soon as he pulls up, he leans across the seat and cranes his neck to see out the passenger window.

"You sure this is where you want to get out?" he asks. The nearest house is yards away.

"Yeah, this is it."

Which isn't exactly true, of course. There's just no way I'm popping out of a cab directly in front of the Handlers' house.

I pay the fare along with a generous tip. After exiting the car, I walk toward the nearest house to determine how close I am to the Handlers'. The numeral "2" is on a porch column, which means I have just a few blocks to go. I tighten the belt on my coat and start walking.

Only a few minutes later, I'm standing across the street from number 57, an attractive white center-hall Colonial. On the same lot, also of white clapboard, is a much smaller one-story structure. Though I can't see a number, I assume it's 57b, Alison's studio.

Except for a fixture burning above the stoop, the main house is dark, but light streams from the studio windows. Alison must be at work inside. And Handler? Chances are he's still on campus, attending one of the many evening events that probably demand his presence.

For a minute I simply stare at the two buildings. There's no view into the backyard from here, but it's easy to imagine students back there years ago, lolling on the grass and soaking up Handler's words.

I also try to picture Handler and Alison at home here. At the dinner on Tuesday night, they'd seemed fairly in sync, but if his relationship with her began as an extramarital affair, it must have crossed her mind since then that his head could be turned again, and that might be a source of tension. Maybe her unnerving painting of the horse at the kitchen table and a plate piled with wax lips hints at what their evenings at home are really like.

I tell myself that it's time to go, that I've seen what I wanted to. But I don't leave. Instead, before I even know what I'm doing, I dart across the street to the sidewalk in front of the studio. The building is set farther back on the lot than the house, tucked among fir trees, but there's a narrow flagstone path leading to the door. I check behind me, find no one there, and though I know I'm being stupid, I turn back around and start slowly down the path.

Despite the light seeping from the studio windows, it's dark back here, not something I relish. Still, I keep going, oddly curious. Once I get closer to the building, I push up onto the balls of my feet so I'm practically tiptoeing.

Nearing the front door, I pause and listen. I'm close enough that if Alison is working in there, I should be able to hear her moving or speaking on the phone. But there's suddenly wind in the fir trees, swishing the branches, and that's the only sound I hear.

I step off the path and move toward one of the windows. *This is insane,* I think, but that doesn't stop me from peering cautiously inside.

The studio turns out to be an open space with several large paintings hanging on a far wall and others leaning against it. There's a big easel in the middle of the room, as well as an array of rolling carts overflowing with art supplies.

Though several lamps are on, Alison doesn't seem to be around. Unless the door in the back wall leads to another room in the studio and she's working in there.

I step even closer to the window. From where I'm standing, some of the paintings aren't much more than a blur of color—blues, greens, and yellows, punctuated in places with black—but I have a good view of one directly across the room from me, resting on the floor. It features a pretty, long-haired woman in a white dress, floating Chagall-like in midair. *Beautiful,* I think, and then shudder as I register more details. The straw basket in the woman's hand is overflowing with fat brown mice, some of which are scurrying down her legs.

Another "dream," I suppose. The deeply unsettling kind that still gnaws at you as you brush your teeth.

"Can I help you?"

I nearly leap out of my skin. I spin around to find Jeffrey Handler just a short distance away on the path. He's the tiniest bit out of breath, like he might have hurried on foot from wherever he's been until now.

"Oh, hi," I say. That's all I come up with in my flustered state.

He simply stands there without saying anything, and even in the dim light, I can detect the tight set of his jaw.

"I was looking for Alison," I add, scrambling. "She invited me to drop by her studio."

He squints as if confused.

"Alison isn't here," he says. "She's out for the evening."

Has he guessed that I've fudged the truth? Hopefully he'll tell himself I'm simply a jet-lagged, grief-addled woman, unsure of which end is up.

"Ah, okay. No worries."

"It *is* worrisome, though—that you've come all this way for no reason. It's not like Alison to forget a meeting."

"She didn't forget," I say. I move away from the window and plant myself back on the path. "We hadn't set up a specific time. I just took a chance she'd be here."

"I see. Well, do check with her first if you find the time to stop by again," he says. He shifts position slightly, and thanks to the direction of the light, I can see his face better now. He looks slightly vexed, like I've tapped his bumper with my own in a parking lot. "I'm sure she'd love to show you her work, but she's quite busy lately, and there's no guarantee she'll be in the studio on any given day."

"Will do."

He goes quiet again and seems to study me.

"I take it you've had a busy week so far," he says finally, his tone softer now.

"Fairly, yes . . . And, oh, I got the copies of *The Muse*. Thank you for your help on those."

"Happy to do what I can."

I take a breath, no longer quite as flustered. "At dinner, you also mentioned that you might have some of Melanie's work in a file at home. You probably haven't had a chance to look yet, though."

He clears his throat. "No, actually, I did look at lunchtime today and was going to email you. Unfortunately, I didn't find anything."

"Well, I appreciate the effort," I say, disheartened by the news. "And—and there's no other place her work might be?"

A beat passes. And then another.

"I'm afraid not."

"Good night, then. And sorry to disturb you."

"Wait," he says as I start to brush past him. "Would you like me to call you a cab? You can come in the house while you're waiting."

Instinctively, I glance in that direction, where the only light burning is over the stoop. A faint ripple of fear runs through me. *No,* I think. *I don't want to go into that house with you and wait for you to call a cab.*

Chapter 19

"Thank you, but that's not necessary," I say. "I'm in the mood for a walk again."

"See you tomorrow night, then," Handler says. "Shall I mention to Alison that you dropped by?"

Maybe he thinks I don't want her to know I was peeking in her windows, and that I'd be grateful if he kept it between us.

"Yes, please. Tell her I'm sorry I missed her, but it's my fault entirely."

As I make my way up the path, I feel his eyes on my back. I turn left at the sidewalk, then walk rapidly—almost jogging, really—until I'm back at the corner of Birch and Oak Street, the spot where the taxi left me. Since Craig mentioned he was calling it quits for the night, I order an Uber and sigh gratefully when I see the wait will be only five minutes.

So, what's Handler doing now? I wonder, still winded. Flicking on the house lights and deciding to call Alison to see if what I told him was true? She'll probably say she *had* extended a welcome for me to visit but that I'd shown little interest, and we'd certainly never discussed a possible time. She might even wonder if I'm a little batty.

I'm not even sure myself why I felt the need to peer through those windows. Alison intrigues me, but it's Handler my mind keeps landing on. Though I still don't have any real sense of him, there's one thing I *do* know: I make him uncomfortable. I felt it in his office, I felt it at dinner, and I certainly felt it tonight.

And then there's the fact that he still didn't come clean about the archive. Even if Mel hadn't uploaded material there, it seems Handler should have at least mentioned it to me. I need to check whether it's still in existence without him knowing what I'm up to.

I also need to learn more about *him*, particularly his reputation when it comes to female students. Maya certainly wouldn't be forthcoming, and it's hardly a question for Chip. But there *is* someone who might be able to shed more light.

When I enter the inn a short time later, the lobby is empty except for Shelly, puttering silently behind the front desk. There's a murmur of male voices from the parlor, though—and one of them is Logan's. Curious, I peer inside.

It's all cozy in there right now. Only the table lamps are burning, creating soft puddles of light around the room, and the gas fireplace is on. Logan's sitting in a wingback chair facing the door, and he straightens as he sees me, then lifts his chin, a signal of some kind, though I'm not sure what it means.

And then I get it—because of the long legs extending from the chair across from him. They must belong to Jack Lawler. Logan had said they were meeting for a drink, but I had no idea that would happen here.

"Oh, Bree, come in," he calls out. "I'm sorry not to phone you back, but now you'll see why."

I proceed into the parlor.

"You remember Jack, don't you?" Logan says next, and a second later my daughter's ex has twisted around so he's facing in my direction.

"Ms. Winter, so nice to see you again," Jack says, starting to stand.

"Please don't get up," I tell him.

"I was just about to anyway." He rises fully, dressed in a tight-fitting black V-neck sweater, slim black jeans, and spiffy black-and-gray sneakers. He takes a couple of steps in my direction and shakes my hand. "I'm due to meet a friend for dinner."

Up close, I see that he's even more attractive than he was in college. His face—clean-shaven now—has filled out in a good way, softening the lines a little, and the short haircut draws attention to his features instead of distracting from them the way the long tousles once did. As I take him in, I can't help but think of poor Mel, forever frozen as a college junior. Occasionally, I've dared to wonder what she would look like as an almost-thirty-year old, but mostly I spare myself the anguish of going there.

"A friend from Carter?" I ask.

I couldn't care less who it is, but I'm stealing time. Logan will fill me in about Jack later, but I need to take a measure of him myself before he splits.

"Yeah, a guy who decided to stay in the area," he says with another smile. "I haven't seen him in ages, so it will be good to catch up."

"And how nice of you to come to the reception."

"It's my pleasure, actually," Jack says. "I was so impressed when I heard about the scholarships and the new *Muse* office. I figured this was a way for me to pay tribute to Mel. I still think about her a lot."

He always had presence, but he's got poise now, too. Gone, I notice, are the self-soothing gestures I remember so vividly from when we had coffee with Mel and him—he would frequently tug at his chin or rake his fingers through his hair.

It unnerved me a little, especially the way it contrasted with the confident, unentangled way he performed his roles onstage.

"I appreciate that," I tell him. "It helps to know people still think of Mel."

"Of course," he says, and runs a hand along the side of his head. So not *completely* unentangled now.

"Well, I should let you get to your dinner. Enjoy your evening."

"Thanks. And see you both tomorrow night."

Logan's risen by now as well, and Jack offers him a quick handshake goodbye, thanks him for the drink, and then strides into the lobby, leaving a trail of musky cologne. For a half minute Logan and I stand nearly motionless until we hear the click of the front door over the insistent hum from the fireplace.

"I didn't realize you were meeting him here," I say, not accusing, just curious.

"It was a last-minute decision. I had a hunch it might give me a leg up to do it on my turf, instead of in some bar."

"And?"

"There's some stuff worth sharing, but, God"—he shoots a hand from the sleeve of his zippered cardigan and glances quickly at his watch—"I'm starving. Have you had dinner yet?"

"No."

"Want to grab a bite somewhere? There's a little Italian restaurant I discovered about twelve, fifteen, minutes from here. The food's nice."

I hesitate. Sitting at the table with him in Uruguay had been both awkward and sad, and I'm not sure I want to repeat it. But I'm hungry myself, and the brief conversation with Jack has only added to how churned up I feel tonight. Maybe a glass of wine and some comfort food will help, even if I'm eating across from Logan.

"If you prefer, I can order something for you while I'm there and drop it off later," he says, clearly sensing my ambivalence.

"No, I'd like to go. Can you give me a few minutes, though? I want to run upstairs."

"Sure thing."

As soon as I'm in my room, I follow the plan I made on the street corner, placing a second call to Harry Kronish.

"Hey," he says in lieu of hello. "What's up?"

"Sorry to trouble you again, Harry. But I had one more question."

"No problem."

"You said you thought Mel might have been seeing someone new but she never volunteered a name. Any idea at all who it could have been?"

"None whatsoever. Like I told you, there seemed to be something a little clandestine about the whole thing."

"*Clandestine?*" I feel goose bumps race along my arms. "I don't recall you using that word before."

"I think I said she seemed like the cat that ate the canary, though clandestine works, too, I suppose. It's so long ago now, but I remember sensing she wanted to keep it secret, even from me for the time being."

Mel had been secretive with Logan and me since she was thirteen, but in time I learned she could be that way even with her friends. I've never forgotten a comment made by her pal Sara at the high school graduation party we threw for Mel in our loft. I asked her what she'd miss the most about the city once she left for college, and after she'd listed a few things, I inquired—always greedy for even a morsel about my daughter—what she thought Melanie would miss. Sara shrugged and said, "Gosh, I'm not sure. You know, Mel. She's always kind of a mystery."

I take a breath. "Could the guy have been a professor?"

"A *professor*? Uh, gee, it's possible, I guess. It wouldn't have been the smartest thing, but she seemed kind of restless after Jack, like she wanted to, you know, shake things up. She even wondered one night if she should have gone to a bigger college."

Something else I didn't know about my daughter.

I exhale slowly, thinking. I hate being a flamethrower, but if I want to get anywhere, I'm going to have to light a match.

"Do you remember Jeffrey Handler from your time at Carter?" I ask.

"Of course—I had the guy for a couple of classes. Wait, are you thinking it might have been *him*?"

"I'm just posing the question for now. Did she ever talk about him?"

"Well, I know she loved the classes she took with him, but she never hinted at anything more than that, at least to me."

"Just one more question, and I promise to let you go, Harry," I say. "Were there ever any rumors about Handler sleeping with students?"

"Students, no, not from what I know."

"What do you mean by 'students, no'?"

There's a pause, and I sense him weighing his words.

"I don't think I've ever told this to a soul, because I figured it was none of my business, but the summer before junior year, I saw him once in a restaurant with another woman. She was attractive, blond, I think, and maybe thirtyish, so definitely not a student. And definitely not his wife because I knew what Mrs. Handler looked like."

I bite my lip, letting the image form in my mind.

"Could it have been a colleague? Or a friend?"

"Nah, they seemed flirty, and at one point he had his hand on top of hers. The location was kind of a red flag, too. They were in Rhinebeck, my hometown. That's an hour and a half drive from Cartersville, which made me think they were on the down-low."

So, from the sound of it, Handler *does* step out on his lovely second wife. Or at least he did in the past.

"Okay, thanks, Harry. Just so you know, I don't have a good reason to suspect Handler of anything, so please don't breathe this to a soul."

"Got it. Just promise you'll let me know if there's any news."

"Promise."

I've been gone at least fifteen minutes by now, and Logan is probably pacing the lobby, ready to eat the drapes, but I take a minute to pull my thoughts together. Though the woman Handler looked tight with in the restaurant hadn't been college age, he might be open to the idea under the right circumstances, just as he was with Alison. There was the little scene in his office, after all.

Of course, it's a big leap to think he was involved with Mel, and yet if he's got a preference for young women, I can certainly see him being drawn to someone like her—smart, pretty, intriguing, and with a level of New York City–born sophistication that might suggest she could be discreet.

Would she have been game? I'd be disappointed to learn she'd been involved with another woman's husband, especially in light of my own situation, but I can picture Handler's allure back then: the supposedly brilliant, erudite, accomplished poet, and a way to, quote, "shake things up" after Jack. Besides, she was only nineteen, an age known for making regrettable choices.

I finally force myself off the bed and swap the blouse I've had on all day for a fresh one. I make a quick attempt to fluff my hair. It's so slicked to my head that I look like a small dog who's just emerged from its bath.

As I start for the door, my mind remains stalled on Handler. If he does pursue college girls, he's probably damn careful about it. Being caught sleeping with a student would not only cost him tenure but also make it really tough for him to secure another teaching job.

What if he *thought* he was getting away with it and then realized the secret was in danger of being revealed, that a girl who initially seemed like the model of discretion was starting to blab to friends or reveal the affair in poems and short stories—or even worse, threatening to accuse him of misconduct?

How far would he go to protect himself?

Chapter 20

Rather than wait for the elevator, I take the stairs to the ground floor. My phone rings just as I step onto the first landing.

"Thirty seconds," I say when I answer, certain it's Logan.

"Shall I hold, then?" a male voice asks. Not Logan's. When I check the screen, I see it's an unknown caller.

"Who is this, please?"

"It's Chip, Chip Conway. We met at dinner last night."

This is not a call I want to be dealing with right now.

"Oh, hi, sorry," I say. "I'm just running out for dinner. Can I ring you tomorrow?"

"Um, sure. But if you've got even half a minute, I wanted to give you a heads-up."

"Okay," I say, now on alert.

"I heard from the reporter again, and it looks like he's preparing a second story, saying there've been several recent developments regarding your daughter's case."

I pause on the steps, catching my breath. Someone in law enforcement has clearly leaked information.

"Is he aware of what those developments are?"

"If he is, he didn't share them with me. Is there anything you can tell me, Ms. Winter? I feel slightly on the back foot here."

Back foot. What does he think this is, a game of pickleball?

"Chip, I appreciate the heads-up, but I'm not free to speak about the case at this time. I'll let you know if and when that changes."

"All right," he says, sounding less than pleased with the response. "The more information we have, the better we can be at dealing with the press."

Maybe he sees nosiness as part of his PR role, but it's starting to get on my nerves.

"Have a good evening" is all I say, hoping to drive home that it's pointless to pressure me.

Logan is in the lobby now—but not pacing. He's standing by the front windows, staring out to the street. Perhaps time has taught him to wait with greater patience.

He turns as I approach him and smiles. There are a few guests congregated by the fire in the parlor now, so I hold off on telling him about the call from Conway until we're outside.

"Well, good," he tells me. "As we've said before, this probably helps our cause."

Once we're cocooned in the car, I find myself finally decompressing a little. For the first minute or two, I simply stare out the window at the endless clapboard houses we pass, many lit inside right now with only the muted glow from a TV screen.

"So," I say finally, "tell me your impressions of Jack."

Logan nods, his eyes still on the road.

"As I'm sure you noticed, he's abandoned the *Inside Llewyn Davis* look. He's all cleaned up now."

"Well, if he's out auditioning for parts, he's got to keep up with the times."

"Exactly. And believe it or not, his career might be taking off."

"Are you serious?" I say, more than a little surprised.

"This is all according to him, of course, but he just shot a pilot for a series with some big-deal—what do they call them?—*showrunner*, and it looks really promising. He's not the lead, but he'd be a regular, in every episode."

"I thought you said he was waiting tables."

"He is, but just till the show gets the green light."

So now, eight years later, Jack Lawler might be closing in on his dream, something never allowed to happen for Mel.

"Okay, good for him," I say as Logan navigates a turn. We're now on the outskirts of Cartersville, traveling a two-lane highway. "But that makes it an even bigger surprise that he took the time to drive up for the reception."

"You don't buy the 'paying tribute to Mel' stuff?"

"Like I said, I could if tomorrow night was a *memorial*, but it's not . . . What . . . what if this trip is really about the show and his red-hot future?"

"I'm not following."

"There's a lot on the line for him now, so maybe the whole point of him coming was to meet with you face-to-face and make sure there aren't hard feelings that could backfire on him."

"He's covering his ass in some way?"

"Yeah, maybe," I say. "I'm not exactly a *People* magazine reader these days, but I've seen stories in the news about male actors on the brink of major stardom who get dropped by agents and studios if there's even a hint of impropriety in their dealings with women. If Jack's career takes off, and reporters investigate his background, they might learn he was on police radar following the murder of his former girlfriend."

Logan nods, fully catching my drift. "And now that he's met with us and made nice, he's probably fairly confident we won't malign him in any way."

"Yup . . . But *should* we be maligning him? Do you think there's any chance he did it, Logan?"

He pulls back a little in the driver's seat, obviously surprised by my comment. "As of now, I'd have to say no, I guess. I mean, Riley's story—if it checks out—pretty much leaves him in the clear." He glances over. "Why? Are you still having trouble believing her?"

A sigh escapes my lips. "No, not anymore, actually. The reason I tried to reach you earlier is because I had a visit today with Morgan Kroll, the woman Riley said she spoke to."

"*What?*"

I tell him about tracking down Kroll and meeting her at the diner—going alone at her insistence—and how she explained that Riley divulged the same story all those Mondays ago. My eyes are trained on Logan. Even in the dimness of the car, I can see that he's taken aback.

"Christ, that confirms it, then," he says.

"Are you shocked I contacted her?" I ask. Because he's still looking stunned.

"Yeah, but not as much as Halligan's going to be. I'm glad you did it, though. At least we have corroboration now."

I'm grateful for his response. This would all be so much worse if we didn't see eye to eye.

Logan slows the car suddenly. "Okay, here we go," he says. "I almost overshot the place."

The restaurant, Nino's, is in a white stucco building set back a little from the road.

"I know, it looks pretty old school," he tells me as we make our way from the car. "But I swear it's good. And I know you're a fan of southern Italian."

He says it with complete confidence, not like a man who hasn't been to a restaurant with me in close to a decade and knows almost nothing about my life since then.

Based on the modest exterior, I'm half expecting red-and-white-checkered tablecloths and wine bottles in straw flasks hanging from the wall, but the dimly lit room, with a long wooden bar at the end, is more formal than that. All the tables are set with crisp white linens and have a small, glowing lamp in the center. There's currently a dozen or so diners, though many look close to finishing their meals.

We're led to a quiet spot in the back and handed two huge leather-bound menus, the size of something you'd pack for a weekend trip.

"I'm almost too tired to look," I say after the maître d' steps away. "Can you Sherlock the menu for us?"

I regret the suggestion as soon as it's out of my mouth. That was something I used to say when we were married because, after all, Logan knew all the games restaurants played. But if I don't want him referencing the past, why should I?

"Sure," he says. He pulls a pair of reading glasses from his shirt pocket and quickly peruses the menu with the glasses perched midway down his nose. He looks as exhausted as I feel.

When the waiter arrives, Logan orders a Caesar salad to share, two chicken piccatas, and two glasses of Chianti classico.

"Sounds good," I say when we're alone again.

"You're not secretly craving some Uruguayan blood sausage and a plate of empanadas?"

I laugh and tell him no, but at the same time I wonder if even coming with him tonight has been a mistake. I swore to myself that I wouldn't give Logan any reason to think we were friends, that I had no intention of sharing another meal with him, and yet here we are sitting together in a dimly lit restaurant. And looking like a middle-aged couple out on date night, no less. What would Bas say if he saw me now?

I need to course correct after tonight.

"So," Logan says, letting his body find the back of the chair. "Where does this leave us?"

His question completely throws me. What's he asking—whether we really *can* be friends now?

"In terms of what?" I say.

"In terms of Riley. Are you really over your reservations?"

Okay, good. I've simply mistaken his meaning.

"How can I *not* be over them?" I say. "Morgan Kroll confirmed every word of the story."

"So, we're back to what we believed years ago? That Ruck killed Melanie?"

I shrug. "I guess."

"Wait, what's going on?" he asks.

And for the first time since I spoke to Morgan, I realize that something about the meeting with Riley has continued to pester me. It's like a shimmer of light on water, tremulous enough for me to see but impossible to grab hold of.

"I'm convinced now that Riley was attacked," I say, "and that she almost died. But I still can't let go of the way she came across at times. Maybe . . . maybe the evasiveness I picked up has to do with Ruck."

"That she's mistaken about him?"

"Yes. It would have been such a relief for her back then to discover her rapist had been apprehended, and so maybe she convinced herself that Ruck was the guy. But at the same time, she might have niggling doubts about him, and those leaked out when she was talking to us."

Logan cocks his head. "Well, his mug shot was all over the news, and the power of suggestion could have taken over."

"Right, you hear about that kind of thing happening. Look, I want to believe Ruck did it, but what if he was never on any kind of rampage in Cartersville?"

"But what would that mean, then?" he says. "That there was some other serial killer in the area that weekend, and he attacked both girls with the same MO as Ruck's?"

"You're right. That makes no sense at all."

Logan rests an elbow on the table and exhales into his fist. "What we need is a follow-up with Halligan to see where he stands on all of this. It's late, but let me text him and say we want to talk tomorrow."

I watch as he digs his phone from his pocket and taps out the message. I'm glad I confessed my lingering worries about Riley and wonder, sitting there, if I should also tell him about my encounter with Handler and all my concerns on that front. But I decide against it. As I told Harry, I don't have a good reason to suspect Handler of sleeping with Mel, so why inject that ugly thought into Logan's head tonight?

The salad arrives, and then, as soon as we finish, the chicken piccata appears. Logan digs in with relish as if we've driven to some far-flung Michelin-starred restaurant where it's taken months to get a reservation.

"See, it's quite good, isn't it?" he announces after a few bites. "They haven't dredged the damn thing in a ton of flour and turned it into a congealed mass."

"Delicious," I say, though under the circumstances, it's hard to really relish it.

"Remember that period when Mel was nine or ten, and all she seemed to want was chicken piccata?"

"Yeah. She'd beg you to make it every week, sometimes twice."

"But then she'd order it out, too. Always when we went to Monte's, that place on MacDougal."

I look off, feeling a swell of emotion and hoping I can contain it.

"God, I loved the Monte years," I say. "That was before Mel decided she hated me."

"Bree, she didn't hate you. How can you say that?"

"Come on, Logan, you were *there*. Whatever connection we'd had when she was young was gone by the time she was thirteen. From then on, I could do almost nothing right in her eyes."

He swipes at the air with his hand, dismissing the idea. "That was all about her being an adolescent. Of course Mel loved you, but like any teenager, she sucked at showing it."

"The adolescent Mel didn't have any trouble showing *you* she cared."

"Well, that's because I was her father, not her mother. I'm no shrink, but I know it's supposedly a whole different ball game between mothers and daughters."

It's more or less the same wisdom he used to impart years ago, when he was working hard to reassure me. I have to hand this to my ex: he never gloated about his own closeness with Melanie, never found any way to rub in my failure.

"Maybe," I say.

"Not maybe. I'm sure everything would have changed once Mel was an adult. She had a total love of words and books, just like you. Think of what you two would have shared."

"I can never be sure of it, though, can I?"

My voice has cracked as I've been speaking, a warning from my body that it doesn't like the topic.

"Yes, you *can* be. Bree, I can't let you think this way."

We're sitting catty-corner, our forearms only a few inches apart on the table, and suddenly he's laying his hand over mine.

And without any warning at all, I'm overwhelmed with a rush of desire.

Chapter 21

I know I shouldn't leave my hand there. It's too strange to have mine under Logan's, and he might even feel how fast my blood is pumping through my veins. But if I jerk away, I'll send a weird message.

After a short while, I tap his hand a few times with my free one, like I'm petting a dog who's put his head on my knee, and then slowly slide my fingers out from under his.

"That means a lot," I say.

I feel ill at ease with Logan for the first time this evening, unnerved by how aroused I was by his touch. I know he'd probably like an espresso now—he sometimes drank them until midnight without a problem—but I tell him I'm tired and would like to get back to the inn.

"Of course," he says, and then signals to the waiter for the check. "I'm tired, too, and I want to look over my remarks for tomorrow night before turning in."

I try my hardest to make the waiter accept my credit card along with Logan's, but my ex insists on paying the bill, saying it was his idea to come here. As we depart the restaurant, I thank him in the polite tones I might use if I were one of his work colleagues—though not one he's fucking—and I keep a few feet between us on our walk across the parking lot. We stay quiet on the car ride back. Not the kind of companionable silence from years back but an awkward one, as if I've dragged my discomfort from the end of the meal into the car with us.

Does he sense what happened to me back there? I hope this was the first time in his life that he couldn't read the room.

We turn into the inn parking lot. Before Logan climbs out of the car, his phone pings.

"A text from Halligan," he announces. It's the first he's spoken since we left the restaurant. "He wants to do a call with us at half past noon tomorrow."

I nod, relieved at the news.

"There's a small meeting room at the rear of the inn," he says. "I'll see if I can reserve it for tomorrow, and then we can put him on speakerphone."

"Good idea. Though, gosh, by now he's probably heard I met with Morgan Kroll. I bet he's really pissed."

"He'll get over it."

Logan pauses at the front door and studies me intently. I pull back ever so slightly, worried that, God forbid, he's about to offer a comforting hug.

"Are you going to be okay until then?" he asks.

"Yeah, thanks. I'll probably walk over to campus at some point and peek at the new *Muse* office."

He smiles. "It's not quite finished yet, but you'll get the picture. And I think you'll be impressed."

Good ol' Shelly glances up as we enter the lobby, tells us "Good evening," and returns to her busywork. If she's curious about what happened to the third player in our sad little drama, she's not letting on.

"I think I'll grab a sparkling water from the bar," I say to Logan.

"Good night, then," he says, offering a wan smile.

As soon as the elevator starts to ascend, I take the stairs to my room. I kick off my shoes, peel off my clothes, and after getting into pajamas, I perch on the edge of the bed, hoping to quiet my thoughts.

What I'm not going to do is beat myself up over the twinge of desire I felt at the restaurant.

It says nothing about my love and desire for Bas. Obviously, it was just some kind of muscle memory, triggered—thanks to a stupid decision on my part—by being in such an intimate setting with Logan. Sex, after all, had been a vivid part of our relationship, an almost ever-present erotic hum, even when we were livid with each other and barely speaking.

Of course, not during our last year together. We seldom even kissed through those crushing months. In late summer, when I finally reached out for Logan in bed—when I thought sex might, at the very least, help stave off my desire to die—he had no interest. Or rather, as I soon learned, he had no interest in sex with *me* at that time.

And it's not like I still feel anything for Logan, other than gratitude for having him as my ally this week. If I'm being honest with myself, there've been stray moments when I've *recalled* my feelings for him and how much they defined such a huge chunk of my life. But that's the same as being in an old, ramshackle house and sensing the ghost of someone who died before their time or even against their will.

I just need to be more mindful, I think. That means avoiding dimly lit settings and not getting into conversations with him about stuff like chicken piccata and bistros we once escaped to on frigid nights. This trip is all about Melanie, and that's the only thing that matters.

I grab my phone and send a quick text to Bas, even though I'm certain he's sleeping now, trying to fight off his cold.

Hope you feel better by the time you get this. Miss you terribly.
xoxo

Though my unsettled state seems to permeate my dreams, I wake feeling resolute—and within minutes I have a solid plan for the morning. As I told Logan, I want to see the *Muse* office, but there are now several things ahead of that on my list.

For starters, I'm going to try to learn more about Handler this morning. It might not matter in the bigger scheme of things, but if he was Mel's secret crush or lover, I want to know.

I also intend to find out if the creative content archive still exists and whether it contains any of Mel's work—and I've decided to solicit the pesky Chip Conway's help on that front.

And I'm going to make a trip this morning to Mohegan Park, where Riley was attacked. Maybe if I survey it with my own eyes, and everything is just as she described, it will be a final verification for me.

Sitting at the desk in my room, I do a Google search on Handler, just to see if there's anything more to find online. He's not on social media, so nothing to go by on that front, and there's no media coverage of any scandals in his past—he wouldn't be at Carter if there were. Mostly what I end up with are reviews of his poetry books, and the occasional profile accompanying them.

Interestingly, he speaks in one article about the need for a poet to live freely. *Live freely to do what?* I wonder.

It's after ten when I finish, and time to phone Chip, though I end up with only voicemail. I ask him to call me as soon as possible. He's going to mistakenly think I've decided to fill him in about the case, but that's okay. Whatever it takes to have him get in touch.

After grabbing a coffee to go in the lobby, I order an Uber to take me to the park. While in the back of the car, with the cardboard coffee cup gripped between my feet on the floor, I send a text to Bas, one I've been mulling over since I woke up. Until now I've been so worried about the danger of telling Bas too much that I've failed to see the price I could pay for telling him too little, that it might be creating a gulf between us. I have to take a chance that our relationship can handle all of it.

> Sweetheart, just wanted to say sorry about always rushing you off the phone. Things are crazy here and constantly shifting. Will tell you much more when I can and we'll have lots of time to talk when I'm home. Xoxo

Finished, I finally glance out the window. As we zip down a street of colorful clapboard houses and still barren trees, I realize I'm almost weighted down with dread. I'm going to Mohegan Park, *not* Pebble Creek, a place I forced myself to see once and vowed never to return to, but they're bound to be similar.

I'm wrong, though. Stepping out of the car, I discover that this park bears little resemblance to Pebble Creek, or at the least the one seared in my memory. That park, ironically, was designed to be a woody sanctuary right in the middle of town, a place to simply wander through or view the creek from a weathered bench.

Mohegan turns out to be much more of a recreational park. I spot a large playground, a sandbox, and a turquoise-painted spray pool, all of which send other kinds of memories surging back. When Mel was young, I used to take her after work, and weather permitting, to a small, nondescript playground in Tribeca. She particularly liked the sandbox, but not for any reason other kids did.

"Do you want to build something, honey?" I asked her once when she was probably five or so. "You have your shovel."

"No, that's okay. I just want to sit here and pretend."

"Pretend what?"

"That this is the Land of the Sand. And I'm the ruler."

It's chilly today, and most of the people here are moms or sitters with kids, braving the unspring-like weather to use the playground. I pause and survey my surroundings. An older man is jogging farther ahead of me, and I realize he must be on the path Riley said she was using when her assailant approached her.

I start walking again, and as I near the path, I notice picnic tables in the general area, each tucked under a different maple tree. Riley said that after being struck on the back of her head, she'd been dragged to a table. My stomach turns as I realize it might have been one of these.

The jogging path stretches both ways into the distance, but this seems to be the only spot with tables nearby. Making sure I'm not about to collide with anyone, I dart across the path.

And then, just below me, I spot the creek. The water's only a few feet high, and clear, which means I can see down to the endless gray and black pebbles that line the bottom. I run my gaze along the bank. There's a gentle slope from where I'm standing, meaning someone could scramble down easily enough, perhaps even with their shorts below their knees.

The creek is barely moving, though, which makes me wonder why her attacker hadn't followed her down the embankment and dragged her back onto shore. Surely he would have done anything to keep her from escaping and later identifying him.

But on that Sunday night eight years ago, the creek had been full and moving fast, Riley said, and she was carried off by the current. Her assailant might have assumed he'd never catch her. Maybe he didn't know how to swim and was afraid of being carried off himself.

As I start to retrace my steps, I catch sight again of the nearest picnic table. Against my will, I'm seeing Riley on the table, clawing at the leash around her neck. And then, to my horror, I'm picturing Mel as well—with the life being strangled out of her.

I race back to the park entrance, and when the Uber app shows that a car will take fifteen minutes to get here, I phone Cartersville Taxi, and the owner, Craig, handles the order this time, too.

"I'll be there in five," he says, and thankfully he is. I nearly hurl myself into the back seat.

"You been checkin' out the local sights?" he asks once we're moving.

"Sort of . . ." I say, trying to settle my mind. "Do—do you know much about the water here?"

"Pebble Creek? I know it as well as anyone, I guess. I fish it for rock bass, but farther upstream, where it's not as populated."

"It looks really low right now."

"Ha, just how I like it. That way you can see the holes where the bass are hidin'."

"But does it get much higher sometimes—and move really fast? So fast that it could carry someone away?"

"Oh yeah, sure, depending on the rain. A buddy of mine lost his dog that way last year. One of those little ones that looks like a fox."

Still another detail confirmed. So far, Riley's story has checked out, though I still have no proof her assailant was Ruck.

I've cut things a little close this morning, but I arrive at the inn just in time for the call with Halligan. I dash up to the room to pee and drop off my trench coat, and as I'm about to hurry back downstairs, my phone rings. I answer right away, thinking it might be Chip, but to my shock, it's Morgan Kroll.

"I hope I'm not interrupting you," she says.

"Not at all. Is something up?"

"I just had my follow-up appointment with the state police today."

"How did it go?" Surely she's told Halligan I went around him.

"Well enough. I'd found the notes I made after Riley left the English department that day, and I went over them with the detective—and he seemed to accept that my hands were tied about taking any action . . . There's one thing I wanted to mention, though. The detective, Harrington, or—"

"Halligan," I say and then hold my breath.

"Right. He asked that I keep everything to myself, and I made a split-second decision not to admit the two of us had talked. He seemed so by the book that I was afraid he might be seriously miffed. I wanted to give you a heads-up."

She obviously has more heart than I gave her credit for.

"Thank you so much for that, Morgan."

"And now, I guess, we just try to move on from here. Are you headed home soon?"

"Yeah, in a couple of days."

"Well, best of luck."

"Same to you."

I'm running slightly behind now, and by the time I locate the meeting room, Logan already has his phone on the polished wooden table, and Halligan's voice is droning through the speaker.

"Hold on a sec, will you?" Logan interrupts. "Here she is."

I quickly apologize and take a seat catty-corner from my ex.

"We were just getting started," he explains. "Detective Halligan was saying that he's spoken to two people who've helped corroborate Riley's story. One is the woman from the Carter English department who she mentioned to us."

Logan's phrased his comment to indicate that Halligan doesn't seem to know I beat him to the punch. I'm tempted to confess, and yet if I do, my transgression will not only cast me in a negative light but Morgan, too, since she kept quiet about it. So, I just listen.

"The first person I spoke to actually was Riley's gynecologist," Halligan says. "She said that Riley became a patient about a year and a half ago and revealed that she'd been raped and wanted to make sure it hadn't affected her ability to conceive or carry a child once she married."

I wince at this revelation. Riley's concern was probably heightened because of her engagement, but she may have been tormented about the issue for years.

"But of greater significance," he adds, "was the interview with Morgan Kroll. She confirmed that Riley reported the rape to her the next morning, along with details about how she escaped. And she showed her the bruising on her neck."

"This is very helpful, Brian," I say after giving his words a moment to sit in the air. "And though I admit I had some reservations yesterday, I accept that Riley was attacked exactly as she said she was. But how can we be sure the man who did it was really Ruck? It was dark, she was terrified . . ."

"Right," Logan interjects, "What's to say she wasn't influenced by the photos she later saw of him."

"Well, her description of him that morning couldn't have been closer," Halligan says.

"*What* description?" I blurt out.

"Morgan Kroll showed us the notes she'd made after Riley left her—she'd jotted things down in case she ended up speaking to the police herself. Riley told her the assailant was late thirties or early forties, tall, heavyset, clean-shaven, and with very short brown hair. And she made a point of mentioning that his eyes were set weirdly far apart."

Eyes set weirdly far apart. I can see those loathsome weasel eyes even now, not only looking out from Ruck's mug shot but also staring at me from across the courtroom. I'd never thought to ask Morgan if Riley had described her attacker that morning, only if she'd been sure it was him once she saw his photo.

"That definitely sounds like Ruck," Logan says. He glances over to check my reaction. I nod in agreement—because the description is dead-on.

"I agree," Halligan says. "And since we know now that Ruck assaulted another woman that weekend, it would be an extraordinary coincidence if Melanie had been attacked two nights earlier—and a mile and a half away—by someone with the same MO but who wasn't Ruck."

"So?" Logan says. "You've decided that Ruck killed Mel, just as we've always believed?"

"Yes," Halligan says soberly. "I managed to speak to the analyst late yesterday, and she's of the same mind."

It's what I've been praying for since I boarded the plane from Uruguay, but before I can stop them, David Schmidt's words about Ruck echo in my mind: "He wanted credit where it was due and not where it wasn't."

I lean in toward the table. "And he lied to his lawyer about Mel *because* . . . ?"

"As the analyst pointed out, even when these bastards *do* confess, they sometimes try to manipulate investigators."

"But what about the inconsistencies you brought up on Monday?" I say. "How do we now explain those away?"

"As the three of us discussed, Ruck might have been interrupted by a noise when he was attacking your daughter, but the woman I spoke to offered an additional theory. Serial killers like Ruck generally keep a homicidal fantasy going in their heads, and they need everything they do to match it. But something might not have gone as planned for

Ruck in Pebble Creek Park and so he abandoned parts of his MO. That would explain why there was no sexual assault and no postmortem bite to any of Melanie's fingers. It might even explain why he felt compelled to attack another woman two nights later—so he could make things right this time."

My pulse is racing now. I long to surrender the doubts Halligan raised on Monday, but for some reason, I'm still resisting, still hearing Schmidt's words.

"And there's no chance at all that Ruck attacked Riley but someone *else* killed Mel?"

"Like I said, it would be such a huge coincidence."

"But what if—what if it wasn't a total coincidence? What if someone Mel *knew* had gotten wind of what happened to Sailor Abbott and tried to make Mel's murder seem like the work of a serial killer? And that person got lucky when Ruck was arrested."

I'm thinking about Jack, the rejected boyfriend. And even Handler, who might have been Mel's lover.

I see Logan straighten in his chair. Does he think I'm sounding like a lunatic, or at the very least beating a dead horse?

"A copycat is always worth considering, but I double-checked with Plattsburgh, and the crime scene details from Sailor Abbott's case—like the use of a dog leash—were kept tightly under wraps until well after Ruck's arrest."

I sigh, sinking into my chair. So I *am* beating a dead horse—into a bloody pulp. And I've got nothing else to add. Logan drums his fingers on the table.

"That's it, then?" he asks.

"I'd say yes. It might not bring a lot of comfort, but I believe your daughter's killer was apprehended and died in prison."

"Okay, thank you, Brian," Logan says. "We appreciate everything you've done."

"Do you think Riley will be okay?" I ask. I don't want to lose sight of her in the middle of this.

"I hope so," Halligan says. "I think she's felt good getting the truth off her chest."

He signs off then, wishing us the best. For a few seconds I sit motionless in my chair, absorbing what I've learned. I came here for the truth, and Halligan says we now have it.

Which means it's time to go home.

Chapter 22

"So?" Logan asks, jerking me from my thoughts. "Are you okay with this?"

I shrug. "I have to be. Halligan's confirmed what he could, answered all our questions . . . and in the end, it's hard to make a case against what he says."

"I wish you didn't look so distressed."

I offer a rueful smile, grateful for his perception. "I think I'm just exhausted from the roller coaster this week, believing one thing one minute and something else the next, and on and on and on."

"It *has* been a roller coaster. But it's bound to be better once we get the hell out of this town."

"Yeah."

"What?"

"I'm just worried that even when I leave, the doubt about Ruck will stay with me. Like it's permanently stuck in my mind now."

"You've got to unstick it, Bree."

"Okay," I say, as if that's enough to make it so.

Logan shoots an arm from the sleeve of his sweater, checking his watch. "Why don't we grab some lunch, have a glass of wine. I've got work calls to make this afternoon, but it would be good to try to decompress first."

I'm famished, but what I want more than food is to plan my trip home and provide more of the details to Bas. To finally have a full conversation with him and, as promised, share more of the news from here. To make the distance between us seem like less than five thousand miles.

Besides, going out to lunch with Logan would be repeating the mistake I made last night. Though I've appreciated his support, it's time to recalibrate and put the old boundaries in place.

"I should go back to my room. I need to take care of a few things."

"Sure." He checks his watch again as if forgetting he did that ten seconds ago. "Why don't we plan to meet in the lobby at five thirty. The reception starts at six, but I'd like to show up at Boyd Hall a few minutes early."

He's expecting me to go with him, and I really should. After all, he gave Lisa the boot on my account, and it seems unfair to make him arrive alone. But I don't want to walk in there practically arm in arm. We seem unified at this moment, but it's only in grief and outrage. Anything else is an illusion.

"Thanks, but I'll probably be coming from another direction. Not the inn."

He nods, his expression inscrutable. I say goodbye, promising to see him shortly after six.

Back in my room, I wolf down a small bag of potato chips from the basket on the dresser and settle at the desk to check flights for tomorrow night. I wasn't expecting an issue at this time of year, but the one route to Montevideo that doesn't involve a huge layover is sold out. I had no intention of spending one more minute than I had to in Cartersville, but holing up in my room here for an extra day seems like a better option than an eight-hour wait in the São Paulo airport—at least based on how slightly fragile I feel.

I book the flight for Saturday night instead, which means by midday Sunday, I'll be at the chacra, eating lunch with Bas and drinking espresso afterward with my feet in his lap. I grab my phone and place a call to him, but it goes to voicemail.

"Bas, hi," I say. "We just met with the police, and they've decided everything points to Ruck in the end. I'll be there Sunday morning at ten forty. Can't wait to see you, sweetheart."

A wave of fatigue almost knocks me off the desk chair. I rise, stumble toward the freshly made bed, and stretch out across it on my back. Right above me on the ceiling is a carved plaster medallion where a light must have hung during another decade. As my gaze traces its outline, I feel something seeping through me, quickly weighing me down. I'm not just tired, I realize. I'm . . . *disconsolate*, like I've been swallowed whole by sadness and can barely move.

I should never have gone to Mohegan Park today. In the end it offered nothing new, and what it's done instead is stir the ghastly images I've worked so hard to bury: Mel brutalized, suffering beyond words, possibly pleading for her life. And unable to escape.

Opening my eyes, I realize I've passed out cold. And when I glance at the bedside clock, I discover, to my shock, that it's after four. *Shit.* The reception is less than two hours from now.

I check my phone to see if I've missed any calls or messages. There's nothing, not even one from Bas. Maybe his cold has laid him low.

I take my second shower of the day, hoping to jolt my senses, and then slip into the lavender silk cocktail dress I brought, pairing it with silver kitten heels and a matching clutch. I chose it for tonight because one of the rare compliments Mel paid me after age thirteen was that I looked nice in lavender.

I wasn't really deceiving Logan when I said I'd be coming from elsewhere. My intention is to finally check out the new *Muse* office before heading to Boyd Hall.

Though there's still light in the sky as I make my way to campus, the air is raw, and I shiver inside my trench coat. I should have made time earlier in the day for this, but at least going now means I won't have to come back to Carter College again before I leave town.

Arriving at the campus, I find it looking oddly deserted. The students I do pass are all hurrying, eager, I'm sure, to get to their dorm rooms or one of the dining halls.

I'm halfway across the quad when Chip finally returns my call.

"Ms. Winter, sorry to be late getting back to you," he says. "How can I be of assistance?"

I explain what I've heard about the archive and my hope to find Mel's writing there.

"You heard correctly," he says. "There *is* a creative archive."

"Wow." I'd been sure that with my luck so far, it didn't exist anymore. "How do you happen to know?"

"Because I stored some stuff of mine there ages ago."

"Oh yes, Maya mentioned you worked on *The Muse*—and that you knew Melanie back then."

"Yes, I did. Like everyone else, I was devastated by what happened. She was a wonderful person."

I give him the chance to expound a little, to offer a tiny nugget about her that my always greedy hands can snatch away, but there's only silence. I don't blame him for wanting to be done with the topic.

"Is writing still a passion of yours?" I ask.

"Uh, not anymore. I used to dabble now and then, but my stories were never—in a manner of speaking—much to write home about . . . Let me see what I can find out before the reception. And if there's stuff of Melanie's stored on it, I'll get you a link."

"Thank you, Chip. I've already asked the English department for help on some matters, and I don't want to bother them another time."

I'm hoping my last comment will guarantee he won't go through Handler about this.

"Understood . . . You must be heading over to Boyd Hall soon, right?"

"Yes, in a bit. I'm going to check out the *Muse* office first and then make my way there."

By the time we sign off, I'm chilled. I pick up my pace until the humanities building looms ahead of me. Though the first-floor classrooms are all dark, there are lights shining from some of the arched second-floor windows, probably a sign of faculty working late.

My gaze flicks to the very end, where I know Handler's office is located, and to my surprise I see the backlit shape of a man standing right against the window, obviously staring out at the quad. Is he simply lost in thought, or looking at something? Is he even looking at me?

I reach the building and push open the door, nearly colliding with a dark-skinned girl in cornrows, zipping a hooded Carter sweatshirt.

"Oops, sorry," I say and offer a smile. "Would you know where I can find the *Muse* office?"

"Yeah, it's down one flight," she says, kicking up her chin toward the nearby stairwell. "And then all the way to the end. But I don't think it's finished yet."

"That's okay, I'm just here to see how it's coming."

She smiles distractedly as she exits, wishing me good night. Once she's gone, I seem to have the floor to myself.

I descend to the lower level, the clicking sound of my heels echoing up the stairwell. Pushing open the fire door at the bottom, I find myself in a brightly lit corridor with classrooms and meeting rooms on either side. I hesitate for a moment. It appears deserted on this level. But after hearing muted voices coming from one of the rooms farther down, I start along the corridor. Once I reach the room with the voices, the window in the door offers a glimpse of several people sitting around a meeting table.

Finally, I near the end of the corridor, where the door facing me has a work permit taped to the outside. Against the wall on the left is a metal worktable with a large roll of brown paper on top. To the right of the door, there's a brass plaque. It says, "In Memory of Melanie Chase."

So here it is, Logan's other gift to Carter College. I wait for a swell of pride and/or pleasure, but there's only dead calm—which I guess shouldn't surprise me. Mel isn't here to see her name on the door and never will be.

I'm pleased to find that the door's not locked. Once I've pulled it open, I smell fresh paint, but it's too dark to see anything. I carefully pat the inside wall until I find a switch, and seconds later the space floods with light from a recessed ceiling fixture. I step across the threshold, taking everything in. The office is still partially cluttered with stuff like tarps, a couple of sawhorses, and paint cans, but it's far enough along for me to see how impressive the final results will be.

I glance behind me down the empty corridor. The group must still be in the meeting, so I'm not alone on the floor. And since there seems to be no harm in taking a closer look around, I lay my evening purse on the top of one of the sawhorses, unbutton my coat, and step farther into the office. I'll just have to mind the wet paint.

The first part of the space is taken up by the conversation pit that Handler described at the dinner party, and beyond that there's an open area with six modern-looking workstations. To my left as I walk is what looks like a meeting room, and beyond that are two glass-walled rooms that will probably be the podcast studios. I picture each of them with a table and mic and students conducting interviews, maybe dreaming of their own shows one day.

Bravo, Logan, I think. When I was on the literary magazine in college, we worked as a group at a dented metal table in an otherwise empty room, and that was just fine for us, but I see how a place like this could be exciting for students, providing them with a sense of being on a real publication. And it will certainly be an impressive feature on campus tours.

Footsteps stir me from my thoughts, the sound of someone in the outside corridor, possibly headed this way. As I twist my head, the overhead light blinks off and the room goes partially dark.

"Hey," I call out, spinning around. It must be a worker or custodian who thinks the lights have been left on by mistake. From where I'm standing, I see the main door start to close, so fast I can't tell who's on the other side. "Someone's *in* here," I yell.

A second later the door slams shut, and I'm standing in total darkness.

Chapter 23

My heart skitters.

"*Hey,*" I call out again, even louder now.

No one responds this time, either, but a second later I hear the faint scrape of metal like something's being dragged along the corridor outside. What the hell is going on?

"Open the door, please." I'm nearly screaming now. "I'm *inside* here."

I slap at my thigh several times, fumbling for my purse, and then remember I brought the clutch tonight, and it's on the damn sawhorse by the door, with my phone stuck inside it.

By now fear's foaming inside me. The lower level is windowless, so there's no light coming from anywhere. After grabbing the doorframe of the podcast studio, I move cautiously along the wall for a couple of feet.

I try to picture the setup in my mind. There were two additional rooms before this one, I think—the other podcast studio and the meeting room—and if I walk along the outside of them, hugging the wall, I'll reach the front, and I can feel my way toward the sawhorse. But there are booby traps on this side of the space—paint cans and rolls of tarp. It might be better to walk more in the center until I reach the workstations. Then navigate my way around them.

I start with baby steps, sliding my kitten heels across the tile floor with both arms stretched out in front of me, still seeing nothing. It's like I've been submerged in a tank of quivering blackness. I take a deep breath, feeling my panic come to a boil.

Finally, my left thigh connects with something hard—the first workstation, I realize. I grasp the edge of the desktop with my hand and inch along the side of it. I do the same with the next two desktops until I'm finally at the end.

Sweat is nearly pouring from me now, soaking the armpits of my dress. I gulp air, assuring myself I'm almost there. And sure enough, my eyes spot a thin, faint ribbon of light along the ground. That must be where the door is, with the sawhorse just ahead of it.

I start baby-stepping again, aiming for the ribbon of light. And then, horribly, the ground gives way beneath my left foot, and I go pitching forward. For a split second I seem to be falling in space before landing on the ground with a hard thwack.

The conversation pit. I must be at the bottom of it now. Groaning, I slowly pull myself up on an elbow. Both my left hip and wrist sting from breaking the fall, but all I care about right now is getting out of the dark. I crawl around until I find the edge of the seating area, hoist myself onto it, and struggle to my feet.

The ribbon of light is now only feet away. I limp in that direction until my hand finally makes contact with my purse, and once I have it, I dig out my phone and turn on the flashlight. Training the beam toward the wall, I locate the light switch and flick it on.

Almost instantly my panic starts to subside.

I stand there for a moment, getting my bearings and finally focusing on my body. My hip and wrist are throbbing, but neither seems seriously injured. My dress is another story, however. Not only is it wet from perspiration, but there's also a huge smear of dirt on the lower half. Though it will mean being late for the reception, I'll have to return to the inn and change.

Yet when I press the door handle and push, nothing happens. I try again, this time using my unbruised hip. The door budges only an inch. Something is blocking it.

I flash back to the scrape of metal I heard minutes ago... and then picture the table I saw in the corridor. Maybe that's against the door now. Did the workmen come back and place it there for some reason, not knowing anyone was inside?

Or did someone do this to me on purpose?

I feel my panic start to simmer again. I need to call Logan and have him send someone to get me out. I quickly tap his number on my phone, only to see that there's no cell coverage or Wi-Fi signal down here yet.

Fuck. But I tell myself to calm down. At least it's not dark anymore, and hopefully the people I heard earlier are still on the floor. Besides, if I keep pushing hard enough, I can probably force the table out of the way on my own.

After setting my phone back down, I start on the door again, using both my good hip and hand to shove. It's obvious after a dozen miserable tries, however, that there's no way I'm going to dislodge the table more than a couple of inches. It feels like one end is jammed into a corner of the hall, creating an unbudging wedge.

But at least there's enough of an opening for my voice to be heard.

"Is anyone out there?" I yell with my cheek against the door. "*Please*, I need help."

I call out several more times, but no one comes.

My hip is hurting even more now, so I drag a metal folding chair toward the door and slowly lower myself onto the seat. I start calling out again, taking small breaks in between. No response. I double-check my phone, hoping a signal has miraculously appeared, but it's still a total dead zone.

Then I notice the time: 6:22. The reception has already started. Logan is there, of course, vaguely wondering where I am by now but probably assuming I didn't want to arrive too early and have to mingle. But remarks are due to start at 6:30, and they're only going to wait so long for me to arrive.

What if I miss his remarks? What if I miss the whole reception?

I struggle up from the chair and start yelling even louder than before, until my voice is strained. Why would someone *do* this to me?

I need to make more noise. The people who were meeting down here earlier are obviously gone, but there still might be professors in their offices on the second floor. I glance around. Lying by the far wall are a couple of barrel-shaped metal rods. After hobbling over and grabbing one of them, I start pounding on the door with it. It makes an almost deafening sound, and before long I've not only chipped paint off parts of the door but also covered the top half with dents.

Minutes pass, then more minutes. I keep pounding, pausing now and then to listen and praying for the sound of footsteps—*friendly* ones. Maybe by this point, the building has completely emptied.

Chip, I suddenly think. I mentioned to him that I was going to stop here. But I doubt he'll waste much time wondering where I am.

As I start to pound again, I feel tears welling in my eyes. I'm going to miss the reception, and Logan will assume I chickened out, that whatever change of heart I experienced about going was overridden by my initial instinct to stay away. Beyond that, I'll be entombed here all night, forced to pee in a corner. Has someone done this to mess with my head?

And then, in between the repeated clangs of metal on metal, I hear it: footsteps, then someone yelling, "Hold on."

Seconds later, whatever has blocked the door is being dragged away, making a long, earsplitting screech. At last, the door swings open. A fortyish man in gray coveralls is standing there, looking both wary and baffled at the sight of me.

"Thank you," I blurt out, setting the rod down. I spot the table right behind him, which confirms that was the barricade.

"What happened?" he asks. "What are doing you in here?"

"I was looking around, and someone shut the door, then pushed the table in front. Who would have done that?"

He glances behind him at the table as if the answer is sitting on top of it.

"The workers, maybe," he says, looking back at me. "To discourage people from sneaking in here."

People like me, he probably means.

"But why not check first to make sure no one was here?"

He shrugs. "They must have thought it was empty."

Maybe.

"I'm so sorry for any damage to the door," I say, grabbing my phone and purse. "I'll—I'll speak to President Williams about having it repaired. Thank you again for finding me."

"You're okay?" he asks as I move past him to leave.

"Yes, okay." But that's not true at all.

I have no time now to go back to the inn and change. As I race toward Boyd Hall, I use a tissue from my coat pocket to wipe my face and then attack the dirt on my dress, which proves to be futile. When I finally reach my destination, I have a stitch in my side, my hip hurts even more, and my heels feel nearly raw. I enter the building and find myself in a large wood-paneled foyer, with the reception happening in a room just to my left. I steal a frantic glance at my phone: 7:14.

There's a rolling clothes rack by the door, and a handful of people are already tugging their coats from hangers, preparing to leave. Deciding I don't even have time to find a restroom, I approach the reception area. It's a beautiful, high-ceilinged room, its walls hung with gilt-framed oil paintings. About thirty guests are still gathered inside, though the vibe is of a party that's past its prime.

Almost instantly, I discover Logan standing in a cluster of people. Seconds later, he shifts position slightly, spots me, and stares across the room. There's a look of bewilderment in his eyes, not an expression from his usual repertoire.

I slip out of my coat, drape it across my arm, and smooth my hair with my better hand. I step into the room and start toward Logan, but before I've gone far, someone is touching my shoulder. Turning, I see that it's Alison Handler. She's dressed in a flowy cream-colored skirt and pearl-buttoned cardigan of the same hue, almost like an image from one of her paintings.

"Bree, good evening," she says. "And congratulations on the reception."

"Thank you," I say, half in a daze by now. "Thank you for coming tonight."

"I looked for you earlier, but it was so crowded during the first hour, I didn't see you, and now I'm off to dinner with a friend."

She obviously assumes I've been here the whole time and simply opted for a slightly disheveled, sweat-drenched look for the evening.

"I'm sorry to have missed you yesterday," she adds.

"That's my fault for not contacting you first," I fumble. "Your husband said you were out for the evening."

"The shame is I was actually in my studio, but in the back room, reading on my daybed. I must not have heard you knock."

There's no way I'm going to admit I didn't knock, that I was simply peering into her window like a Peeping Tom.

"Oh, too bad."

"Why don't you come by tomorrow," she says, holding my gaze. "I'll be there all morning for sure."

Is there any point in returning there? Right now, I'm too discombobulated to decide.

"Thank you, but I probably won't have the chance before I leave for Uruguay."

"Well, just in case, here's my phone number." She quickly extracts the card from her purse and presses it into my hand. "You can text or call me."

She smiles, then hurries away. I take a few breaths to steady myself and half hobble across the room in Logan's direction. As I close the distance, he steps out from the group he's talking to and waits for me in the middle of the room.

He doesn't say a word when I reach him, just stares with his eyes now dark as slate in the dimness of the room. He looks both hurt and confused.

"I'm so sorry, Logan," I say. "I didn't do this on purpose. Something happened to me."

He reaches up to touch my left temple, and I pull back in surprise.

"Is that *blood*?" he asks, withdrawing his hand.

Instinctively, I press on the same spot and then find a smear of red on my fingertips.

"I fell," I say. "And worse than that, I've been locked in the *Muse* office for the last hour and a half."

"Christ, Bree, what happened?"

"I'm not sure. But, look, let's save it for later."

"Are you okay, though?"

"Mostly just shaken. I feel terrible about missing your remarks—all of this."

He glances back toward the group he'd been standing with. "Can you give me a little time to finish up with a reporter?"

"Was there a good press turnout?"

"Yes, including a feature reporter from the Albany paper who wants to do a big piece on Mel and the scholarships. Give me twenty minutes to nail down a game plan with him and say goodbye to people, and then I can drive you back to the inn."

I start to nod in consent but realize I don't have the psychic energy to stay any longer.

"I think I need to go back right now," I say.

"Are you sure you'll be all right on your own?"

"Yes, I just didn't want you to think I wasn't coming."

"I'll call you soon as I'm done here."

I nod, then retrace my steps across the room. If Jack's still here, I don't see him, and there's also no sign of Maya or anyone from the dinner Tuesday night. But as I exit the reception room, I nearly collide with Chip Conway, buttoning his coat.

"There you are," Chip says, and his eyes quickly scoot to the side of my forehead where Logan noticed the blood. "I've been looking for you—because I've got some good news."

I stare at him, slightly dumbfounded. What good news could there possibly be tonight? And then I recall our conversation from earlier.

"I found Mel's stuff," he adds.

"That's fantastic," I exclaim. I barely revel in this news before I see Jeffrey Handler approach the coatrack, too. I certainly don't want Chip saying anything more in front of Handler. "But I'm in a terrible hurry right now," I add. "Can I call you first thing tomorrow?"

"Sure, sure, whenever works for you. Why don't I simply text you a link with directions on how to download the material." To my dismay, he also notices Handler and smiles in greeting. "Hey, Professor Handler. Ms. Winter was wondering if some of Melanie's writing might be in our creative content archive, and sure enough, I located a bunch of things."

Chip returns his attention to me. "Don't let me hold you up anymore," he says. "I'll send you the link tonight."

I mumble a thank-you and start to back away, but for a moment I'm immobilized, pinned in place by Handler's gaze. He's just learned I'm going to have access to Mel's writing, and he doesn't seem the least bit happy with the news.

Chapter 24

I don't bother to hear what either man says next. Instead, I hurry out of the entry area and limp down the steps of the building. I order an Uber, which ends up taking thirteen minutes to show. It probably would have been better to wait for Logan.

By the time I arrive back at the inn, the best I can do is stagger to the elevator and then to my room. I ease my shoes off with my right hand and nearly rip off my dress, which smells like I've spent most of the day digging trenches. In the bathroom I lean across the sink, examining my face in the mirror. Despite my earlier efforts with a tissue, my eye makeup is smeared and there's dried blood along a small gash in my forehead, obviously the result of face-planting into the conversation pit.

I tell myself to focus on all that's good about tonight. Mel was celebrated, even without me being there. And, according to Chip, there's more work of hers waiting for me, which I might have already read but maybe not. And *if* not, it might provide a fresh glimpse of the girl I struggled so hard to know.

And yet I feel unnerved. And ragged, too, as if I'm coming apart at the seams.

I'm suddenly desperate for the sound of Bas's voice. As I grab my phone to call him, it strikes me that he still hasn't responded to my text from the morning or the call I made. Which must mean he's seriously under the weather and might even be sleeping. I send him a text instead of calling.

Hey, hope you haven't been felled by your cold. If you're still up, give me a call, okay?

I wait a minute or two for a response, but none comes. Is it possible he found the text I sent this morning dismissive, me saying that I'd wait until I returned to fill him in?

I carry my phone into the bathroom, lay it on the counter, and fire up the shower. The hot water ends up bringing minor relief to both my wrist and my hip. Once I'm done, I slip into the complimentary terry-cloth robe and wander back into the bedroom, dabbing antibacterial ointment from my toiletry bag onto the cut on my forehead.

A knock on the door makes me jerk in surprise. Before I can respond, a voice comes from the other side.

"Bree, it's me, Logan."

"Uh, give me a sec," I call out. I shrug off the robe, grab the nearest clothes, then wince as I pull the jeans over my bruised hip. When I finally open the door, I find Logan with flushed cheeks—from either the wind or hurrying or both. He's carrying two plastic bags.

"Can I come in?" he says. "I want to see how you're doing. And I brought you something to eat."

"Sure, and thanks. The only thing I've eaten since breakfast is a bag of chips."

He heads for the small round table by the armchair and begins to unpack the bags. It's obviously food from the reception: crackers and cheese, a napkin full of boiled shrimp, and a plastic container of cocktail sauce. He's also got a bottle of red wine, which I assume he grabbed from the parlor downstairs. He pours us each a glass, using the two goblets on the dresser.

Okay, there's no world in which we should be sharing wine and jumbo shrimp in a hotel room, but I need to fill him in, and more than that, I can't bear the thought of being alone. Someone came after me tonight, and I don't know who. I've booked my trip home, but none of the answers I'm going back with make me feel any better. And though

I'm responsible for the disconnect with Bas—and maybe his failure to get in touch today—that's no consolation.

"Is your head okay?" he asks.

"Yes, seems to be."

"Here, sit," he tells me, nodding toward one of the chairs by the table.

As I fall into the chair and help myself to a piece of shrimp, Logan slips out of his navy blazer and sits down himself.

"Now please tell me what the heck happened," he says.

I toss the shrimp tail onto a paper napkin. "Okay, I went to see the *Muse* office, as planned, and while I was in there, someone turned off the light, shut the door, and dragged a worktable in front of it so there was no way I could budge the door open."

Logan stares at me, aghast. "How did you manage to get out?"

I explain about hollering and banging until the custodian finally responded.

"Could it have been a mistake?" he says. "Someone not realizing you were in there?"

I give my head a shake. "That's what the custodian said—that someone from the work crew must have done it. But don't you think it's odd they blocked the door with a table? Why not just use a key to lock it?"

"Maybe there's no working lock yet. Besides, who in the world would want to trap you like that? Who would have even known you were there?"

"Jeffrey Handler might have known," I say. "He happened to be watching the quad from his office window when I walked into the building, and I think he saw me."

He furrows his brow, not sure where I'm going with this. At last I divulge what I've experienced with Handler this week—his apparent unease with me, his failure to share the information about the archive, and how I didn't help matters by being caught sneaking around his property in an attempt to learn more about him.

"Why would he be uneasy or act weird about you seeing Mel's stuff?"

"Okay, I know this might sound far-fetched, but hear me out. From what I've put together, Handler's a cheater, and I keep wondering if he might have been Mel's secret crush, the one Harry mentioned."

I wait for his eyes to widen with incredulity. Instead, he steeples his hands and exhales a ragged breath into his fingers.

"I wondered the same thing once," he says.

"*When?* On this trip?"

He shakes his head. "When Mel was here."

"Was it because of something she said?"

If so, why hasn't Logan ever told me?

"No, nothing she said. It was a few weeks before she died, that Friday I was in the Albany area for work and I drove over to see her. We had an early dinner in town here and ran into Handler afterward while we were walking to the car. As you know, she'd always raved about him, but the conversation was oddly stilted, like there was something hanging in the air."

"And you thought *affair*?"

"Yes, but not for more than a millisecond. I told myself that, Mel being Mel, she probably felt a little awkward running into him with a parent—and so it never seemed worth bringing up."

In some ways I've made the same decision myself over the past days, not wanting to turn a molehill into a mountain about Handler. And what could I have done with the information if Logan *had* told me? Certainly not raise it with Mel, because she would have said, as she had more than once, that her love life was none of my damn business.

"In hindsight, though, do you think it's a possibility?"

Logan takes another long drink of wine, nearly tipping the glass upside down to drain the contents, then slowly shakes his head. "Frankly, it's hard to imagine, and that's another reason I dropped the idea so fast. Yeah, Mel always went for creative types—just look at Jack—but Handler seems like a guy with a stick up his ass."

I stare off into the middle distance, considering his comment.

"Still, he's an attractive man in his own way and a successful poet, with plenty of allure on that front," I say. "Of course, if they had a fling, he would have been terrified about anyone finding out."

"Exactly. Don't you lose tenure over things like that?"

"Absolutely."

Logan pulls back, suddenly sensing where I'm really going with this. "Whoa, you're not suggesting Handler killed Mel, are you?"

I stare back at him, saying nothing.

"Bree, *Ruck* killed Melanie," he says. "You've got to let go of your doubts and stop torturing yourself."

"I know, I know, you're right," I say. Because he *is*.

"Regardless, I'm going to do what I can to find out how you got locked in that room."

"I'd appreciate that."

I bite half-heartedly into another piece of shrimp. I'm famished, but at the same time I still can't summon any interest in food.

"I haven't even asked you about the event," I say. "Are you happy with how it went?"

"Very. Maya spoke, followed by Eileen Zhao—the head of donor relations—and then I gave my little talk. I choked up once but otherwise kept it together."

"I'm so sorry not to have heard it. Can you email me a copy of your remarks?"

"Sure thing."

He reaches for the bottle of wine, ready to pour us each another glass, and I hear a warning siren go off in my head. It's felt good to have someone here for a while, but we need to wrap this up.

"Do you want to take that back to your room?" I say, lifting my chin toward the bottle. I slowly rise from the table. "I should probably get to bed soon."

"Uh, yeah, of course," he says. He rises, too, and starts to tidy up the table.

"Leave that, I'll get it in the morning," I urge.

Ignoring me, he stuffs a few more things into one of the plastic bags.

"Have you made your travel plans yet?" he asks.

"Yes, my flight's on Saturday. I couldn't get one before then."

"I could drop you off at the train station that day if you like."

"Thanks, but I can grab a cab or an Uber."

"Well, let me know if you change your mind." He tugs his blazer from the back of the chair and then slips into it. Maybe he's going downstairs for a drink, or back to the Italian restaurant for a decent dinner. Against my will, I feel a strange urge to go, too. To be on a car ride with him again, driving through the dark.

"How come you'll be in Cartersville this weekend?" I ask as we both take a few steps toward the door.

"I have a meeting late Saturday afternoon with the guy who designed the *Muse* office, so I'll head back to the city on Sunday. And then take it from there."

"Take what? Is there still stuff to do with the college?"

"Nah, that's all pretty much wrapped up. I meant dealing with everything else." He waves a hand in the air. "You know, all the stuff we had to face here. This probably sounds a little lame, but I might look up the grief counselor I went to years ago and see if she's still practicing."

"Grief counselor?" I say, taken aback.

"Yeah. I knew this week wouldn't be easy, but it's been worse than I thought. I know for you, too."

"Yes, but wait . . . When did you go to a grief counselor? Not when we were together?"

"No, not then—though I should have. You kept urging me to see the woman you'd been going to." He pats the breast pocket of his blazer as if looking for something but then drops his arm, still empty-handed. "It was later."

I'm stunned by his admission. Had he finally realized that grief was something that couldn't be outrun?

"What made you change your mind?"

"To be honest, the double loss. You and Mel both gone in barely more than a year." He scoffs as if mocking himself. "I actually had one of those panic attacks that makes you think you're in full fucking cardiac arrest, and it was a nurse in the ER who convinced me to finally get some help."

For a few seconds I stand there silently, trying to digest all of this.

"I wasn't very kind then, was I?" I say finally. "I should have made some attempt to understand about the infidelity—so that we could have parted on better terms."

Or—not parted at all? God, am I really asking myself that question after so many years? I certainly didn't ask it back then. I was too shattered and heartsick and furious to listen to any language of grief but the one I spoke myself.

"That means a lot," he says, finding my eyes with his. He inhales deeply, steeling himself, it seems. "I love you, Bree. I've never stopped."

Stunned, I hear my breath hitch. For a few moments we stand motionless, looking directly at each other. Then Logan reaches out, making me blink, and cups my face with his hand. I feel a rush of desire, more than muscle memory this time. Seconds later, we're kissing passionately.

I want this, I realize. I'm about to betray my partner, and yet I'm not pulling away. Maybe it's simply my despair taking over, hoping for an escape on the last of these four awful days—with the one person in the universe whose feelings right now are close to my own—but thinking that doesn't change my mind.

Chapter 25

The next morning, a faint light from the window eases my eyes open. I blink a couple of times until I'm fully awake, and then I remember: I slept with Logan last night. I'm lying on my right side, and as the seconds pass, I become aware of his breathing behind me.

Somewhere, someplace, I sense guilt on the prowl, roaming room by room, but it hasn't found me yet. I've cheated on Bas, a man I know I love, but what I feel—at least for now—is only a lingering elation from last night, from sex that was intoxicatingly brand-new and familiar at the same time, as if I'd gone to bed with a stranger who'd studied my body in a past life and knew everything it liked.

And if I'm being honest with myself, it was more than good sex. There was relief, the kind from having all your saddest, darkest places known without having to explain them. Elation, too, from being allowed entry to a land I'd been banished from and never thought I'd see again.

I hear Logan stir behind me. I have no idea what his reaction will be this morning, but I might as well find out. I roll onto my back and turn my head. His eyes are open. In fact, he's staring at my face.

"Morning," he says, smiling softly.

"Morning."

After wrestling his arm from beneath the sheet, he reaches up and smooths my hair.

"Are you up for some breakfast downstairs?" he says, his voice still deep from sleep. "I'll probably just have coffee and a bagel, but I'll sit with you."

"Sure, but I need some time to get ready."

He plucks his watch from the bedside table and glances at it. "Why don't we meet down there in thirty minutes? I'm going to hit your bathroom first, though, if you don't mind."

After he gets out of bed, finds his boxers on the floor, and pads off to the bathroom, I push myself up to a sitting position. Both my wrist and hip are throbbing lightly, something I managed not to notice last night, even with Logan on top of me, gently holding my wrists.

And now, here it comes at last: guilt nosing its way into the room. My stomach twists, not only from regret but panic, too. I've made a commitment to Sebastian, and sleeping with Logan has been a total violation, one that would cause Bas such pain if he knew. Even set our relationship on fire.

And though last night seemed separate from Bas and me, a type of time travel to a past life unrelated to my new one, surely *Bas* wouldn't see it that way.

I realize suddenly that he's still never responded to my messages from yesterday. Maybe he *did* find my text dismissive. But right now, of course, that doesn't hold a candle to my infidelity.

God, what an awful mess I've made.

I dress quickly and fire up the Nespresso machine on the dresser. From the bathroom comes the sound of the tap running at full force and water splashing. Logan was always noisy at the bathroom sink, cupping water with both hands and tossing it at his face. It's like hearing a song on the radio that I haven't listened to in years and haven't even remembered until now.

He emerges moments later, and I keep my back to him as he finishes dressing. Then I turn and hand him an espresso.

"What do you think you'll do today?" he says.

Yes, what *will* I do, besides trying to swim against the waves of guilt now trying to swamp me? Alison Handler suggested last night that I drop by her studio, but at this point I don't see any reason to. I haven't lost my resolve to find out if Mel had an affair with her husband—and as far as I know, he's the one who dragged the table in front of the door last night—and yet I'm not going to learn anything by looking at his wife's creepy paintings.

"Just answer emails, I guess," I say, starting an espresso for myself. "And read Mel's writing from the digital archive. I'm supposed to be getting the link soon, so I'll pass it along when I have it . . . You?"

"Just tying up some loose ends," he says. "And I want to stop by the *Muse* office while the workers are around, see if I can get to the bottom of things. I'll also talk to someone about repairing the door."

"Great."

He takes a long pull of his drink and narrows his eyes. "I know this sounds crazy, but part of me has wanted to go by Pebble Creek Park while I'm still here. I don't know, maybe being back there will be a release of some kind."

I shake my head as hard as I can. "Logan, *don't*. I haven't had a chance to tell you yet, but I went by the other park, Mohegan, yesterday to see where Riley was attacked, and I've regretted it ever since. It'll stir up all the worst things for you."

"You're right, you're right," he says, massaging the back of his neck. "I think I brought it up so you'd talk me out of it."

The second espresso is finished pouring, and I take a careful sip.

"Were things the way Riley described?" he asks.

"Very much, and that's partly why I came to believe her. I saw the jogging path and the picnic tables, hidden under some trees. The creek was shallow yesterday, but the cabdriver told me it can get full enough to carry someone downstream—depending on how much rain there's been."

"That makes sense." He shakes his own head, not as a no but with a look of dismay. "Remember me saying that Riley's story made me angry? Because if she'd come forward at the time, things would have moved faster here, and Amanda Kline might still be alive. Since then, though, I realized that I also *resent* her. She somehow managed to fight back and roll off the table and throw herself into that raging creek. But none of that happened for our beautiful Mel."

"I know," I say quietly. Because, for the first time, I realize I've felt twinges of resentment as well. Riley got *away*.

And then, seemingly out of nowhere, something begins to paw at my brain—and it's got nothing to do with regret this time. I hesitate, the espresso cup in midair, and though I struggle to hold on to the thought, it beats a fast retreat. It's like I've heard the scuff of a shoe behind me, but when I turn around, no one's there.

Logan drains the last of his coffee without taking his eyes from my face.

"What?" he says, clearly reading my expression.

"Uh, nothing." But it *is* something. The elusive thought has drifted within reach again, and this time I grasp hold. It's really more of a question, one I should have asked myself yesterday.

"See you in a few, then," Logan says. He grabs his blazer from the armchair and swings it over his shoulder. Still a bit of the rogue, even at fifty-nine.

I nod, smiling.

"Bree."

Okay, here it comes, I realize. The "about last night" talk. Something like, "We lost our heads in the heat of the moment. Can we just put this behind us?"

And that's okay for him to say. We *did* lose our heads, and we should never have done what we did. *Right?*

"Yes?" I say. I realize I'm holding my breath.

"I meant what I said last night. I love you. And it's burning a hole in my heart."

It's now seven in the morning, meaning his declaration of love last night wasn't simply one-part seduction and two-parts pining for the past.

But what's he really saying—that he wants us to be together again? How does he imagine that even playing out?

Without waiting for a reply, he lowers his head and moves toward the door. Seconds later, he's gone.

I need to get a grip on how to handle the mess I've made, but not right this minute. Because there's something even more urgent I need to contend with.

I grab the small notebook I've used off and on this week and thumb through it until I reach the notes I scribbled when I first spoke to Harry Kronish.

Mel was "like the cat that ate canary"
Because weather better?
Harry—"New squeeze?"
Mel—"My lips are sealed."

Yes, it's just as I remembered. Before Harry deduced that Mel might be involved with someone new, he assumed her good mood was due to a change in the weather. It had turned sunny and warmish after seemingly endless days of rain.

Suddenly, something doesn't make sense to me.

I flip open my laptop. As I start to type in the search bar, my phone rings, with Maya's name on the screen. Maybe she heard about my experience in the *Muse* office.

"Bree, I'm so sorry I missed you last night," she says. "I looked for you several times, and yet our paths never crossed."

So, she hasn't heard. I should bring her up to speed about what happened—but not now.

"Unfortunately, something came up, and I didn't arrive until very late," I say. "Logan says the event was terrific."

"Well, as you know, we're very grateful to both of you. When do you head back?"

"Tomorrow."

"Is there anything I can do for you before you leave?"

"That's very kind of you, Maya, but I think I'll be okay."

A brief pause follows.

"You sure?" she asks.

There's something about her comment that causes me to sit up straighter.

"What makes you ask that?"

"I've been a little concerned about how you're doing. Professor Handler called me this morning and said you'd seemed quite distressed at the reception, and also when he ran into you outside his house one night. He wondered if there was any way for the school to be of assistance."

I feel my blood start to boil. Handler could care less about my well-being.

"That's very kind of you, Maya, but it's nothing more than normal grief rearing its head. Maybe Professor Handler's been lucky enough not to know what that feels like."

I summoned more than a hint of sarcasm for the last line, which I'm sure has caught her off guard.

"If so, how lucky for him indeed," she says, the perfect response. "I wish you all the best, Bree."

I wish her well, too, and offer a warm goodbye. It will surely be the last time we ever speak.

I give myself a minute or two to stew about Handler. He's got some kind of game going on—trying to paint me as slightly unhinged, possibly barricading me in the room last night. Is it all a defensive move, in case I start making accusations about him and Mel? As Logan keeps reiterating, it was Ruck who killed Mel, and yet Handler might have secrets he wants kept under wraps.

But I need to table that right now and return to the task at hand. After briefly searching online, I end up on a site that provides the weather history for any place in the US. I type in "Cartersville, NY," and then find my way to the October Mel died. I've done my best since yesterday to quell any vague, lingering doubts about her murder, but I'm not going to ignore a possible discrepancy. What I'm looking for are the weather conditions not only on the night Riley jumped into the creek but also on the days leading up to it.

The information is surprisingly easy to interpret. There's a graph for each day of the month as well as an accompanying summary, covering details like the temperature throughout the day, dew point, and wind speed, but the only thing that matters to me is precipitation. As I go through the month one day at a time, I jot details down in my notebook and create my own little chart.

Just as Harry reported, the first half of October was incredibly rainy. There was at least some precipitation on eleven out of those fifteen days, and the temperature never reached sixty.

The Sunday before Mel died must have been particularly miserable. It apparently poured the entire day, with an accumulation of over two inches. But everything, I see, shifted on Monday. According to the graph, there was zero precipitation that day or during the days immediately following. The temperature climbed into the high sixties. Indian summer, just as Harry said.

Which meant it was practically balmy when Mel walked to the park that night after dinner.

I recall next to nothing about weather conditions upstate during the days after she died, though it must have turned cool again since I was always in a coat, a lightweight camel one that I tossed in a dumpster as soon as I arrived back to Tribeca.

It doesn't matter, however, that I've forgotten the details because all I need to know is right here on my computer screen. The temperatures in Cartersville did indeed begin to dip again on Saturday, but—and this is the part that interests me most—the skies remained clear. There wasn't a drop of precipitation again until the following Tuesday.

I finish drawing my own little chart and stare at it, reiterating the question I asked myself as Logan was about to leave my room: *Can a creek be raging if it hasn't rained in days?*

Probably not, I think, but I'm out of my league here. What I need is a consult with someone who knows waterways, but since I certainly don't have access to anyone like that, I call Cartersville Taxi and ask for Craig, who seemed savvy about the creek.

"Yeah, hi," he says after I remind him who I am. "Are you at the inn? I'm jammed up now, but I can have someone else pick you up in fifteen."

"I don't need a ride. I just want to ask a question about the creek."

"You thinkin' of taking a boat out on it?"

"Not quite," I say, hearing myself laugh in spite of everything. "I was just wondering how much the creek might change during a given week. Like yesterday, it looked low and slow, but you said that it rises after it rains."

"Yup, exactly."

"And then how long would it take to go down again once the rain stopped?"

"Not long. The creek's what they call flashy."

"Flashy?"

"It's how they describe a stream or river that rises fast when it rains but decreases almost just as fast afterward. It's all got to do with the watershed."

"So, if it was pouring one weekend but the rainfall stopped completely by Monday morning, would the creek be low, like, six days later?"

"If there was no more rain? Oh yeah, it'd be just pokin' along by then . . . That all you need for now?"

"Yes, yes, thank you."

My heart is racing as I set down the phone. Based on what I've learned this morning, there's no way Pebble Creek could have carried Riley downstream that Sunday night.

Which means I'm staring at a gaping hole in her story.

Chapter 26

I'm still convinced Riley was raped and almost killed—but she seems to have lied about one aspect of that night: either the date . . . or the fact she escaped in swift-moving waters of the creek.

It seems odd she would make up leaping into the creek. Why would she include an almost improbable-seeming detail that could undermine the credibility of her story?

So that leaves the date as a lie. It now seems possible that Riley was actually attacked at least several days earlier than she told us, when the creek was still high from days' worth of rain—and that's why she seemed evasive to me. It certainly doesn't discount Ruck as her assailant. He'd been at his sister's house for about six days before Mel was killed, which means there's a clear window for him to have attacked Riley earlier than she claimed.

But why deceive us? As I sit motionless at the desk, I suddenly see, with gut-wrenching clarity, what her motive was. If she admitted to being raped days earlier, we'd be holding her partly to blame for our daughter's death. Mel would never have taken a meditative stroll in a park one night if she'd heard there was a rapist on the loose.

In the end, of course, such a lie wouldn't alter the bigger truth I've come to accept: Ruck killed Melanie and he also attacked Riley. It just would have been in reverse order.

Still . . . unease has a grip on me and won't let go. If Riley lied about that, she might have lied about other things—things that matter.

I send a text to Logan, telling him to start eating without me, that something's come up that I need to deal with. Then I tap the number I have for Morgan Kroll. My call goes straight to voicemail, so I leave a message asking for her to phone me as soon as possible. She'll probably groan as soon as she hears my voice. She wants all this behind her.

But a few minutes later, as I'm pacing the room, she calls me back.

"Can I pick your brain for a couple of minutes?" I ask.

"Okay, but two minutes tops," she says briskly, sounding like she's on the move. "I've got an eight-thirty class this morning."

"Understood. Look, I know that Riley was brutally attacked. But—is there any chance she could have misled all of us about the timeline?"

"The *timeline*? That's not something the two of us really discussed. I think she said she was in the park at eight or so, but she didn't get specific about the length of the assault or how long she was in the water, any of it."

She's misunderstood my question.

"Sorry, what I meant was the timeline in terms of the night she was attacked. Is there any chance it happened *before* that Sunday? Like five or six days before?"

A long pause follows.

"Wow, that's a weird thought," Morgan says finally. "Needless to say, I didn't give her a lie detector test, so I can't be a hundred percent sure, but she definitely said it had happened the night before. And based on her demeanor, it seemed like she was still in shock."

"Hmm," I say. Her shock, of course, could have lasted for days.

"And why would she need to lie about that anyway?"

"Because if she'd been raped earlier and hadn't reported it, we'd be holding her partially responsible for Mel's death."

"Okay, I see what you're getting at," she says, and I sense her stopping in place, finally absorbing it all. "And you'd be justified in blaming her. But where's this idea coming from?"

"From some records I found about the weather that month. The creek level is related to rainfall, and it was probably too low that Sunday night to carry her away from the park."

"But it was high enough days earlier?"

"Uh-huh." Though I'm almost past the two-minute time limit Morgan gave, I glance down at the chart I've sketched, letting ideas take shape as I'm speaking. "It rained hard on the *previous* Sunday, so the creek would have been high that day and also on Monday. Probably Tuesday as well. I think that's the time frame it happened in."

"So you're saying she out and out deceived me."

"Just about the date, not the horror of the assault. Let's say Riley was attacked on Monday night instead of the following Sunday. She might have flagged down a ride just as she described and decided to try to get on with her life without going to the cops. But then on Friday, Melanie was killed only a short distance away, which would have triggered a huge amount of guilt and anxiety. Up until then, she might have convinced herself she could still manage school but then realized she couldn't. That's why she finally went by the English department to see about getting extensions. And she misled you about the time frame so that no one could blame her for Mel's death."

Another pause.

"I suppose it's possible," Morgan says after a couple of beats. "But wait . . . she couldn't have been lying about the date. I saw the bruises on her neck."

I'd completely lost sight of that detail. How stupid of me.

"You're right," I say, bewildered.

"Are you sure the information you found about the creek is correct? Or maybe it *was* low, and she still managed to paddle downstream."

Not only are my thoughts in a jumble by this point, but I'm also embarrassed. I've dragged Morgan Kroll back into this because of a theory that now seems baseless.

"Yeah, maybe," I say. "I'm so sorry to have held you up. As you can tell, this is all really fraught for me."

"That's understandable, but—and excuse me if this sounds rude—isn't it time to let the girl get on with her life? She was wrong not to contact the cops earlier, but she's finally done that. And though maybe she hasn't remembered or presented every detail perfectly, the bottom line is that the past eight years have been a shit show for her, and she needs some closure."

Her comment smarts, but I let it go. I sign off saying I appreciate her taking the time to talk.

The call over, I flop onto the bed and stare up at the carved plaster medallion. Maybe my theory about the date of the attack *is* wrong and I'm being totally unfair to someone who suffered an indescribable trauma. And as Morgan said, the bruises on her neck were proof of the date.

I jump back off the bed and return to my laptop, typing, "What are the stages of a bruise?" into the search bar. A bunch of links pop up, and I open the first one, to an article on WebMD.

As a bruise heals, the piece says, the hemoglobin in the blood breaks down to other compounds and the color gradually changes. It's red for a couple of days after the injury and then converts to purplish or black and blue. After five to ten days, the bruise finally turns green or yellow and then eventually a light brown.

So, if Riley *were* attacked five or six days earlier, the bruise might have been purplish on the following Monday, instead of red, but it's possible it looked fresh to an untrained eye offered only a glimpse. Meaning my earlier deduction could be right. By the time Riley spoke to Morgan, she might have been living with the rape for nearly a week.

She must have suffered horribly during that time, reliving the assault in her mind and how close she'd come to dying, and also terrified she might be pregnant. Unwilling to confide in her parents or seek professional help, had she unburdened herself to a friend at the college then? If so, that person would know the truth about the date.

A thought stirs in me. If she told someone other than Morgan, does that matter in a way I can't see? The only one with answers is Riley, which means I'm going to have to find a way to speak to her alone—and get her to open up.

I check the time. I'm now seriously late for breakfast, and I decide to skip it altogether, which is for the best anyway. Staring across the table at Logan will only add to my anguish about my betrayal.

Sorry, I can't get away now after all, I text.

A reply comes within seconds.

Is everything okay?

Yes, just something I need to check out. I'll fill you in later.

There's no point in sharing anything until I know more.

I return to my laptop and find my way to a website for Hilary Brown, who turns out to have her own boutique law firm in Loudonville, a town probably twenty-five minutes away. It appears to specialize in contracts, meaning she's out of her comfort zone advising Riley. But she might be doing it as a favor for someone Riley knows.

I dial the number expecting to reach a receptionist, but I get voicemail instead. I take a breath and speak.

"Hi, Ms. Brown, it's Bree Winter. I'm heading back to South America soon, and I wonder if I could touch base with you briefly before I leave. Logan and I really appreciate your help in this situation, and Riley's, too, needless to say."

I'm using her to get to Riley, which isn't very nice, but it's the only way to have a shot at the real story.

I give it fifteen minutes, but Hilary doesn't call back, so I finally take a shower with the phone on the sink once again and then dress for the day. While I wait in the bedroom, still praying to hear from her, I open my emails to see if Chip Conway has sent the link to the archive yet—and I'm startled to spot an email from Sebastian, sent late yesterday. We generally communicate only via WhatsApp when we're not together.

"Thoughts," the subject line read. *Thoughts?* Is he about to share a concern about our relationship, based on how elusive I've been this week? God, what if he sensed I was going to cheat on him even before I did?

I open the email and nervously start to read.

> Bree, hi. I decided to put some thoughts in an email since WhatsApp seemed like the wrong place.
>
> I realized since we spoke that I've been pestering you every day for updates, but I see now how hard it must be to give them with all that's going on. This is such a terrible time for you, cariño, and things seem to be in constant flux. You have to stay focused on the situation there and make sure you learn the truth. Call if you need any moral support but otherwise don't feel you have to take me through everything right now. You can share when you get home, and I will be eager to hear and provide whatever support I can. I'm sending you all my love.
>
> And Poco sends his love, too.

My stomach pricks almost painfully with remorse. The man I've violated has been thinking only of me, sensing from five thousand miles away how tough it is to be both living this nightmare and sharing it over the phone.

Adding to my misery, I can picture him on the galería as he wrote the email, drinking an espresso and sometimes glancing out at the fields with his deep-brown eyes.

I've no clue yet how to deal with what I've done, but I reply to the email right away.

Thank you for understanding, Bas, and sorry to just be responding now. I haven't been checking email. How is your cold? Did you get the voicemail about my flights?

A reply comes almost immediately.

Yes, sorry on my end, too, cariño. My cold leveled me most of the day and I was in bed by nine. But much better now. Can't wait for Sunday.

Me too.

But what do I do when I get there? Do I confess my unfaithfulness and beg him to understand? If I do, there's a good chance he won't forgive me, just like I refused to forgive Logan for *his* faithlessness. Which means I stand to lose everything—Bas, my lovely life with him, those endless rolling green fields. If I were smart, I'd get on a plane tonight, no matter how long the layover, and figure out how to fix it. But I can't go now, not before I understand the goddamned hole in Riley's story.

My phone rings, startling me from my troubled thoughts. It's Hilary Brown. I answer and tell her how grateful I am for the call.

"Of course," she says. "I'm sorry I didn't have the chance to say this the other day, but I feel just terrible about what you and Mr. Chase have been through."

There's a refreshing folksiness to her speaking style.

"Thank you, that means a lot," I reply. "And it's certainly helped to have Riley come forward."

"I'm pleased to hear that," Hilary says, "and I know Riley will be, too."

"Actually, is it possible for me to tell her that myself—over the phone? As I mentioned, I'm leaving soon, and I'd love to thank her directly."

This is one deception I *can* forgive myself for. Riley's the one with the truth, and she needs to share it with the rest of us.

"I don't see why not, but let me check with her. She's still in the area actually, staying with me until her fiancé—who happens to be my nephew—can drive here tomorrow from Buffalo and pick her up."

So that's how Riley ended up with Hilary as her lawyer.

"You're in Loudonville, I see."

"My office, yes, but my home's just outside the town of Edgerton. I decided to try country life after my divorce. Let me reach out to Riley and get back to you."

I pace some more and open a bottle of sparkling water, guzzling it down. Fifteen minutes later, my phone rings. I groan in frustration when I spot "Unknown Caller" on the screen and not Hilary Brown's name, but when I answer, I'm in for a surprise. It's Riley herself.

"Riley, hi," I say, almost deliriously relieved. "Thanks for calling. I just wanted a chance to say how much I appreciate you talking to us on Wednesday."

"You're welcome," she says haltingly. "I'm sorry it took me this long to speak up."

"Well, you've done so now, and that's what counts. As you can imagine, it's been devastating for us to lose Melanie, but thanks to you, we've been able to add some missing pieces to the puzzle."

"I'm glad."

"Before I let you go, there's something on my mind that I was hoping you might help me with. Uh, a small detail I'm still confused about."

"Okay," she says, her tone suddenly wary. I need to tread carefully.

"I've been thinking a lot about what you went through, and it's so good you were able to get away, but as I was reading about the creek during those days, I discovered that it was very low that Sunday. I was wondering if somehow you got confused about the night that everything happened. I mean, you must have been beside yourself and maybe disoriented and . . ."

I'm rambling stupidly and finally force myself to shut up. An excruciating silence follows. I'm about to try again when I hear a sob catch in Riley's throat.

"I need to talk to you," she says. "About what you just mentioned, you know—about the date."

"Okay," I say, barely breathing.

"But, uh, not on the phone. In person."

"In Loudonville?" I ask, thinking she means at Hilary's office.

"No, at Mrs. Brown's house. It's in Edgerton, um, 4204 Bonner Road."

"Shall I come right this minute?"

Please, I think. *Please say yes.*

"No, now isn't good. My fiancé and I are supposed to talk in a little while when he has a work break."

"Just say when."

"Four o'clock, I guess. That would be okay."

"Great, I'll be there. And thank you, Riley. I'll be so grateful for whatever you tell me. And no judgment on my part, I promise that."

"Okay," she says.

"See you in a few hours, then. Oh wait, please just one more question. Right after everything happened, did you tell anyone? So that someone else back then knew the real date, too?"

For a few moments there's only silence again, this time a chilling one.

"Yes," she says at last. "One person."

She ends the call before I can say another word.

Chapter 27

I jump up from the chair, swiping my hands through my hair. So, Riley *did* lie. She didn't come right out and say so just now, but she made clear it's the reason she wants to meet.

And she told someone right afterward, days before she blurted out the story to Morgan.

I wonder now if I should reach out to Halligan. But after he finished chewing me out for going around him, he'd probably say what I've already concluded, that in the end this doesn't change a thing—Ruck still committed both crimes.

But *did* he? I'm yanked back to the idea of a copycat, a concept that initially seemed far-fetched. What if the person Riley told her awful story to—or a person he or she told—was someone who hated Mel and wanted her gone from the earth. This could have given the murderer the perfect way to kill her without throwing suspicion on himself.

If things actually played out this way, Mel's killer must have hoped Riley would eventually go to the cops so that they'd suspect a serial rapist, and yet in the end it didn't matter. Ruck was arrested in Plattsburgh less than a month later, and soon after that he was linked to Melanie's murder.

Is Jack the killer after all? Carter College is a small school, so it's possible Jack heard about Riley's rape through someone. Or she might have known Jack herself and told him.

My thoughts rush toward Handler next. It's possible that Riley, an English major, told him about her experience, hoping to get some guidance about handling school in the aftermath. Maybe when she broke down in front of Morgan, she'd only gone by the English department office in the hope of following up on an earlier conversation with Handler.

Maybe, maybe, maybe. I really have no clue.

I force myself back to the present. I call Craig's number and book a ride for later to Edgerton, explaining that I'll need the driver to wait for at least thirty minutes.

It's not even noon yet, so I have several hours to kill before leaving. I told myself earlier that I wasn't going to take Alison Handler up on her offer to see the studio, but I've changed my mind. Though taking a closer look at her paintings isn't likely to tell me much, maybe talking to her will provide a tiny bit of insight about the Handlers' world—and marriage.

I find her business card and shoot her a text, asking if it would be possible for me to drop by in the next hour.

Yes, that would be lovely, she replies soon afterward. *You know the address, of course.*

Hopefully Handler is hunkered down on campus today. Regardless of whether or not he locked me in the *Muse* office, I don't want to run into him.

Even though my hip still aches a bit, I decide to go on foot to Birch Street. It's been days since I had any real exercise, and besides, walking might help me outpace my guilt for a while and keep thoughts about Bas and Logan at bay for now.

I grab my coat and head out from the inn. Fifteen minutes later, when I'm near the north end of the campus, Chip Conway calls.

"Have you got a minute?" he asks.

"Is it about the archive? Because I never received a link."

"I know, I know, I'm sorry about that. Melanie's stuff is there, but I ended up in meetings all morning. Give me until later this afternoon, and I promise to get something to you."

"Great," I say, eager to be done. But when he coughs briefly, I realize he's not going anywhere.

"While I've got you, I wanted to mention that I've had yet another call from that reporter from the Albany *Times Union*, the one on the crime beat I told you about."

"Right. Well, you just have to keep repeating the same message, Chip—that we still have nothing to say about Melanie's case."

"Understood. But I'd do a better job at staving him off if I had more information to go on. He's always throwing something new at me and catching me off guard."

"New?" I'm on alert now.

"Yeah. Does the name Riley Reynolds mean anything to you?"

Damn. Someone with the police must have leaked information about her. Riley is going to be badly rattled if her name ends up in the news.

"I know she was a student at Carter once," I say. He's not getting anything more from me than that.

"Yes, but she left in the middle of the fall term—the same year Melanie died—and never returned. And she's supposedly back in the area now. You haven't heard where, have you?"

"Chip, you really need to speak to the state police about any questions you have," I say, irritated again by how much he's pushing. "I'm not the correct person to be commenting on any of this."

"Sure, sure, of course."

As I hang up and fully focus on my whereabouts again, I realize I'm already on the corner of Oak Street and Birch, and five minutes later I'm in front of Alison's studio. I start quickly down the path, hoping that if Handler *is* at home, he won't have noticed me.

The door swings open only seconds after I knock. Unlike her husband, Alison hasn't taken her sweet time to respond.

"Ah, welcome," she says. She offers a smile that's both inviting and enigmatic, as if she's pleased I'm here but still savoring a secret from earlier in the day. In the daylight, I notice that her hazel eyes are flecked with gold.

"I hope I'm not throwing off your schedule," I say.

"Not at all. Please come in."

It's the smell I notice first: a rich mix of woodsy scents like cypress and cedar with a hint of something minty, maybe eucalyptus. It's almost like I've stepped into a hidden forest, something magical or dreamlike.

The look of the studio is enchanting, too, even more than I realized when I snooped through the windows. I'm closer to the paintings now, with their vivid yellows and blues, but I avoid fixating on their disturbing images.

Instead, I soak up the rest of the space with my eyes—the large easel in the middle of the room, the rolling carts overflowing with brushes and paint tubes, the antique-looking wooden worktable against the wall on my right. The door to the back room is open, and I spot a daybed inside and a rattan ceiling fan rotating above it. Is that room just for reading and afternoon naps, or does Alison escape there some evenings, fretting about a husband she senses might be a cheater?

"What a lovely workspace," I say. "You must enjoy coming here each day."

"I do, very much." She's dressed in a white turtleneck sweater and flowy moss-green pants, like the mistress of this tranquil forest, and her hair is in a loose knot, with tendrils framing her face. "When we were first looking in the area, we couldn't find anything with a suitable outbuilding, but someone at the college knew this house was about to go on the market and told Jeffrey about it."

"Is Friday a busy teaching day for him?" I ask, hoping to confirm he's on campus.

"No, Fridays are when he writes, though today he's having lunch in Albany with a friend . . . Please take a look around. And I'd be glad to answer any questions you have."

I don't have any choice now but to absorb the artwork. For the first time I wonder if she views me as a potential buyer, and my decision to stop by has totally misled her. How thoughtless of me not to consider that.

I approach the painting of the woman with the basket full of mice, and as I fully take it in, I admit to myself that the image might be unsettling but it's also gripping. Still, I'd never want anything like that hanging in my living room.

I force my gaze to the painting to the left. In this one a woman sits at a kitchen table, echoing a painting on Alison's website. There's a horse in this one, too, but it's tiny, the size of a toy figure, and it's perched on a dinner plate. The woman is about to cut into it with her knife and fork.

And next to that is one with slightly different colors. There's a woman in a white dress again, but she's dark haired and holding a baby doll with bright-orange flames shooting out of its head.

"What do you think?" Alison asks evenly from behind me. "And please be honest. I'm very thick-skinned about my work."

"I have to admit they're disturbing, but also very arresting," I say, turning around. "And I love the colors you use."

"Thank you, that means a lot."

"Are these actual dreams of yours?"

"Not dreams I've necessarily had. But ones I can imagine myself having."

"I see," I say, though I'm not sure I do. Perhaps she's afraid of mice and conflicted about not having children and assumes those thoughts might haunt her sleep if given half a chance.

"Can I pour you a cup of herbal tea? I made a pot just before you arrived."

"Yes, please, as long as you're having a cup, too."

She smiles serenely and heads toward a wooden stand next to her worktable, where an electric kettle sits along with a large clay teapot and several mugs.

"I'm working on something now that I'd love your thoughts on," she says, glancing over her shoulder. "It's at the other end of the room."

I wander to the opposite side of the studio, where another easel holds an unfinished work. Next to it is a wooden storage rack with about ten pieces of art tucked into the slots. As I stop to examine the new work, I spot a flash of silver in one of the paintings on the rack. Curious, I slide it out a foot or so. I think it's the painting of the woman with three zippers running up her arm from her wrist.

"This one's on your website, right?" I call over to her. "Do you mind if I take a better look?"

"Um, sure," she says, and her comment is followed by the quiet tread of her suede flats on the laminated floor. Suddenly, she's standing right next to me, empty-handed, as if the plan for tea has been abandoned.

Does she not want me to see this one? Perhaps, I wonder with a start, this work reflects suicidal ideations on her part, and she'll feel uncomfortable showing it to me.

She slides the painting out and leans it against the wall. It's indeed the painting from her website, with a young woman lying prone on a kind of trapeze or swing, her face in profile and her right arm dangling over the side. Three zippers run side by side from her wrist to the elbow. And the colors in this work seem more somber than those in the other paintings I've viewed.

"And this is a dream, too?" I say. "I mean, one you can imagine yourself having?"

"Perhaps. It's an older painting of mine, and I don't remember everything I was thinking of at the time."

"Is it about self-harm?" I ask, surprised that I've dared to go there.

"No, no. I can see how it might come across in such a way, but that's not anything I've ever considered. It's—just based on something someone told me once."

I finally tear my gaze away from the bright silver zippers and glance upward. Since the young woman is lying with her face in profile, it's hard to get a good sense of what she looks like, but I study the image more closely than I did the other night on the website: the slightly wavy brown hair cascading over the side, the blue-green eyes and high cheekbones, the full lips turned upward in the tiniest of smiles. All suddenly so familiar.

I let out a small gasp.

"Is this—*Melanie*?" I say.

Behind me there's only silence now, as if Alison has exited the room, but when I spin around, we're only inches apart. She's biting her lower lip, clearly caught by surprise.

"Yes," she says quietly. "Yes, it is."

My heart has begun to thrum.

"She told you she hated buttons? That's why you painted the zippers?"

"Yes." Alison has composed her face so that it's now a total blank.

"And—and did she actually *pose* for you?"

"For several sessions. And I also worked with photographs I took of her."

In my mind, fragments of thoughts trip over each other: Mel being secretive when Harry asked if she had a new squeeze; her acting awkward around Handler when she and Logan bumped into him; the words "returning to birch" in her haiku.

"Were you and Melanie *lovers*?" I blurt out.

Alison lowers her gaze, her lips pressed tightly together, and then she looks back at me.

"I'm not going to lie to you," she says finally. "We were lovers, yes—that last fall before she died."

Chapter 28

My hand flies to my mouth, and I press it hard against my lips. There's a whooshing sensation in my head, like I've bent down to the ground and come up way too fast.

"Your daughter wasn't gay, if that's what you're thinking," Alison says. "She was just, uh, curious, I think . . . experimenting. We'd felt a strong connection at the end of her sophomore year, and as soon as she got back to campus, it turned into something physical."

I step backward toward the center of the room, grappling with the revelation. I might as well be in one of the paintings here, this moment as surreal as a tiny horse being served for dinner or flames shooting from a baby doll's head.

"Actually, that's *not* what I'm thinking," I say, feeling my anger spike. "Mel was her own person, and I don't care whether she was gay or bisexual or whatever. What I *am* thinking is why in God's name didn't you come forward when she was murdered."

"For obvious reasons," she says and quickly tucks a tendril of hair behind her ear. "What good would it have done anyway?"

"What *good*? You might have been able to help the police."

"That's highly unlikely," she insists. "Your daughter was a very special person, but what we had was simply a two-month fling, which I was about to end anyway."

I shake my head again, bewildered. My thoughts are spinning so fast I can barely see them, but one finally takes shape.

"Did your husband find out about you and Mel?" I demand.

She looks off, silent for several beats. I watch her chest rise as she takes a breath.

"Yes," she says finally.

That explains Handler's awkwardness toward me, as well as his failure to divulge where Mel's writing was stored. He might have feared something in Mel's work would unveil the affair.

"Let me guess," I say, not caring how snide my tone is. "He wasn't happy with the news."

She doesn't bother arguing my point.

And surely Handler wasn't merely unhappy. He must have been *livid*. Not only had his wife cheated on him, probably a no-no in his book despite his own infidelities, but she'd also made it a million times worse by choosing a Carter College student.

"Did it not occur to you that your own husband might have killed Melanie?" I ask. "In a jealous rage?"

"What?" she exclaims, her face now pinched in distress. "Of course not. Jeffrey wasn't jealous about the relationship."

"Oh please, how could he not have been?"

She looks off briefly again.

"Because we have an open marriage," she says. "It's been that way from nearly the beginning."

I part my lips in surprise, totally taken aback. So, she's not the cuckolded, possibly wounded spouse I imagined her to be.

"And he didn't mind that you chose one of his students for a fling?"

She hesitates for a second, and I sense her picking her words.

"That was clearly a mistake on my part, and it's why I'd decided to call it off," she says, crossing her arms over her chest. "An open marriage needs rules and boundaries, and for us that's always meant only one outside person at a time, and no students or anyone else close to home. I came clean with Jeffrey, promised to end the relationship, and he forgave me."

"Just like that?" I say. It's hard to believe he'd be so sanguine.

"Yes. I'd been having a really difficult time with my work the previous months, and it caused me to get sloppy with the rules more than once, about seeing only one person at a time and who was off-limits. When I confessed everything to Jeffrey, he understood that it was about me losing my way for a while, not about him. I've never broken the rules again."

I won't judge her about her marriage, that's her business, but I can't stand how self-absorbed she sounds, talking about her sloppy phase as if she'd gotten tipsy at a couple of dinner parties. She seems oblivious to the fact that there could have been serious repercussions besides those impacting her and her husband.

"You implied you had nothing of value to tell the police, but initially they were looking at people in Mel's orbit, and as far as you knew, you had information that could be important to them."

"That's not true. Mel and I talked about art and poetry, about the books we were reading, and not a word about our personal lives. There was nothing for me to contribute."

She bites her lip again, the mistress of the forest now suddenly ruffled, as if she's sensed there's danger in the dark between the trees. The most staggering part: she's incapable of seeing her failure to act as wrong.

I shake my head, disgusted, and hitch up the strap of my shoulder bag, more than ready to get out of here.

"Why in the world did you encourage me to come today?" I say.

I notice that her pale cheeks are now slightly flushed.

"I wanted to show some kindness—because I can tell how difficult it is for you to be back in the area. And because of Melanie. I cared about her, and to be honest, her death was quite shattering for me."

Not so shattering that she wanted to help the police find the murderer. Right now, I can't stand the sight of Alison Handler.

"I see I've upset you," she adds. "I'm sorry."

"Don't worry, I'm sure you'll get over it."

I start for the door, leaving her behind me, and then spin back around just as I'm about to reach for the handle.

"Does the name *Riley Reynolds* mean anything to you?" I ask.

Alison gazes back at me with a baffled expression.

"Reynolds?" she says and shakes her head. "I don't know anyone by that name."

I have no idea whether she's being truthful or not. I tug the door open and slam it hard behind me.

☙

I end up at the little diner I've stopped at before, having come on foot from the studio. I need to call Logan and loop him into every crazy thing I've learned this morning, but first I have to think through Alison's revelation and decide what it might mean.

She said Handler wasn't jealous, but there were other things at stake for him. If the college found out that his wife had taken one of his students as her lover, it would have been a real embarrassment for him. I doubt either Alison's fling or the couple's open marriage would have violated the moral turpitude clause of Handler's tenure contract, but the indiscretion might have impacted him in other, smaller ways that added up over time.

According to Alison, she assured her husband she was going to break things off with Melanie, but he had no guarantee she'd keep her word—or that Mel would stay quiet.

And there's something else, something that's making my pulse race: If the other person Riley told about her experience *was* Handler, he might have known all the details—the blow to the head, the dog leash, everything.

Wait, is this really where I'm going? Seriously wondering now whether Handler killed Mel? It seems like a stretch to think he did it to derail gossip about his wife and a student—unless there's part of the story I'm missing.

I take a sip of the iced tea I've ordered along with a plate of chicken salad and try not to get ahead of myself. Surely I'll know more once I've spoken to Riley, so it's pointless to speculate until I get there.

I wish I could call Bas right now and talk this through with him. But I'd feel like a fraud—which will be the case until I figure out what I'm going to do about my infidelity.

I force myself to finish my food, not wanting to skip another meal. The revelation from Alison has added to how crumpled I feel. I meant what I said to Alison about Mel being her own person and me not caring if she was gay or bi or simply experimenting. But it's shown once again how in the dark I was about my daughter. The list of things I never knew refuses to stop growing, even this many years after her death.

Plus—as if I needed to add to my angst—I pretty much have proof now that Mel's haiku about birches, the sliver of joy I held on to for so long, was not about the two of us. There was never a longing on her part to reconnect with me.

I need to pay the bill and get moving. As my eyes search the room for the waiter, they're snagged by a familiar face. *Jack.* He's standing at the front counter, accepting food in a white plastic bag. So, he's still in town. Though the smile he flashes at the cashier is perfectly charming, it sends a shiver through me.

As I watch him leave and vanish down the street, I catch sight of Craig's white cab idling on the curb outside. I'd called him on my hurried walk from the studio, switching my pickup address to the diner. It's finally time to meet with Riley.

"So, you're takin' quite the tour of the area," Craig says as soon as I slide into the car.

"Yeah, sort of," I say. I'm tempted to add "a tour of the *underworld*" but instead sink back into the seat. The ride, I've determined, will take about forty minutes.

As soon as we depart, I see I've missed two texts from Logan wondering what's going on, so I type out a reply.

> Can't speak right now—in a taxi. But I've pretty much confirmed Riley was not attacked the night she said she was. Will know more soon. Please stand by and don't say anything to Halligan yet.

It's only seconds before I hear back from him.

What? You cant call me? I need to know what's happening

There's no way I can discuss any of this in front of Craig.

I promise to call as soon as I can.

Right on schedule, we pull into the tiny town of Edgerton and soon after turn onto Bonner, a fairly rural road. There's a mix of houses along it, some a bit ramshackle, and others newer and suburban in feel, but they're all set fairly far apart, with plenty of trees growing between them. So, this is what Hilary meant when she said she wanted to give country life a try.

Craig comes to a stop at number 4204. The house, up a slight incline, is an attractive, average-size grayish-beige ranch with a stone foundation and an attached garage. The front lawn is dotted with young trees, obviously planted after the excavation.

I reiterate to Craig that I'll be finished in thirty minutes or less. I'm positive Riley will want to get this over quickly, and I'm not going to belabor things, though I hope I can talk her into calling Halligan while I'm here.

I reach the porch and press the doorbell, the kind with a camera lens just above it. From inside come two melodious dong sounds, almost like church bells. I inhale deeply, waiting for footsteps to follow. But they don't come. I give it almost a minute before trying again. Nothing this time, either.

Has Riley gotten cold feet? No, that can't be the case, it just can't be. I felt her sense of urgency as we spoke on the phone.

I back off the porch and traipse through the flower bed until I've reached one of the front windows. I peer inside. The curtains have been pulled closed, but there's enough of a gap for me to see a small, sparsely furnished bedroom. It looks like a guest room, possibly the one Riley is staying in, though she doesn't seem to be in the room. The curtains on the other window are too tightly closed to see inside.

She's probably in the rear of the house, I decide, where the living area must be, and it's possible she has earbuds in and didn't hear the bell. I scroll through today's calls and tap her number. For a second, I think I hear the faint sound of a ringtone, but it could be my imagination. The call goes to voicemail, which makes me growl in frustration.

"Riley, hi, it's Bree. I'm out front. I'm really looking forward to speaking with you."

I return to the porch and try the doorbell again. Nothing. I jiggle the door handle. Locked.

Okay, so maybe she's simply out for a walk, and then I instantly realize the absurdity of that thought. After being brutally raped in a park, Riley Reynolds has probably never ventured out by herself for a walk since then, let alone on a deserted road.

I decide my only option now is to call Hilary Brown, though if Riley hasn't told her about the meeting, I'll be tipping my hand, and she might try to nix the whole thing. This time Hilary picks up right away.

"Hilary, hi," I say. "Did Riley tell you she'd invited me to your house to talk?"

I hear her sigh.

"Yes," she says. "And, Bree, I must tell you that I advised her to cancel the invitation, at least for now. I know you're looking for answers, but if Riley wants to discuss things with you, she'll need to do it once I'm home and can be in the room with her."

"She never canceled," I explain. "I'm at your house now, but she's not answering the door."

Brown sighs again, a mix, it seems, of frustration and empathy. "I'm sorry you drove all the way out there. She might have felt skittish about calling you back to cancel, and now just isn't responding."

"I can understand your wish to be part of the conversation," I say, "but . . . what if you call her and conference me in?" I'm grasping at straws, desperately hoping not to leave empty-handed. "I would let you take the lead, of course."

The line goes quiet for a moment.

"Hilary, please," I add, nearly begging now. "I don't think Riley was completely honest with us, and we need the truth from her. Otherwise, we'll never know what really happened to Mel."

"All right," she says. "Give me a minute to try her and I'll ring you back."

I lean against the wall of the recessed porch. It's utterly quiet out here, not a car, bicyclist, or jogger on the road. The silence is suddenly broken by the faint ringtone of a phone, coming from deep within the house. I'm close enough now to really hear it.

The second ring cuts off midway through. I strain to pick up Riley's hello, but nothing follows.

Seconds later Hilary phones back.

"She didn't answer," she says.

"I could hear it ringing in the house. Maybe she didn't pick up because she's seen me out front and knows you're reaching out on my behalf."

"No, that's not like her," she says bluntly. "Something's wrong."

Chapter 29

Unease ripples through me. "What should we do?" I ask Hilary.

"I'm coming back there," she says.

"Do you want me to try to get inside?"

"No, it's locked up like a drum. But just stay there, *please*, in case she finally answers the door. I'll see you in twenty minutes."

As I drop the phone in my bag, I catch sight of Craig leaning across the front seat and powering down the passenger-side window.

"Everything okay?" he yells.

"Uh, yeah," I call out, traipsing back to the car. "But it's going to be longer than I said. Maybe up to an hour."

"These things happen, I know, but I'm gonna have to come back for you or send another driver. I got an airport pickup I can't be late for."

I groan internally. It would be so much better to have a car waiting here so I could quickly exit no matter how this plays out today.

"Okay," I say. "I'll call when I'm ready."

He starts the car and drives off, leaving me totally alone on the empty road. The sky has darkened since I set out from Cartersville, and it's cooler now. Tightening the belt on my coat, I head back up toward the front porch but instead decide to walk around to the back. Maybe I can get a glimpse of Riley, reassuring myself that she's okay.

Rounding the rear corner of the building, I see that Hilary has taken pains with her backyard, too. Adjacent to the house is a small, nicely designed stone patio with a bird feeder standing at the far end.

The rear lawn is as manicured as the front one, though it quickly gives way to a thickly wooded area that seems to extend for miles. Some of the trees have buds already, but no leaves yet, and a few of the closest ones have blue bird boxes tacked to them.

I step onto the patio. The large window at the back of the house has its drapes open, and after peering inside, I realize I'm looking into the living room with a dining area on the far left. No sign of Riley.

I return to the front of the house and plop onto the porch chair. My disquiet seems to swell by the minute, not helped by how strange it feels to be out here all by myself. Finally, I hear a car approach and soon spot a silver SUV barreling up the road. The vehicle makes a sharp turn into the driveway, screeching a little as it comes to a stop only inches from the garage door.

Hilary Brown bolts from the car.

"Any sign of her?" she calls out to me. Her apple-green coat is unbuttoned, and the sides flap as she hurries in my direction with her house key already in hand.

"None," I say.

She jabs the key in the lock and quickly opens the door. I follow her into a small corridor.

"Riley?" she says, raising her voice a little.

We're greeted by silence, along with the lingering smell of room spray, one of those scents that's supposed to remind you of rain or fresh linen.

Hilary takes a few steps in her sensible-looking pumps and stops at the first door on the left, pushing it open. We're now staring into the guest bedroom I saw earlier from the front window.

"Is this the room she's staying in?" I ask.

"Yes."

As she strides toward the en suite bathroom and glances inside, I survey the space. The only belongings I spot are a pair of black-and-tan ballet flats by the closet door.

Hilary starts moving again, back to the living room, with me right behind her. She calls Riley's name twice more without getting a response.

Our eyes seem to fall simultaneously on the large glass coffee table, where a smartphone in a turquoise case lies next to the TV remote.

"That's hers," Hilary says, though its presence is hardly reassuring. Riley's phone might be here, but where in the world is *she*?

Hilary ducks into a small kitchen just behind the dining area. It's empty, too.

"That's odd," Hilary says, returning to the living room. The muscles in her face are taut with worry.

"What?"

"The dishwasher's warm. She must have run it, but I didn't ask her to."

So, Riley's taken the time to tidy up.

"Could she have gone back to Buffalo sooner than planned—and forgotten her phone?"

"No, I checked the Ring camera on the front door before I left the office, and she hasn't been in or out of the house. And it's not just her phone that's here. All her toiletries are still in the bathroom."

My unease shape-shifts into a low-grade dread.

"Maybe she left in a rush and went out the back," I say as my gaze lights on a door from the dining area to the outside. "She could have panicked about speaking to me—because she knew I had doubts about the date she was raped . . . Did you know, Hilary? That it didn't happen when she claimed it did?"

She shrugs out of her coat, tosses it on the table, and turns to face me, her expression grave.

"Yes, she told me on the phone today—after she talked to you."

So, there it is: my nagging suspicion finally confirmed.

"Did she say when it *did* happen?" I ask.

"On the previous Monday night. I'm sorry—I had no idea until today."

I fight off a swell of emotions, a chaotic mix of anger, frustration, and unbearable sadness. Just as I told myself before, if she'd reported the crime, Mel would surely be alive.

"I'm glad she admitted it to you," I say finally, "but it seems she's decided to take off rather than explain herself."

Hilary shakes her head. "She said she wanted to tell you the whole truth, and I said fine, as long as I was here at the time. I can't believe she left without any word."

"What if you call your nephew? He might know what's going on."

"Right, but"—I see her eyes flicker with a thought—"let me check the den first. She sometimes reads in there. Maybe she's fallen asleep."

She hurries off again with me still following, and I realize we're headed down a short corridor to the other room that faced the flower bed, which I'd assumed was a bedroom.

The door is closed.

She raps lightly and calls Riley's name again. Nothing. For a moment, Hilary hesitates as if gathering her nerve. Then she slowly pushes open the door.

We see her at the same time. I gasp as my knees buckle. Hilary lets out a wail of anguish.

Riley is sitting slumped over on the floor with her back against a partially open bathroom door and her neck wound with orange electrical cord. The cord extends from over the top of the door and seems to be tied to the handle on the other side. Her head has dropped onto her chest, but I can see enough to tell that her eyes are closed and her pretty face is dark red, like someone's held a blowtorch only inches away.

We lurch in unison toward Riley, and each of us grabs hold of an arm. Somehow, we manage to hoist her into an upright position so that the cord finally slackens. My cheek is almost touching Riley's, but I can't hear her breathing.

Let her still be all right. Please, please, please.

"I'll keep her lifted," I say, panting. "Can you unknot the cord?"

"Yup."

I feel Hilary working on the other side of the door, and from the way the cord jiggles, I can tell her hands are shaking.

"God dammit," she yells. "I can't get this."

"Do you have something to cut it with?"

Riley is too heavy for me to hold much longer, and I'm scared I'll drop her and that the cord will tighten around her neck again.

"Yeah. No, wait . . . I've got it."

I feel the cord slacken even more, and as I lower Riley back to the floor, it slithers quickly down this side of the door. I lay her on her back and loosen the cord enough so that it isn't choking her. An angry red bruise is circling her neck.

"Do you know CPR?" I ask as Hilary stoops down next to me.

"God, no, I don't."

"I do, kind of. Call nine-one-one and I'll try."

As Hilary races out of the room, I kneel to the floor, tear open Riley's pale-blue blouse, and start chest compressions, aiming for a hundred per minute. With my arms aching, I reach one hundred, then two hundred.

"They're on their way," Hilary yells from the doorway. I hear her come up behind me. "Please tell me she's alive."

"There's no sign she's breathing," I say, still working desperately. "Can you take her pulse?"

She drops to the floor, shoves up the sleeve of Riley's blouse, and shifts her fingers around until they're finally resting in one place.

"I can't feel anything," she says, her voice breaking.

I glance closely at Riley's face for the first time. Her mouth is slack, and every inch of her skin looks burned. Instinctively, I reach up with one hand and touch her forehead. Despite the fiery color, it's cool to the touch.

"I think it's too late," I say hoarsely, letting my hands drop to my sides.

Hilary moans, and we both sink back onto our heels.

My own hands are shaking now, partly from doing the compressions, and the rest from despair. Riley is dead, has died within hours of speaking to me. She will never return to her job or her fiancé, never have children like she wanted, never slip her feet into those black-and-tan ballet flats again.

I swallow hard and fight off the urge to dry heave.

"Why would she *do* this?" Hilary exclaims, pressing her temples hard with her hand. "She said she was ready to put the past behind her."

But I'd pushed her, hadn't I? Was she terrified about people learning of her failure to come forward and then judging her harshly? Shaken, I realize she might have put off the conversation with me today just to buy herself enough time to end her life.

"Did she sound distraught when you spoke to her?" I ask.

"No, just a little nervous about admitting the truth," Hilary says. "Besides, Riley was a *survivor*. I can't believe she'd give up and do this."

I gasp.

"Hold on," I say and stagger to a standing position. "Maybe she *wouldn't* do it . . . Does the cord belong to you?"

"Uh, it must have been in the garage with stuff that got left by the previous owners."

"But you're not sure?"

"No . . . Are you saying she was *murdered*?"

Instinctively, I glance down at Riley. Someone could have surprised her from behind, strangled her with the electrical cord, and strung her up over the door.

"Yes, maybe. Even if she wanted to take her own life, would she have chosen to die like this—in the same horrible way she was attacked years ago?"

"Oh dear . . . then we need to get out of this room," Hilary says, rising now, too. "I'm not a criminal lawyer, but I know we shouldn't be tramping around in here any more than we already have."

We back out of the den, then hurry to the living room. As I stand nearly shell-shocked in the center of the space, Hilary drifts to the back door and stares hard at it.

"The bolt's not on," she says. "And it was when I left this morning."

"So, someone broke in from the back?"

Hilary shakes her head. "No, there's almost zero way to pick the lock . . . And I can't picture Riley opening the door to a stranger."

I shake my own head, bewildered. "What . . . what if it wasn't a stranger?" I say finally, chilled as I utter those words. "We know Riley lied about the timing of the assault, and maybe somehow that caught up with her in a way we don't understand."

"For God's sake, how?"

"When Riley and I spoke on the phone, I asked her if anyone knew the real date besides her, and she admitted that she'd told someone right afterward. Did she say anything to you about that?"

"No, we never got that far."

"Maybe that person found out she was going to tell the truth, and it would have been bad for him."

"But how could that be bad for anyone?"

I press a hand to my head, trying to force my thoughts.

"Uh, because it might have exposed him somehow . . . or because it meant that the world would know Riley was attacked before Mel, and *that* threatened him—because of what he did with the information."

There, I've said it. What's been knitting together since I spoke on the phone to Riley: Someone used the details of Riley's attack to kill Mel.

"And then," I say, "that person showed up here today, pretending to want to talk or offer support but really intending to silence her."

Hilary gasps, then darts into the kitchen. Perplexed, I follow behind her. After tugging down the right sleeve of her blouse so that it covers her hand, she yanks open the dishwasher, releasing a small gust of warm air. The machine is nearly empty, except for three upside-down coffee mugs on top and a couple of spoons in the caddy on the lower shelf.

"So, what are we looking at?" I ask, still confused.

"I used one of those brown mugs for coffee before I left," she says. "And the white one is the mug Riley's been using each morning. I don't know what the other brown one is doing here."

"Could it have been used last night?"

"I emptied the dishwasher before I even had my coffee this morning. And why would she run it with so few dishes?"

Hilary swivels and stares at the bright-red Keurig coffee maker on the countertop, then opens the trash can in the corner.

"There are four capsules in here," she says. "Riley and I each had a cup of coffee this morning, so how do you explain the other two?"

"She definitely had a visitor, then."

Someone who'd steered clear of the Ring camera on the front door. Someone who'd been invited in for coffee. Someone who clearly put their mug in the dishwasher and ran it so there'd be no fingerprints or trace of their DNA.

Chapter 30

The EMTs arrive first, followed only minutes later by two gray-uniformed state troopers, who take brief statements from us in the hallway. Hilary wastes no time in telling them that we have reason to believe this could be a homicide. They herd us back into the living room, informing us that a detective will arrive shortly and that we're to sit apart from each other without speaking or making any phone calls.

Per instructions, Hilary and I sit silently, forced to overhear the awful sounds from down the hall—people shuffling and murmuring, one man saying, "Yeah, yeah," every minute or so. My stomach turns as I picture Riley's lifeless form in there, awaiting someone from the coroner's office.

This is what it must have been like for Mel that night. Total strangers tramping around her body, pawing at her in latex gloves, snapping photographs—in her case, with her pants around her ankles.

I retch and take several long breaths, exhaling through my nose.

"You okay?" Hilary calls over in a whisper. The flip's gone out of her hair, and her makeup is slightly smeared from her efforts in the den. It must be taking everything she's got to hold herself together.

"Yeah, sorry. It's just so devastating."

Could I be partly to blame for this? Because I wouldn't stop asking questions? I was doing it for Mel so that the truth would come out, never guessing there might be collateral damage.

I lean forward and whisper across the room to Hilary, "I know the troopers said no calls for now, but are you okay with me texting Logan? Just to let him know where I am."

But I've got an even more urgent motive than that.

"Sure. I just wish they'd let me call my poor nephew. He and my sister will never be the same."

I slide my phone out from my purse and type quickly, keeping one eye on the corridor.

> At H. Brown house in Edgerton. Found Riley dead. State police here now. pls get hold of Halligan ASAP. Apparent suicide but we think she was killed.

Seconds later the phone rings, Logan calling, of course. I quickly silence it and frantically send another text.

> They won't let me use phone now. Please call Halligan!

I've barely dropped the phone back in my purse when a tall man in a dark-blue suit and tie enters the living room and introduces himself as Detective Pendergrass. He's about forty-five, a little husky, with blond hair styled in a buzz cut. Hilary quickly describes her relationship to Riley, our concerns when she didn't respond to phone calls, and our efforts to save her. She offers up the reasons we both have doubts she took her own life, including the detail about the mugs.

Pendergrass nods, not giving anything away.

"I'll need to speak to each of you at much greater length," he says, "but it's best if we can do it at the station. Plus, we'll be better able to examine the scene once you've vacated the premises."

Hilary's body sags in frustration. She reiterates that she's an attorney and nearly begs him to let us give statements at the house so she can call her nephew from here the moment she's able to. She asks if the two of us can wait on the patio until he's ready to speak to us.

The detective relents, and after Hilary grabs her coat, we exit through the main bedroom and take seats at either end of the patio. And then we wait—endlessly, it seems. *Who did this to Riley?* I keep asking myself. *Will we ever know?*

It's twilight by the time we see Pendergrass again. He asks Hilary to come inside first and tells me he'll be back in a bit. I'm left to hang out alone in the chilly air, staring into the darkening woods and doing my best not to lose my mind. Bas must be sitting down to dinner right now, with a fire blazing in the hearth. What a fool I was to come to Cartersville without him. I might have been a fool to come at all.

Pendergrass finally returns for me, shows me to a seat back in the living room, and opens his notebook. He's courteous enough, but at the same time he seems slightly wary of me—and how can I blame him? Hilary must have explained who I am and why I showed up here. He starts by asking me to describe the scene in the den, what I touched, and what my CPR efforts consisted of. I answer carefully, trying to keep my emotions under control, but a couple of times my voice quavers.

As we're speaking, Hilary's voice suddenly intrudes from the bedroom. She must have been given permission to contact her relatives, and I overhear not only her anguished words but also faint cries of despair from the other end of the line.

Pendergrass plows ahead, now asking about my relationship with Riley, and I relate the reason I came today. I end by urging him to call Halligan, who, I explain, has been handling the investigation regarding Mel.

"Detective Halligan has no idea you showed up here today?" he asks, practically scowling.

"I hadn't alerted him to my concerns yet," I say. "It seemed premature."

Finally, mercifully, Pendergrass says I'm free to go. Hilary has emerged from the bedroom, her face stained with tears, and as soon as I'm up from the couch, I approach her and ask if she's going to be okay alone here.

"A friend is picking me up and taking me to her house for the night," she says.

I nod and touch the edge of her sleeve, heartbroken for her and still churning with a vague sense of guilt. Is this somehow all on me? "Let me know if there's anything I can do," I say. Though I can't imagine how I could possibly help.

Pendergrass leads me out, and I avert my gaze as we pass the corridor to the den. Stepping outside, I see that the ambulance is gone, though there are several police vehicles parked in the driveway. I pause on the lawn to take a breath and then call Craig, who miraculously says he can have a driver here in twenty minutes.

Next, I try Logan, who answers on the first ring. "Bree, please tell me you're okay," he demands.

"Yeah—just really shaken. I went to meet with Riley this afternoon, and Hilary and I found her hanging from a door."

I choke a little over the last words.

"Christ. You're still there?"

"Yes, but all done with the police now."

"Let me come get you."

"I've already ordered a taxi, and he's closer than you. Have you reached Halligan yet? He needs to know about this as soon as possible."

"I've left two messages, but I haven't heard back yet. You really think this was a homicide?"

"Yes, and . . . I think it could be related to Mel's case."

"How?"

"I'm not sure, but like I told you in the text, Riley lied about the date of her attack. It happened six days earlier."

"So that's why she seemed evasive to you."

"Right. And she apparently told someone right after it happened—maybe a friend or someone with the school, and that person might have told people, too. Which means the details about her assault were out there four days before Mel died."

He's silent for a couple of beats, probably worried I'm still struggling to accept the truth.

"Are we talking again about a possible copycat? About *Jack*?"

"Uh, maybe. Him or somebody else."

I need to tell Logan about Mel's affair, but I'll do that when I have more time to explain.

"Just get back here, okay?"

"I will, but *please*—keep trying Halligan."

As I hang up, I assure myself that even if we don't hear back from Halligan, Pendergrass will contact him tonight. But what if there's no evidence pointing to murder? I have to figure out who Riley spoke to right after the rape.

I dial Morgan next.

"What now?" she says instead of hello.

"I'm sorry, but I have some terrible news. Riley is dead—a suicide, it seems. She was found this afternoon."

Pendergrass made it clear that I shouldn't share specifics about the scene, and other than with Logan, I don't intend to do that.

"My God, that's horrible," Morgan says.

"I know. Look, I've been a total nuisance so far, but can you meet with me one more time? There's something important I need to ask you."

I could ask now, of course, and make everything easier for myself, but this needs to happen in person, I think. Morgan must be sick to death of me, maybe ready to blow me off, and if I talk to her face-to-face, it will be easier for me to press if I have to.

"Is this really necessary?"

"Yes, *please*."

I hear a sigh of frustration. "All right, then. Where?"

I have nothing in mind, but then I remember Craig mentioning in the car that Edgerton wasn't far from Barrow, the town where Morgan and I had met.

"Any chance you can meet me at that diner again?"

"Bea's? Yeah, I suppose. But not till around, uh, eight forty-five or so."
"That's okay. I'll head there and wait."

As soon as I arrive at the diner, I order a grilled cheese sandwich and coffee from the twentysomething waiter. I've arranged for a taxi to come back for me at 9:15—because I can't imagine Morgan wanting to give me any more time than that.

My phone's low on battery, so I update Logan by text rather than calling.

> Back at 10 or so. I have some new questions for Morgan Kroll and we're meeting in a few minutes.

> WHAT questions?

> Pls just be patient. I'll explain later.

The diner is only a quarter full, people finishing what, for the region, might be a late dinner. I think again of Bas, perhaps getting ready for bed. I feel desperate again to call him and describe this new hell, but what right do I have at this moment to ask for any comfort? What if that right is gone for good? It's quite possible I've ruined things with him, with no way to repair the damage—and I won't know for sure until I get back to Uruguay.

I quickly shoot him a text on WhatsApp that I know he'll see first thing in the morning.

> Hope you're still on the mend. So much happening here. Will call early tomorrow. I love you.

At 8:50, Morgan pushes open the diner door and strides in my direction. She's in blue jeans, a tight black turtleneck, and a thin black puffer vest. As she nears the table, I see she's not wearing her red lipstick tonight, so I've probably dragged her here from home.

"I can't believe it," she says, sliding into the booth and shaking her head. "Though maybe I should have seen it coming."

The waiter returns to the booth immediately, and this time Morgan orders a Diet Coke.

"You bet," he says, "but just so you ladies know, we close at nine."

I have even less time than I thought, but I give the waiter a chance to move away before I lob my first question.

"What do you mean by 'should have seen it coming'?"

"When Riley called me earlier this week, she sounded like a total wreck. She said she was proud about finally going to the police, but I could tell it was going to bring everything to the surface for her again—in the worst way possible."

"Things got even more complicated since I talked to you last," I say. "You know how I asked if Riley might have misinformed us about the date of the attack? Well, it turns out she did. She was actually raped the previous Monday night, almost a week before she spoke to you."

Morgan straightens in her seat, clearly taken aback. "What makes you so sure now?"

"She more or less admitted it to me over the phone, and she told her lawyer straight out."

"But what about the bruises she showed me?"

"I did a bit of research, and it might have been hard for you to tell they were nearly a week old."

"Fuck. Why would she lie about which night it was?"

"Because of my daughter, I assume—not wanting to be blamed for her death."

Morgan's Diet Coke has arrived, along with the check, and she stirs the straw around and around in the glass, making the ice clink. "Wow, I got played for a fool, didn't I?"

The bitterness in her tone surprises me.

"Don't think that way, Morgan. Look, I'm furious about Riley keeping quiet, but I get the reason for it. She was frightened and ashamed."

Based on her expression, I'd say my comment hasn't mollified her.

"Are you worried again that this might blow back on you professionally?" I ask.

She keeps stirring her Diet Coke.

"Yes, because it *could* blow back," she says finally. "I couldn't have saved your daughter, but if I'd convinced Riley to report the crime or gone to the police myself, I might have saved that second girl in Plattsburgh."

"Surely people will understand why you made the choice you did."

"Only time will tell, won't it?"

She stuffs a hand in her jeans pocket and fishes out a few dollars, obviously eager to split. I can't let her go without asking the question I came with.

"Please, here's the reason I wanted to see you, and then I promise—you never have to hear from me again."

She drops the bills on the table and leans back in her seat.

"Shoot."

"When I spoke to Riley today, she admitted someone else knew about the real date, someone she told right afterward, but she didn't say who it was. Did she give any hint who it might have been?"

Morgan shakes her head. "Like I think I mentioned, she said she'd been alone the night before, so I figured I was the first to know, but I suppose she might have told someone—especially if there was all that time in between."

"Can you picture her telling Jeffrey Handler?"

"*Handler?* Why in God's name would she go to him?"

"Maybe she went by the English department the next day—the *real* next day—to ask about extensions and ended up running into Handler and telling him what happened, then dropped by the following Monday to check in with him again, but she ran into you instead. So you were the second person to hear the story."

She shakes her head. "I can't imagine her sharing the story with him, even if she'd been locked in a room with the man. You just have to read his poetry to know that the only thing he gives a shit about is stuff like crows and rock croppings."

The lights in the diner flash, startling me. I notice we're the only customers still here, and the remaining staff must be signaling that it's time for us to wrap up. I push the bills back toward Morgan.

"Let me pay," I tell her. "I appreciate you coming all this way tonight."

As I quickly take care of the bill, I feel my heart sinking. I've been praying Morgan held a piece of the puzzle, but she doesn't. Though I might *sense* that Riley's lie led to her death and that it's related somehow to Mel's murder, I have no proof whatsoever.

Chapter 31

Once we're outside, Morgan and I follow the short concrete sidewalk to the edge of the parking lot, which runs adjacent to the diner. She stops to dig a key fob from her jeans pocket and then continues ahead, the wind tousling her short black hair.

"I'll say goodbye here," I call out from behind her. "A taxi's picking me up in a few minutes."

That's not exactly true, though. I'm going to have to shiver by myself in the parking lot for a while, along with my anguished thoughts.

"Oh," she says, turning back to me. "Uh, why don't you wait in my car?"

I'm touched by the offer, but I need to let her go. She's had enough of me to last a lifetime.

"That's very thoughtful, Morgan, but I'll be fine."

Behind us, the diner lights switch off, one section at a time, and then, all at once, those in the parking lot do, too, except for a single security light. I take a second to glance around. The stores on either side of the diner—as well as those across the road—seem to be locked up tight for the night, and there's very little traffic right now. It's not going to be any fun waiting here alone.

"Sure?" Morgan asks. "I don't mind hanging around a bit longer."

"Well, if you really *don't* mind, I think I'll take you up on your offer. But just so you know, the taxi actually isn't due for fifteen minutes."

"Not a problem."

I follow her halfway down the darkened lot to a shiny black SUV. A plastic bag skitters across the tarmac, chased by the wind, and then stops dead. There was a fleeing bag like that in the state police parking lot when Logan and I went to meet Riley. Was that only on Wednesday? Because it seems like decades ago.

We reach the car and Morgan unlocks the doors. From the back of the diner comes the sound of a metal door slamming shut, followed by the murmur of voices, the click of car doors opening and shutting, and the sudden purr of an engine. Seconds later, just as I'm opening the door, a sedan with two people appears from behind the restaurant and exits the lot. The last two staffers obviously sharing a ride.

The SUV is spotless inside, and it still has a slight new-car smell. To my surprise, Morgan suddenly fires up the engine.

"Wait," I exclaim. "What—"

"Just turning the car around so we can see the cab when it gets here."

She does just that, backing up the SUV and then pointing it nose forward. She keeps the motor running, I guess so we have light from the dashboard.

"This is very thoughtful of you, Morgan," I say. "You must have work to do tonight, papers to grade."

"Fortunately, I'm done with that for the day. I always save the later part of the evening for my own creative work."

"Writing poems?" At our first meeting, she mentioned she'd studied poetry as part of her MFA program.

"Not anymore, no," she says, glancing over. "I write book reviews for some online sites. And I dabble a little in painting—just watercolors, really."

"What a nice hobby."

"As some wise man once said, it's silent poetry. So maybe I haven't completely abandoned my former passion."

Before I'm even conscious of a thought, I feel my face wrinkle in confusion.

"I heard someone else say that recently," I tell her. "It's part of a longer quote, right?"

My mind flickers for a couple of moments until the person who made the comment materializes in her black velveteen dress: *Alison*. We'd been discussing how she used to sit in on some of her husband's backyard classes and share her thoughts on the similarities between art and poetry.

Did Morgan hear Alison quote Plutarch when she was helping Handler? She mainly worked remotely, she'd said, but perhaps the two women met in passing. Or even became friendly with each other.

"Who?" she asks flatly.

"Um, an editor friend who I've known for years."

I'm not sure why I don't want to admit it was Alison. But my heart has begun to skitter like the plastic bag, which I see from the window is now on the move again.

"You were in publishing?"

"Yes—though, since Melanie's death, I've only worked freelance."

Another remark of Alison's swims to the surface in my mind. She said she'd been sloppy with the rules more than once during that period years ago, meaning Mel might not have been the only lover who didn't fit within the boundaries the Handlers established for their open marriage.

Could Morgan be someone she once got sloppy with? Surely professional colleagues of her husband would have been off-limits.

And there was another rule Alison admitted violating, one about overlap. Meaning she'd allowed herself two lovers during the same time frame.

There's now a weird rumbling in my head, as if I've picked up the early sounds of a stampede of horses and if I don't get out of the way, I'll be knocked to the ground and dragged in their wake.

"Is everything okay?" Morgan asks, staring across the front seat at me.

Maybe she can tell, even in the dimness of the car, that the blood has drained from my face. All I know is that I don't want to be sitting here anymore.

"I'm fine," I say. "But—but I should let you go. I hate holding you up this way."

"I said it's not a problem."

As I fumble for the door handle, Morgan reaches across me and grasps my right arm. I can feel the pressure through the sleeve of my coat.

"Don't be crazy," she says. "It's deserted out there."

She tightens her grip, and it takes all my strength to wrench my arm away.

"I don't *care*," I exclaim. My fingers finally find the handle, and then I'm nearly hurling myself from the vehicle.

Within seconds, I'm at a full jog, moving across the blacktop toward the front of the lot and starting to gasp for air. There's no taxi in sight.

God, where is he? I see a truck barrel down the road in front of me but nothing else.

I brace myself for the sound of Morgan's car heading toward me. But what comes next is the double click from the car door opening. My breath freezes in my chest. Seconds later, I hear the scuff of boots on the blacktop. She's following me on foot.

"Bree, what's going on?" she calls out through the darkness. "Are you all right?"

I'm almost at the road, but there's not a single car passing by. I fish desperately in my purse for my phone, finally grabbing it.

Then, almost out of nowhere, a white taxi rumbles into view and pulls up in front of the restaurant. I wave frantically at the driver, who nods when he sees me. I rush toward the car and yank the rear door open. Before diving in, I turn quickly back. Morgan is retreating to her car and is soon enveloped in darkness.

"Everything okay?" the driver asks, eyeing me in the rearview mirror.

"Yeah, I just need to get back to the inn as soon as possible."

Was I being totally irrational just now? Maybe I'm so distraught about Riley that I'm not thinking straight. But no, something feels very wrong, and I'm not sure exactly why. I have to make sense of what just happened and let Halligan know.

I quickly text Logan, my palms almost too sweaty to type.

Have you heard from Halligan?

not yet. where ARE you?

On my way back. I'll be there in thirty-five minutes.

k. come get me in my room.

I lean back against the seat, drained. Will Halligan even care that I've got a weird feeling based on a Plutarch quote? There's one person, I realize, who can fill in some blanks. *Alison Handler.* Though I can't stand the thought of hearing her voice again, I call her anyway. After half a ring, the call goes to voicemail, meaning she's probably declined it. I can hardly blame her. I suggested her husband might be a murderer.

"Alison, I know it's late," I say, "but I need to speak with you tonight. It's urgent."

To my shock, I hear back from her several minutes later.

"I didn't want to be rude and not take the call, but we can't communicate after this," she says. "It's not fair to Jeffrey."

So now she's a fan of fairness.

"I won't call again if you answer one question."

"One question—and really, that's all." She's speaking at a normal volume, so Jeffrey is either out for the evening or she's sneaked over to the studio to guarantee herself privacy.

"Did you once have an affair with Morgan Kroll?"

I hear the intake of breath, and I can almost feel her weighing whether to answer or not.

"Please, Alison. It's critical that I know."

Silence follows. I wait, praying she has the decency to tell me.

"Yes," she says finally. "But Jeffrey can't know about it. I confessed to him about Melanie, and I told him there was someone else around that time, someone I'd been seeing since the summer, but he never knew that person was Morgan."

My pulse, finally slowed from the parking lot, starts to race again.

"It started when she worked for your husband?" I ask.

Another pause.

"The attraction began before then, if you must know. We'd met on campus—when we were both in grad school at SUNY Albany—and I suggested her for a freelance job with Jeffrey. And eventually one thing led to another."

"It sounds like the relationship overlapped with Melanie."

"Why is that relevant?"

"Just *tell* me."

"Yes, for a while. But as I made clear before, I'd lost my way as an artist. I finally broke it off with Morgan once things intensified between Melanie and me."

I swallow, trying to calm myself.

"And how did Morgan take it?" I say.

A few seconds pass before she responds.

"First, I need you to know, I'm not an unprincipled person. I'd always been clear with Morgan that our relationship was a casual thing, but she'd convinced herself otherwise. When it ended, she was furious—furious at me, furious at the idea there might be someone else. She even stalked me for a while."

I don't even say goodbye. I just end the call and let the phone drop in my lap.

Morgan Kroll had been replaced as Alison's paramour, sending her into a rage. Maybe while stalking Alison, she saw her with Mel, and started stalking her, too.

And then, around that time, Riley stumbled into Morgan's life. Riley with her crushing story about being raped and almost killed by a sexual predator.

What if the "one person" who Riley said knew the real date of the attack was simply Morgan? Perhaps the morning Riley showed up in the English department really *was* the next day, meaning that Tuesday morning, not almost a week later. No wonder her bruises looked fresh and she seemed "in shock."

This would mean that Morgan learned everything she needed in order to get rid of her rival without anyone guessing who the killer was.

Chapter 32

It can't be true, can it? But as the car thumps along the dark road, I realize it all makes horrible, terrifying sense.

And if true, it means I *am* responsible for Riley's murder, tapping the first domino when I called Morgan and shared my concerns about the timeline. She must have made contact with Riley soon afterward and found out by midday that Riley was going to come clean. And she couldn't let that happen. My stomach turns as I imagine her driving to Hilary's house, plotting to take Riley's life.

The ride seems interminable, but finally I'm knocking on the door of Logan's room. He ushers me inside and immediately pulls me into an embrace. I feel my eyes well up against the threads of his sweater.

"Bree, what the hell is going on?" he says.

"I think I know who killed Mel," I say, pulling back. "And it wasn't Ruck."

"*What?*" I can tell from the expression in his eyes that he thinks I've gone down a rabbit hole again.

"Please, Logan, it's going to sound crazy, but you need to hear me out."

"I will, but just *tell* me. I'm going out of my mind."

From a quick glance around, I realize I'm in the sitting room of a suite rather than a bedroom. I move quickly to the couch and collapse on it, while Logan takes a seat in the armchair directly across.

Peeling off my coat, I start with what I discovered this morning about the creek water, my call afterward to Riley, and then my visit to Alison's studio and what she confessed about her affair with Mel. Logan's eyes widen, and he begins to pepper me with questions, but I hold up my hand, asking him to let me finish first because the worst is yet to come.

Next, I describe the heart-wrenching scene of finding Riley's body at Hilary Brown's house and how our suspicions became aroused. Finally, I tell him about my meeting with Morgan, her comment about Plutarch, and the admission from Alison when I was on my way back.

By the time I finish, Logan's jaw has dropped in shock—though not, it seems, in total disbelief.

"My God," he says, roughly massaging the back of his neck. "You're saying Morgan Kroll killed Riley—and Mel, *too*? That Ruck told the truth after all?"

"Yes, I think so."

"That fucking bitch."

"You don't think I've lost my mind?" I ask.

"No . . . I mean, we need more information, but it sounds like she had a motive, and this would explain the inconsistencies Halligan originally insisted we shouldn't ignore, like Mel not having a bite mark. All Morgan would have had to work with was what Riley said she'd experienced before she escaped."

"It also explains why half of Mel's clothes were torn off but there was no sexual assault."

I hate how matter-of-fact I'm being about the brutal death of my child, but it's the only way to sort through this without my head exploding.

"So, it was all about jealousy, then?" Logan says as the crease deepens between his eyes. "Kroll killed Melanie to eliminate a rival?"

"Yes, that's what my gut is telling me. Alison said Morgan was furious, and she might have already thought about killing Mel. Then when Riley confided in her about the attack, she suddenly had a way to do it and make it look like a sexual predator was on the loose."

Logan shakes his head in disgust.

"Christ, Bree, she might have killed you, too—if the cab hadn't come along."

Had I really been in danger? Even in the safety of this room, I shudder at the memory of Morgan's hand gripping my arm and the sound of her footsteps after I fled her car.

"Maybe. It would have been a risk for her to try something in a public setting . . . and yet she'd done it before. And she obviously thought nothing of killing Riley."

"But why, for God's sake? That's one part I don't get."

"Because—and I'm just wrapping my head around all this—she found out Riley was going to change her story and tell the real date."

Thanks to me, of course, and my stomach clenches at the thought. I'd vowed not to fawn this time and instead kept digging and prodding, with Riley as collateral damage.

"But wouldn't Morgan have *wanted* Riley's attack to seem like the first of two in the area?" Logan says.

"Initially, yes. And that must be the real reason she called Riley a week or so after the assault and pressed her again to go to the cops. That way they'd know there'd been a similar crime before Mel was killed. Then Ruck was arrested, and everything fell into place for her without Riley's help.

"But now, eight years later, the landscape had shifted, and she probably felt a lie would actually protect her. She might have even talked Riley into it when they first spoke this week, telling her that if she said she'd said she was assaulted *before* Mel, she'd be excoriated for not going to the authorities."

"But how was the lie any protection?"

"First, think about how Morgan was probably feeling this week. For years she'd thought she gotten away with murder, and then out of the blue, Riley surfaces. Morgan probably felt freaked about it and maybe even paranoid, worried that since so much time had passed, the cops might be more curious about her than they would have been before and wonder why she'd held on to the secret all this time. They might have started looking into her time at Carter."

Logan nods. "So now it seemed better for the cops to think Riley was attacked *after* Mel died," he says. "That way they'd never wonder about her being privy to the MO."

"That's what it seems like to me. She must have told herself that she'd be perfectly fine if she just kept her cool and did her best to back up a lie about the date.

"But then," I continue, "she finds out that the truth was in danger of coming to light. And if she *had* pressured Riley to lie, and Riley told Halligan about it, that would have seemed highly suspicious. It might not have taken forever to find a link between Morgan and Alison and Mel . . . And this must be why Morgan was willing to talk to me and stay in touch. She was keeping tabs on things."

"How do you think she heard Riley was about to change her story?"

I shake my head, uncertain. "I'm not sure how it played out. Riley might have called Morgan and told her that she'd decided to tell me the truth, or maybe after Morgan talked to me this morning, she just assumed things were about to come to a head. One way or the other, she went to see Riley, probably all nice and friendly, and then she must have slipped something into her coffee to make it easier to set up the hanging. And then ran the mugs through the dishwasher so there'd be no trace of her DNA."

"Christ," Logan says. "We just have to hope she left some other trace of herself."

But what if she didn't? This is still only my crazy theory, based on not much more than a quote from Plutarch. There might not be any real evidence connecting Morgan to Riley's death.

I exhale, spent from sharing everything. But there's still something else I need to say.

"You realize, don't you, that I'm partly responsible for Riley's death? I called her and questioned the date and pretty much forced her into telling the truth. I triggered *everything*. How can I possibly live with that?"

"You can't beat yourself up over it, Bree," Logan tells me. "You had every right to look for the truth and challenge her story once you saw the holes in it, and I'm sure Halligan will feel the same—if he ever fucking calls."

Nothing Logan said makes me feel any better. If I'd thought it through, talked to Halligan first, there might have been a way to get at the truth without costing Riley her life. Noticing there's a half-empty bottle of wine on the console, I get up and pour myself a small amount. Maybe it will stop my pulse from racing so fast.

"Not that I gave you much of a chance earlier," I say once I'm seated again, "but you haven't commented about Mel and Alison Handler."

Logan shrugs. "It took me by surprise, but it doesn't shock me. Mel was a free spirit, an adventurer . . . open to all sorts of things. We always knew that about her."

"I just wish I felt better about the person she chose. On the surface, Alison is enchanting, but she's one of those people who move through life doing exactly as they please and not minding who they hurt in the process."

Logan's face goes taut with anguish.

"I'll tell you what really bothers me," he says, "and what could leave me undone if I thought about it too long. The fact that our daughter made a seemingly harmless choice that might have cost her life."

I nod, because that could leave me undone as well. There's a part of me that just wants to unspool right now, to let grief and despair have their way, but I need to keep my head clear for what's ahead.

And then finally my phone rings with Halligan's name on the screen.

I answer on speaker, laying the phone on the coffee table and explaining that I'm with Logan.

"I've just gotten off the line with Detective Pendergrass," he says, sounding not at all happy. "You should never have gone to see Riley Reynolds today. You need to stay out of this and let us do our jobs."

"Can you wait and chew me out later?" I ask. "There's something critical I need to tell you."

I relate the entire story just as I did with Logan. Halligan lobs a few questions at me but mostly listens.

"I want you to come in tomorrow and make a full statement," he says finally, his voice still stern. "Ten o'clock. Until then, you're to do nothing. Is that understood?"

"Yes, understood," I say, chastened. "Good night."

I reach down and tap the red button with my finger.

"He clearly listened," Logan says. "And it sounds like he took you seriously."

"And now what?"

"Let's wait and see. It's probably going to be a day or two before we know anything."

My flight, I think suddenly.

"Even if I'm done with Halligan before noon tomorrow, I'll be worried about making it to JFK on time. I'll have to change my ticket—I guess to Sunday night."

Of course, that will delay being with Bas, but it's critical to follow through with things here.

"That makes sense," Logan says. "And I'll go with you to headquarters tomorrow."

I glance at my watch and see that it's almost midnight. This is all the talk I can handle tonight. When I look over, Logan's staring intently at me.

"Bree, please stay tonight, okay?" he says.

I'm not going to have sex with Logan tonight. Even if I tell myself it's just *one last time,* it will dig me even deeper into wrongdoing. And yet for the second night in a row, I can't bear being alone. Logan won't be able to ease the guilt I'm feeling or distract me from my fear over losing Bas—I'm on my own with both of those—but his presence is helping with the other part of the nightmare: Mel's senseless death and how close we came to not knowing the truth. He's the only one who's traveled the same dark roads of hell that I have, so nothing about that journey has to be decoded for him.

"We can just hold each other if that's what you want," Logan adds, picking up on my hesitation.

"Yes, that's all I can handle tonight."

Logan gives me an extra toothbrush from his dopp kit, and after washing up, I swap my clothes for a T-shirt he offers from his suitcase. When he comes out of the bathroom himself, I notice he leaves the door ajar so that the glow from the night-light reaches the bedroom.

"You remembered," I say, touched by the gesture. Is he hoping that somehow we can be friends from here on? But there's no way that can happen. If I do manage to salvage my relationship with Bas, I can never have Logan as an active presence in my life.

"Yeah. I figured that even if you were over your fear of the dark, it surely came back this week."

As soon as we're in bed, he pulls me to him, and as I lie in the crook of his arm, I hear his breathing slow until it's coming from a place deep within his chest. But I'm not so lucky. My brain is flooded with more troubling thoughts than it seems able to handle—the awful truth about Mel's death, my role in Riley's murder, the likelihood that I've wrecked things with the man I've recharted my life with. It's raining out, I realize, not pouring exactly, just a repetitive, rhythmic drip on the windowsill and car hoods below. I try to use the sound as a distraction, but after a while it's like an earworm I can't expel. I drag a pillow over my head and finally, mercifully, sleep overtakes me.

When I wake, Logan is sitting on the edge of the bed beside me. His hand is on my shoulder, and I realize he's jostled me from my sleep.

"What time is it?" I ask groggily. There's light from the living area, through a partially open door.

"Just past six thirty."

"Is—is everything all right?"

"Yeah, more than all right. Morgan Kroll was arrested early this morning for Riley's murder."

Chapter 33

I bolt up straight in bed.

"How do you know?" I ask, shoving the hair off my face.

"That pain-in-the-ass Chip Conway texted me ten minutes ago," Logan says. "He sent a link to a short news item that went up online around six a.m."

"But what could they have on her? DNA tests still take days, I've heard."

"Fingerprints, maybe? Though it seems too soon for a hit on that, either."

I finally focus on the fact that Logan is fully dressed—in jeans, a collared shirt, and a blue zippered cardigan.

"How long have you been up?"

"Since five. I couldn't fall back to sleep, and once I saw the story, I figured I'd better dress to face the day in case all hell breaks loose."

"I need to see the piece. Can you forward me the link?"

"Sure—or come see it on my laptop. It's still open to the story."

I nearly vault out of bed, trail Logan to the living room, and settle there to read the story.

> Early this morning New York State Police arrested Hudson River Community College professor Morgan T. Kroll, 35, of Springtown, for the murder of Riley Reynolds, age 29. Reynolds, a former Carter College

student, was found dead yesterday at a home in Edgerton. Police have not released details of her death or a possible motive, but it's been reported that Reynolds was in the area in conjunction with a renewed investigation into the death of another Carter College, student Melanie Chase, eight years ago.

So, it's true. Morgan killed Riley. Which means she must have killed Mel, too. There's a couple of moments when I feel I might be sick, that I might hurl whatever's left in my stomach. I sat in the same booth and the same car with her, acting all deferential, when she was the person who strangled my smart, talented, beautiful daughter with a dog leash. I don't want her to rot in prison. I want her to burn at the stake.

"She's as much of a monster as Ruck was," Logan says.

I take a deep breath, forcing my stomach into submission. "But what if all the police have is circumstantial evidence, based mostly on what I said? I'm going to go insane until I know more."

"Maybe Halligan will loop us in when we see him this morning."

"He's so pissed at me, we'll be lucky if he tells us anything."

Logan scoffs. "As far as I'm concerned, he has no right to be annoyed. Where would we be if you hadn't dug the way you did?"

I'm glad I dug. I'm glad, in the end, that I came here hoping for the truth. And yet Riley's dead because of it. And Bas might be lost as well.

"I should get moving," I say, and start for the bedroom to grab my clothes. As I reach the doorway, I pivot to Logan.

"Speaking of all hell breaking loose, I wonder if the Handlers have heard. Alison said she told her husband about Mel, but never Morgan. She'll be forced to now."

"This is going to knock them on their asses," Logan says. "There's going to be some ugly gossip over the next few months—at the very least."

"Though maybe Alison can put it to her advantage. She can do a painting of the two of them with flames shooting out of their heads."

"Speaking of Handler," Logan says, "I was so thrown last night, I forgot to mention that I checked with the contractor for the *Muse* office, and he said that the crew is gone every day by four. So, they didn't pull the table against the door, and apparently no one in maintenance would have done it, either. Which leaves Handler as a possibility. But *why?*"

I flip a hand over. "We know now that he wasn't sleeping with Mel, but he might have been afraid I'd find out about her and Alison and go to Maya about it. And he wanted me to look slightly unhinged."

"Yeah, could be. But we'll probably never know for sure."

I finally retreat to the bathroom, wash up a little, and quickly change into the same grungy clothes from yesterday. I need to call Bas as soon as possible and share the news with him. And in the next two days, I need to determine what to do about my infidelity. The thought almost knocks me over with dread.

When I return to the living area, I find Logan staring at his laptop screen.

"Is there an update?" I ask.

"Nothing to speak of. They've included one new detail, that the home belongs to attorney Hilary Brown."

A thought suddenly blooms in my mind. "Wait. If the police found evidence at Hilary's house, she might be privy to what it is."

On the one hand, it seems unfair to ask her, considering what I've set in motion, but she's also seemed sympathetic to my need for the truth. I dial her number with the phone on speaker. Just when I think the call is about to go to voicemail, she picks up.

"I take it you've heard the news," she says.

"Yes, just now."

"I'm gobsmacked. And I frankly don't understand why this woman would do it."

"I think what I said yesterday—that Riley's death might be connected to our daughter's—is true. It seems Morgan Kroll must have used the details she learned about Riley's assault to murder Melanie several days later, and she couldn't afford for Riley to change her story about the date."

A few moments of silence follow. I cringe, wondering if she's now calculating the part I played in Riley's murder.

"Oh heavens," she says finally. "This is almost more than I can fathom."

"I know you must be busy dealing with family today, but I was hoping you could illuminate something for Logan and me. Do you have any idea why they arrested Kroll? Because we're concerned the evidence might not be strong enough."

"Oh, it's enough," Hilary says in disgust.

"What do you mean?"

"This is between the two of us for now, okay? The more I thought about it, the more convinced I was that Riley didn't take her own life and that someone must have been in the house with her. At about nine last night, when I was already at my friend's, I remembered the trail camera I'd set up in the woods right behind the house. I went through the footage. The camera was angled enough to catch a woman arriving at the back door around midday, being let in by Riley, and then exiting in a hurry less than an hour later—with Riley nowhere in sight. I sent it to the police immediately, and based on the questions they had for me, I realized it was Morgan Kroll."

I jerk my head toward Logan, and his expression is as stunned as mine must be. I thank Hilary and promise to update her with anything we learn.

"Who would have guessed?" Logan says once I've disconnected. "We've been saved by someone's interest in fucking wildlife."

Without warning, I begin to cry, unable to stay on autopilot for a second more. I'm crying about Riley and everything she suffered, in part because of me. And I'm crying about Mel. Though I'm pretty sure I finally know the truth about her death, she'll always be part mystery to me and her love forever out of reach. Maybe Logan was right that she did love me and, like many adolescents, was simply sucky at showing it, but I'll never know for sure.

He steps forward and embraces me, and for a few minutes we just hold each other, and the only sound in the room is our ragged breathing. I finally pull away.

"Shall I meet you in the lobby at nine fifteen?" I ask, brushing away my tears.

"Sounds good." He levels his gaze at me. "And then come back, okay?"

"You mean tonight?" That's clearly what he's talking about.

"Actually, I mean *always*," he says. "I want to spend the rest of my life with you, Bree."

My breath catches in shock.

"Logan, I have a partner, and you do, too. She moved in with you only a few months ago."

"It's not the right choice for me, though. And I don't see how you think your choice is the right one for you, either, fleeing to the damn Southern Cone."

"But—"

"I made a huge fucking mistake, Bree, and I'm not only sorry, but I also want the chance to finally make it up to you."

I feel shaky. Despite how solicitous Logan has been this week, I never saw this coming. I'm also shaky because I liked hearing him say those words, and I'm not sure what that means. Would I be willing to throw away my new life with a man I love just to be with Logan again?

I do my best to center myself.

"Logan, I'm moved by what you're saying. But please, can we put this subject on hold for now? I feel too overwhelmed by everything that's happened. I need to get ahold of myself before we meet with Halligan."

"Yes, of course. I'll see you in a couple of hours."

Back in my room, I reset to autopilot. I shower, and with my hair dripping wet, I call Bas.

"Cariño, hi," he says. "I was hoping that was you."

The sound of his voice, so *unknowing*, floods me with guilt.

"Please tell me your cold is better, sweetheart."

"Yes, much."

"So glad to hear."

I feel like an evil magician right now, using sleight of hand to hide not only my two-timing but also the weird ambivalence I left Logan's room with. Knowing Bas, he might even sense the trickery.

"You actually caught me at my computer, double-checking your arrival time."

"That's partly why I'm calling," I say. "Something pretty shocking has happened, and I need to spend another day or two with the police here. I'm going to try to switch my flight to Sunday night."

"What's going on?" he asks.

God, how loaded that question really is.

"The girl who I told you about, the victim who came forward? She's been murdered, and we're pretty sure the woman who did it killed Mel, too. That it wasn't Ruck after all."

"A *woman* killed Mel?" he says.

"It's a harrowing story, related in part to a relationship we never knew Mel had. I can tell you much more later, but I need to get ready to make a statement at police headquarters."

And I do want to tell him, every detail I've learned. And my own complicity in part of it.

"Sure, sure, of course," he says. "And please tell me if there's anything I can do. It's awful being so far away and not being able to help you, Bree. But I'm thinking of you every minute."

Hearing those words in his deep, husky voice is like a balm, one I've come to rely on so heavily. Yes, I've held back about Mel and the true impact of her death on my life—but Bas, so good at always reading me, surely has a sense of the woman I am. From nearly the moment we met, there's been a deep, steadfast connection between the two of us, forged in part because of a shared view of the world and similar sensibilities. Maybe the sex will never be as crazily intense as it was during the early years with Logan, but it's good and it's passionate, and on the flip side, there's tenderness and tranquility, things I craved since Mel's death.

"Thank you, Bas. That means so much."

As soon as I've hung up, I go online and switch my flight to Sunday night. I'm going home for sure, though for how long, I don't know. Because after speaking with Bas, I realize I have to tell him the truth about Logan, that keeping it hidden would simply pile onto my betrayal. And there's a more than decent chance that once I admit my transgression, he'll insist I move out.

Before closing my laptop, I scan my emails to see if Chip has sent the correct link to the archives, and sure enough, he has. I click on it. A page opens with the words "Melanie Chase, Selected Writings" on top.

There are about a dozen haikus, one short story, and a scene from a play she must have been working on. I haven't much time, but I race through them anyway, thrilled to have them in my possession and at the same time wondering what Handler didn't want me to see.

The play scene seems really compelling, but it's about two college girls questioning their faith. The short story is one Mel won a prize for in high school, and from what I can tell, she just did some major editing on it after she went to Carter. Perhaps the haikus include a reference to Alison, but at a glance, they all seem to be nature-oriented—reflections about wind and trees and puddles left by the rain, one simply about a snail slithering up a window.

Though most are indeed new to me, there are two that Logan and I discovered on Mel's desk in Cartersville, including the one I led myself to believe was about me. Maybe this was the one Handler didn't want me finding. Funny that he was afraid I'd put two and two together simply based on the words *returning to birch*, and yet, that's exactly how some of my questions began to form.

My phone rings, making me start. Maybe Maya, I think, who's probably heard the news. But the screen says "Unknown Caller."

"Hello?"

"Good morning, Bree."

The voice sounds vaguely familiar, but I can't place it.

"Who is this?" I ask.

"Lisa Perry."

"Who?"

"Lisa *Perry*. Logan's partner."

"Oh, sorry," I say, completely caught off guard. "How can I help you?"

"I thought you should know that I'm not stupid, Bree."

Oh God, has Logan told her, or has she simply guessed?

"I never said you were, Lisa."

"You must think it, though. But I can tell exactly what's going on between you and Logan."

I cringe. She's clearly fishing, and I have to hand it to her: she's more skilled than I was at reading her man.

"Lisa, if you have an issue with Logan, you should discuss it with him."

"But you're the one he's fucking, so I need to be speaking to you, too."

"Goodbye."

"Before you hang up, there's something I thought you should know."

End the call, I command myself, but I'm frozen suddenly. I hear her clear her throat.

"Just so you have all the facts at your disposal, Logan and I actually go *waay* back as a couple. We had our first fling when I worked for him eleven years ago."

Her words are a hard punch to my gut—because, deep down, I sense she must be telling the truth. With a fumbling hand, I tap the red button.

So Logan's infidelity hadn't simply been about grief. He'd had his fling with Lisa three years before Mel died. And that means there were probably others throughout our two-decade marriage.

I married a bad boy, convincing myself I'd tamed him, when that was never the case.

Logan and I say little on the drive to police headquarters. I expect a tongue-lashing from Halligan, but I don't really care. As for Lisa's revelation, I've tucked that away in my mind with other things that don't matter anymore.

We learn when we arrive that Halligan is off for the day, and another detective ends up taking my statement. Though he stresses, like Halligan did, that I need to let the police do their job, he also thanks me for my help. Detective Halligan, he says, will follow up with us in the next day or two.

Once we're back in the car, Logan checks his phone and finds a text from Jack.

"He's back in the city," he says, "but he's read the story."

"I feel a little guilty about thinking the worst of him."

"Yeah, but maybe you don't get to the truth without first thinking the worst about everyone. And like you said, he was probably trying to make sure we didn't do any damage to his blossoming career."

We're quiet again on the way back to Cartersville, Logan perhaps wondering what I'm going to tell him now that we have the police out of the way, and me forming the words in my head. When we reach the inn, I ask if he'll come to my room for a bit.

"Sure," he says, an eyebrow cocked.

Once I've closed the door, I advance into the room and then turn to face him.

"I want to address what you said earlier," I say.

"Good."

"Well, maybe *not* good. Because though what you said really moved me, Logan, I have to say no. And I think that, in time, you'd see that a no was best for you as well."

He shakes his head, looking taken aback. "It won't be."

"Logan, it wouldn't work between us. For starters, though it might not have seemed obvious the other night, I love my partner, and I assume you love Lisa, too. Plus, there's no reason to think it would be good for us again. We might feel slightly giddy at first, but that surely wouldn't last, and we'd lose some of the strides we've each made dealing with our grief. It would always be in the room with us."

He throws up his hands in frustration. "But how will we know if we don't try?"

"Because this doesn't need an experiment. You said you want your old life back, and I've missed that life, too. But there isn't any way to reclaim it. That life died when Mel did."

I don't mention what I've learned from Lisa. Because why give her the satisfaction of thinking she foiled something—and why bother calling Logan out at this stage of the game?

Anyway, it's all beside the point. Though I felt briefly elated at hearing Logan say he yearned for a life with me again, it's Bas I want. If he lets that happen.

And there's something else I've come to understand now, beyond the scope of Logan's philandering. Though he never once made me feel bad about the easy rapport he had with Mel compared to my fraught one, being with him this week has brought so much of that back to me, turned it from a bruise that hurts only when touched to a steady, throbbing ache. I don't want any more reminders.

He's pacing now, massaging the back of his neck in that way of his.

"Will you at least think about it overnight?" he asks.

I shake my head. "No, but what I'll do—and what I hope you'll do, too—is be grateful for parts of these past few days. The scholarships you donated are incredible, and so is the *Muse* office, and I'm really happy I had the chance to participate a little. Plus, we got to be here for the arrest of the person who most likely killed Mel, and support each other through it. And though I can take some credit for the arrest, I kept digging because you honored my doubts."

Logan starts to speak, but I raise my hand.

"And last but hardly least," I say, "we got to say goodbye to each other in a loving way, without any of the ugliness from seven years ago."

A tear forms in the corner of one of his eyes. I feel an almost tidal wave of sorrow, but no regrets.

Chapter 34

When my flight lands in Montevideo early Monday morning, with the plane bouncing along the runway, my heart bounces, too. I'm really here.

On each leg of my journey, but especially on the nine-and-a-half-hour flight from New York to Brazil, I rehearsed the words I would use when confessing to Bas, though more than once I toyed with the idea of *not* telling him. If I stay silent, I get to keep my relationship and make a fresh start of it. And though Bas will surely sense something's off, I could try to make him think it's related to my ordeal in Cartersville—and, in time, my guilt might even subside. But then I'd be no better than Logan: cheater, liar, cad.

I insisted during my last call to Bas that there was no need for either him or Jorge making the nearly hour-and-a-half drive to pick me up, and that I would instead book Umberto, a guy we sometimes use for airport runs. He begrudgingly agreed and said he would have lunch waiting for me.

And that means I won't have to spend a whole car ride faking that everything's okay.

There's always a ton of people meeting passengers at the Montevideo airport, as if airplane travel is still a novelty. When I emerge from customs, I spot Umberto along the edge of the large, jubilant crowd, and he waves at me with a friendly smile. As we head to the parking lot, in the crisp but pleasant air, he asks me in Spanish about my trip, having no idea what the agenda was.

I tell him that it was good but I'm glad to be home. Not knowing, of course, if it will still be my home by the end of the day.

We head east on Ruta Interbalnearia, the coastal highway that connects Montevideo to Punta del Este. Though tourist season is well over, there are still billboards heralding the joys of summer and others touting area vineyards and availability in new bright-white condominiums.

I close my eyes, trying to shut out the world for a bit. Despite my resolve to tell Bas the truth, I find myself resisting again. But even if I convinced him everything was okay, the deceit would be a dangerous fissure in the foundation of our relationship.

Eventually I feel Umberto veer left, and I open my eyes. We're leaving the main road in order to travel northeast. This stretch is far more rural, and the rolling fields on each side are filled with cattle or sheep, and the occasional concrete farmhouse, its tin roof glinting in the sun. Now and then, we catch up with a beret-wearing gaucho riding his horse along the side of the road.

Finally, we make the turn to the chacra. Sebastian must hear the car coming up the long driveway, because by the time we reach the house, he's standing under the portico. My heart swells at the sight of him with a weird mix of joy and anguish. He's in jeans and a beige flannel shirt, his hair slightly tousled by the breeze. Poco is right beside him, ears raised.

As soon as I'm out of the car, we embrace, and Bas kisses me softly on the mouth.

"*Bienvenido a casa,*" he says tenderly.

"Thank you. It's so good to be here, sweetheart."

But inside, I'm roiling.

A flurry of activity follows—me paying Umberto and petting the leaping, tail-wagging Poco; Bas hauling my bag from the trunk—and it isn't until I've washed up and changed that we're finally side by side again, standing alone in the kitchen.

"Where's Maitena?" I ask. Though I see lunch on the counter, there's no sign of her.

"I asked her to make something earlier and then just leave it for us to serve ourselves. I figured it would be nice to be alone together when you got back."

"Yes, of course." I now have no excuse for putting off the conversation we need to have.

With Poco trailing behind us, we carry out platters and bowls to the galería and set them on the table. There's roast chicken, already carved, chimichurri sauce, potato salad, and sliced tomatoes, perhaps the last good ones until next summer. Bas grabs a bottle of *rosado* and another of *aqua con gas*. We take our usual seats at the table, him at the head and me catty-corner. This way we both can enjoy the view.

"You feel like a *copa de vino*?" he asks, smiling. "It's practically required after a flight on GOL airlines."

"Ha, yes, but just a little, okay? I don't want to pass out at the table."

I take a minute before eating to stare out at the landscape. A few small clouds scuttle across the sky, casting shadows here and there on the fields. For the first time, I notice that the milky plumes of the pampas grass have turned almost completely brown.

"You ordered a perfect day for my return," I say, sounding more wistful than I intended.

"I tried," he says. "But you know how fickle the gods can be."

"Oh yes, they certainly can be." I feel a terrible pang in my chest as I say it. Before the day is done, I'm going to know what the gods have in store for me.

Bas has already taken a few bites of his meal but pauses now, setting his utensils down.

"Any news since we spoke yesterday?"

"No. The case seems to be moving, but we might not hear anything new for at least a day or two."

He smiles lovingly at me. "I'm in awe of what you did, Bree—turning over every stone until it led to this woman."

"Yes, but . . . in the end, this girl Riley *died*."

"You feel responsible?"

There, he sees it right away.

"Yes. Partly, at least."

He rubs his hand slowly down the side of his face, looking up to the left briefly. "When I was getting divorced years ago, I read a few things about guilt—because I had my share of it—and I remember a British psychologist saying that guilt occurs when our own moral standards don't match up to what we've done. I understand how you're feeling, but you had no idea that encouraging Riley to tell the truth would cause her any harm. If you *had* thought that, you would have proceeded differently."

"Yes, I see your point. But that doesn't change the outcome."

"Hmm . . . He said something else that might be of help. Instead of feeling stuck with our guilt, we should use it as an energizing emotion. To get us to apologize or atone—or, um, the third one I think he mentioned was to make amends."

"Ah, that's good food for thought," I say. Bas *gets* me; he has from the start. "Maybe there's something I can do for Riley's fiancé or family."

"Yes, that's an idea for sure."

I take a long sip of rosé. It's dead quiet out, no birdsong at all, but the air between us seems to vibrate as if someone is running a wet finger around the edge of a wineglass. I can't wait any longer.

"Bas, there's something else I need to get off my chest. Something not good. I—"

"Before we go any further," he says, interrupting me, "let me ask you a question, Bree." He glances briefly out to the fields and the enormous Uruguayan sky. "Is this *working* for you? Us, this place, everything?"

The questions take me aback, even make me gulp. Does he already know?

"Yes, Bas, it *is* working. Why are you asking that?"

"When you were gone, especially when we talked on the phone, I was struck by the distance between us. And not just in miles. We've spoken so little about some of the most important things in your life—Melanie, her death, the end of your marriage. I blame myself for not asking more, for not helping us create a dialect for those kinds of discussions, but it doesn't feel—at least to me—that you gave me much of an entry. I never even went online and read about the case because I felt I'd be violating your privacy."

I sigh, my breath stuttering a little. "You're right, Bas, I haven't. But"—and to my surprise, I choke on the words—"I want to change that. I made the mistake of thinking it was better for our relationship—and just plain better for me, too, I guess—if I barricaded all the past behind me."

"And it's not because you've only been biding your time here?"

Is that what he really thinks? Has he made a decision about us before I even got back? I can almost hear my heart pounding in my chest.

"No, Bas, I'm *not* biding my time, not at all. I love you and our life here, and I want it to go on and on . . . But it can't go on without me being honest with you."

He lifts his hand slightly from the table, in a gesture for me to stop. *Please,* I pray, *don't let this all fall away.*

"It's not necessary, Bree," he says finally. "I know things were very hard for you in Cartersville, and that perhaps there was also unfinished business."

I hold my breath. So, he's had his suspicions.

"Yes," I say, barely above a whisper. "But not business I want a part of anymore."

He nods and glances out at the landscape again, seeming to study it, but I know he's thinking, *deciding*. He's got every right to be disgusted by my behavior, unfinished business or not, and to send me on my way.

He turns back to look at me. "I'm willing to put it behind us, Bree, if you are, too. And if this is the life you really want now."

"It is," I say, flooded with relief. "For certain."

And not just because of the serenity it's brought. I *did* flee, as Logan claimed, to the damn Southern Cone, because when I'm here, it often feels as if grief has overslept and missed the flight. But it's also because of Bas and the man that he is.

I set my glass down and reach across the table. I grasp Bas's hand and bring it toward me, pressing my lips against his fingers.

🦋

After lunch, I flop onto the bed, falling into the deepest sleep I've had in days. When I finally wake, I can tell it's still daytime, but for a few seconds, I have no clue where I am, and my heart thrums with anxiety.

And then, as I become aware of the soft cotton spread beneath me, I realize: Uruguay. I'm still *here*. In a bed I share with Bas. This is my home for certain, so far away from my old life but where I get to feel of the world again. My eyes well with tears, wetting the pillowcase.

After climbing out of bed and wiping my face, I check in with Bas, who's starting a fire in the great room. I promise to join him momentarily. I grab my laptop from my tote bag and take it to my office, placing it on my desk.

There's a lot to catch up on now that I'm home. I want to email my friend Ellie today and set up a time to talk—and share everything with her—as soon as she's back home from her vacation. And I need to get back to the in-house editor I've been working with, who's written to say she's very happy with the recent edits I did and has another project for me. In a day or two, I'll be ready to jump into work again.

There's something else I intend to do this week. Now that I've got my hands on more of Mel's writing, I've decided to self-publish a collection of her work in book form. Not to sell online. The book will be mainly for me, Logan, some relatives on Logan's side, and old friends of hers, like Harry. Mel dreamed of being published, and now she will be.

The intoxicating smell of woodsmoke wafts in through the partially open door.

As I start to leave the room, my cell phone rings, and I nearly jump at the sound. I've been on pins and needles since I left, wondering how the case against Morgan will proceed.

It's Logan, and the sight of his name makes me flinch a little.

"Hey," I say.

"You settled in yet?"

"Pretty much. Anxious about the investigation, of course."

"Well, that's partly why I'm calling. Turns out Morgan bought orange electrical cord at a Walmart several towns away from Edgerton. She paid cash, but she was caught on a store camera. Halligan had asked to see footage from every place within a huge radius."

Still standing, I feel my knees weaken. This is huge, more than I dared hope for.

"Thank God."

"Wait, there's more. You know the anti-anxiety drug clonazepam? The tox results came back this morning, and Riley had enough in her system to knock her out. The cops didn't find any in her possession, so they think Kroll brought it to the house and dropped it into Riley's coffee, just as you suspected. Apparently, her partner has a prescription for it. Not a slam-dunk piece of evidence, but it's one more thing to put on the list, helping it all add up."

"But nothing yet connecting her to Mel's death?"

"Not yet, but Halligan thinks that might come in time. Alison will be brought in for questioning, of course."

I sigh. We might never have absolute proof, but we'll *know*. And though I still want her burned at the stake, I sense that, this time, my hatred of Melanie's killer won't be able to eat me alive.

"Thanks for telling me . . . Everything okay on the home front?"

Though I never told him about Lisa's call, she's surely confronted him.

"Depends on who you ask. I told Lisa it wasn't working and that we needed to split."

"Oh, Logan. I was a fly in the ointment, but can't you put that behind you?"

"It's not just about you and me. It's about her."

"Did you view her in a different light once the week was over?"

"Yeah. And that damn designer duffel bag of hers started to get on my nerves. I kept thinking she could kill me and stuff my body inside it without anyone being the wiser."

The comment makes me laugh.

"Well, that's probably better than a wood chipper," I say. "And look, I know you'll find someone else."

Someone better, I think, because I do want him to be happy. Maybe the right partner and an aging libido will even keep him faithful.

"I'm not looking that far ahead at the moment."

"I should let you go," I say, and then realize how strange the words are in the context of everything. I need to stay in contact with Logan about the case, especially if it goes to trial, which is highly likely, but at the same time, I have to keep the right distance. It won't be hard this go-around.

"Okay. And, oh, thanks for sending me the links to that other stuff of Mel's."

"No big revelations, but it's nice to have, isn't it?"

"For sure. And didn't you feel better when you saw the haiku about you?"

"What?"

"The one about the pine trees. It's about you."

"But what makes you say that?"

"I remember Mel showing it to me. Well, not *showing* me. She wouldn't go that far. But I found it on the kitchen counter when she was home the summer before she died—and when I asked, she said it was about the two of you at the first house we had on the Cape."

"I had no idea."

"Yeah, read it again."

We wish each other goodbye, and as soon as I've disconnected, I return to my laptop and scroll to the poem, knowing exactly which one he's referring to—which I'd assumed was yet another nature haiku.

Mel was eight and nine when we had the Cape Cod house he mentioned, and those summers were magical for me. After coming back from the beach each day, she and I would read in a hammock surrounded by pine trees. And I sometimes sang her a Scottish ballad my mother had taught me.

I read the poem once more, with Logan's revelation in mind.

> The song in the pines
> Stays with me always, always,
> Without you knowing.

Oh, Mel, I think. *It's stayed with me always, too.*

Acknowledgments

I'm always so incredibly grateful to the people who take time away from their busy schedules to help me with my research, and for this book I offer a big thank-you to the following: Susan Brune, Brune Law; Barbara Butcher, consultant for forensic and medicolegal investigations and author of *What the Dead Know*; Paul Paganelli, MD; Joyce Hanshaw, retired captain from the Hunterdon County Prosecutor's Office; Will Valenza, Glens Falls Police Department, retired; Charlie Melcher, founder and CEO, Melcher Media; Debra Geer; Cheryl Brown; Michael White; Cristina Weiz; Laura Brown; Beth Cushman, Jody Heyward; and Emily White.

Thank you, as well, to my awesome agent, Kathy Schneider of the Jane Rotrosen Agency, for her extraordinary help and guidance on this book. And what an exciting, gratifying experience it's been to work with both my acquiring editor, Liz Pearsons, and my developmental editor, Tiffany Yates Martin. Thanks also to my copyeditor, Michelle Hope; proofreader, Jill Schoenhaut; cold reader, Steve Schul; and production manager, Miranda Gardner.

I want to also express my gratitude to those on my personal team: my social media director, Shany Scharks of Scharks Digital Media; my website designer and manager, Bill Cunningham; and my newsletter editor, Miriam Friedman. I'm so lucky to be working with all of you.

A very, very special thanks goes out my husband, Brad, and my kids, Hunter and Hayley, for always being in my corner as an author.

And finally, thank you from the bottom of my heart to my amazing readers. I get to live such a fun, fulfilling life as a suspense author (*I Came Back for You* is my nineteenth!), and it wouldn't be possible without your terrific support. I've so enjoyed getting to know some of you through social media and at bookstore and library events.

About the Author

Photo © 2020 Jordan Matter

Kate White is the *New York Times* and *USA Today* bestselling author of nineteen novels of suspense, including the stand-alone thrillers *The Last Time She Saw Him*, *Between Two Strangers*, *The Second Husband*, and the Bailey Weggins mysteries. A former editor-in-chief of *Cosmopolitan* for fourteen years, Kate decided to pursue another passion: writing suspense fiction. Her first mystery, *If Looks Could Kill*, was a Kelly Ripa Book Club pick, a #1 Amazon bestseller, and an instant *New York Times* bestseller. She has been nominated for an International Thriller Writers Award, and her books have been published in over thirty countries. Kate is an avid traveler and spends each winter with her husband at their home in Uruguay. She holds an honorary doctorate of letters from her alma mater, Union College, where she gave the 2022 commencement address. For more information, visit www.katewhite.com.